MURDER AT FOLLY BEACH CREEK

CATHY PICKENS

A Blue Ridge Mountain Mystery Book 2

Originally published as *Done Gone Wrong*

Revised edition 2023
Joffe Books, London
www.joffebooks.com

First published by St Martin's Press in 2005
as *Done Gone Wrong*

This paperback edition was first published
in Great Britain in 2023

Cover art by Sasha Alsberg

ISBN: 978-1-80405-800-8

Dedicated to my sisters — my best friends for life.
And always, to my parents and to Bob.

ACKNOWLEDGMENTS

Many thanks to the readers and advisers who try to keep Avery out of trouble: the Doctors Dickinson, Nancy Forbis, Sgt. Henry King of the North Carolina Highway Patrol, Donna Ashley, Tamara Burrell, and — for advice above and beyond the call — Terry Hoover and Paula Connolly. All remaining mistakes and misinformation are mine, all mine.

And with affection and admiration to Ruth Cavin, an incomparable editor whose surgical precision and wry humor always improve both the product and the process.

AUTHOR'S NOTE

Barnard Medical Center sits, in my imagination, on imaginary streets in imaginary buildings close to where an outstanding medical university and hospitals actually sit in Charleston. Nothing and no one in this book portrays any real situation, institution, or person.

Things which are seen were not made
of things which do appear.

Hebrews 11:3 (KJV)

CHAPTER ONE

Wednesday night

What had I expected, coming back to Charleston? I twirled my Waterman pen between my fingers, watching the engraved *Avery Andrews* catch the candlelight, then tossed the pen onto the table, stared out at the sliver of orange-red sun that lit the still marsh grass, and pretended not to notice the waitress glaring at me.

I'd monopolized her best table too long, waiting on a date who had obviously stood me up. The look on her face said it all: *Wise up, honey. He ain't showin' and sittin' here ain't gonna make it happen. Take your portable office and cruise for guys on somebody else's rent money.*

When she finally walked past, I offered her my jury-winningest smile and asked for a cup of she-crab soup. She flounced off. Maybe I ought to abandon ship. No telling what she would do to my soup between kitchen and table.

Where the heck was Mark Tilman? This dinner — and this marsh-bound restaurant on stilts — had been his suggestion, when he'd hunted me down earlier in the day at Jake Baker's law office, pestering Jake's receptionist until she brought him back to my temporary office.

It had taken only a blink for me to recognize him, even out of context. Mark Tilman, Gregg Tilman's little brother.

He was too young for the worry lines that creased his forehead, but they looked fresh, temporary. He repeatedly apologized for interrupting but insisted that he had to talk to me. About something terribly important. This evening, as soon as he finished his medical clinic rounds.

Was it the pleading-puppy look he gave me or the fact that his eyes were identical to Gregg's? Or because I'd have to explain to Mom if I ignored his plea. I'd agreed to meet him at this restaurant off Folly Beach Road, where we could eat early and avoid the crowd. So here I sat, perched above the marsh grass in a weather-roughened seafood restaurant known mostly to locals, wasting time Jake Baker was paying for, waiting on some kid who only looked like somebody I once dated.

For the past hour, I'd alternated between calling Mark's cell phone and staring out the window, sipping ice tea. Deep pink and purple sunset clouds framed a skimming, awkward egret. The stillness of the water-footed grass belied the teeming wildlife nursery beneath it — a nursery dying because too many of us want to live in stilt houses or eat in stilt restaurants and pretend we belong here.

It felt odd to be back in Charleston, the site of my ignominious defeat. No, not defeat — self-realization. My ignominious self-realization. Three months earlier, I'd gotten disgusted with an expert witness in a medical malpractice trial for lying, even though his lies could win my case for me. A case even my client knew we shouldn't win. I'd decided — inopportunely, considering it was the middle of the trial — that I didn't want any part of his lies, and I'd goaded my expert until he exploded, which blew the trial. Threatened with disbarment, I'd headed back to my upstate hometown, out of a job and needing some time to process what had happened. And why.

For the last three months, since Thanksgiving, I'd been hiding in Dacus, but it was now February and I was getting a bit antsy. A small town doesn't offer much in the way of pickings. Divorces, property transfers, wills, car wrecks — all boringly routine. Some numbskull had scrawled my name in the Dacus Law Enforcement Center's intake cell, which had provided not-quite-equal measures of hilarity and heartbreak but not much excitement over the last few weeks. Now that I was here, I realized how much I'd missed the energy of a pending trial — and how much I'd missed Charleston.

Jake Baker had offered me the only thing that could have lured me out of my self-imposed lethargy and isolation — a high-stakes case. Lawyers aren't noted for their humility, and they never ask for help, so when Jake actually pleaded for mine, I admit I was intrigued. He had been trying to talk me into joining his practice since I'd quit — or, more accurately, been forced out of my former law firm. He may have wanted me for my wit and charm, but I figured he really wanted my insider's view from the defense side. Defense lawyers and plaintiff lawyers are oil and water, coming together in the courtroom but never really mixing. Deep down, Jake was hoping he could convert me from the dark side.

I'd repeatedly said no to a permanent job, which, to Jake, only made me more attractive. He isn't used to hearing the word no. Two weeks ago, when he called me about the Uplift case and invited me to Charleston, I turned down his first offer — a room in his house. Jake had a reputation. When he offered the premier suite at Two Meeting Street Inn and some tantalizing tidbits about his case, I packed my bag.

A forklift operator with a semi-automatic arsenal had gone berserk, killing several coworkers and then himself. Tragic, but hardly news. I pictured Jake sizing up the case as any lawyer looking to sue would. He had sharked his way through the list of potential defendants: the shooter? No money. The company? Not much money and protected by an earlier settlement and by workers' compensation payments. The gun manufacturer? Too expensive and unlikely to be successful in South Carolina, a state full of gun-toters. Ah, how about the pharmaceutical company that made the antidepressant the poor schmo was taking? And, for good measure, maybe his psychiatrist. Nobody much liked drug companies. And drug companies and doctors had money.

I balked at first, cynically seeing the case as little more than a bunch of injured folks looking for somebody else to blame — and a greedy plaintiffs' lawyer looking to pay off his beach house. Jake finally hooked me when he explained he wanted me to sit in the courtroom and whisper in his ear. The chance to stage-manage a case intrigued me. He didn't want a "jury selection expert" with a psychology degree. He wanted somebody who'd been on the firing line, who knew what it meant to fight for a client in court.

Selfishly, I realized it would give me a rare close-up view from the plaintiff's side of the courtroom. I'd spent ten years as a defense attorney, defending companies and doctors being sued by guys like Jake. While I was unemployed, why not take this chance to see the other side? And this chance to eat she-crab soup.

Good she-crab soup, too, that tasted like Lowcountry South Carolina: salty, slightly muddy, buttery, foreign. Nothing like the Upstate — especially my hill country, where the air smelled cinnamon-dank and, at this time of year, held a crisp bite.

I'd been absentmindedly staring at a partially submerged log floating in the water, lit by the floodlights, when one of the bumps on the log winked at me and the log sank out of sight. That's another thing we don't have back home: alligators peering up out of the creeks. Nor do we have waving waist-high fields of marsh grass, deceptively land-like, which hide miles of gooey black "pluff" mud worse than any quicksand, full of strange creatures I'd missed eating.

The waitress swooped in for my empty soup bowl. "I'll have the salt-and-pepper catfish." She stopped just short of rolling her eyes.

Still no sign of Mark, but I couldn't keep from glancing at the dining room door whenever someone entered. No point in trying the cell phone again.

4

He'd probably had an emergency at the clinic. That's what doctors do, after all. Emergencies. Still, I couldn't shake some undefined sense of unease. Maybe it had been his newborn worry wrinkles. Or his insistence on dinner despite his tight schedule.

Night had completely swallowed the reddish-purple glow on the horizon by the time I found myself debating how much tip to leave. I erred on the side of unmerited generosity since I'd seen no signs of sabotage to my food. Not that I could easily detect spit.

The seashell tabby parking lot crunched underfoot as I crossed to my vintage red Mustang convertible. Rising behind the restaurant, an apocalyptic moon lit the marsh in a subtly shaded caricature of daylight. I'd never seen a moon so huge. Maybe the full moon had brought Mark an emergency room full of new babies and knifing victims.

My headlights picked out the unpaved road, running along a dike built across the marsh. The moon picked out the sea of grass on either side, waving almost imperceptibly in unseen currents.

After a few hundred yards, the marsh road dead-ended in another road paved in the dark gray sand and crunched seashells common to "dirt" roads in the Lowcountry. I waited on a couple of cars turning toward the restaurant before I turned right onto the road that ran alongside a creek, hidden from the orange-yellow moonlight by a tunnel of oaks. At night and alone, separated from the day-bright moon, this stretch looked primitive and eerie.

The road crooked slightly as it followed the creek and ahead, under the arching oaks, the hysterical circling of police and ambulance lights startled me, popping through the trees and slicing the blackness into bright, frenetic ribbons. The scene would not have been startling or out of place in Columbia or Charleston. But here a simple car accident looked out of context.

Even out here, the accident had attracted looky-loos, including one heavy-set guy standing too far out in the road, dragging on a cigarette and watching someone at work below the embankment. The sight of guys slouching around hoping for some gore always irritates me beyond words. My mind flashed again to Mark and I felt guilty. He was probably occupied with life-and-death drama like this while I pouted about being stood up.

Doctors may have to stop at accident scenes, but I don't like to be confused with the kind of bottom-feeder lawyers who would. I eased onto the right shoulder of the road, past the wrecker with its winch at the ready, and pointed my headlights toward hard-topped road and Charleston's lights.

CHAPTER TWO

Thursday morning

"I've got an appointment to see a Dr. Blaine Demarcos tomorrow."

Jake Baker raised his sand-colored eyebrows. "So you'll miss jury selection."

"Like you need me to seat a jury in Charleston." I'd practiced law mostly in Columbia. Jake had grown up in Charleston, the son of a trial lawyer.

"You got a point there." Jake sat behind a desk roughly the size of Charleston harbor, drawling every sentence in an accent as thick and sticky as marsh mud. "What can Blaine Demarcos do for us?" His words had no r's, just a soft rise and fall like tide on a sand flat.

"A physician friend of mine recommended him." Some friend. Still no word from Mark Tilman, no apology for standing me up. Nothing. I'd have to call him. He'd probably just forgotten our date, but I was a bit worried. "Demarcos is supposed to be the expert in drug research around here, so maybe he can give some background on the approval process for Uplift, whether there were any problems in its history. If nothing else, it seemed smart to get the local guru locked up before the other side decides it needs him."

"Brief me tomorrow then about anything he can give us on Perforce Pharmaceuticals." He scratched notes with a brilliant gold fountain pen and broad sweeping strokes.

I'd worn a bulky cable sweater and jeans, my hair pulled back in a ponytail. Best to dress comfortably when the meeting might last a while. I settled back into the baby-butt smooth leather chair and changed the subject. "Jake, I need to talk generalities. I need more direction about exactly what you think I can do for you."

He looked up, hunched over his blotter-sized note pad. The wry smile at the corner of his mouth said he had a smutty reply in mind, but he hesitated when he caught my "don't go there" expression.

His chair sighed as he settled back. "Truth be told, Avery, I'm just anxious about this one. I don't like getting a case late like this. I like developing my own case. You'd think it'd be easy, just reviewing what somebody else has done. But you can't do that if the SOB handling it croaked and left precious little to work from. 'Course," he shrugged, "following behind Pete has made me realize what a scant road map I leave when I'm working on a case."

I couldn't imagine stepping into a major trial with just weeks to prepare. Jake had been on the periphery of the case and, with his trial experience, had been the logical choice when Pete James, the lead attorney, died suddenly of an aneurysm. An excessive number of continuances had already been ordered in the case, so the judge, with sound logic from his perspective, had kept the case on the trial docket despite Pete's death. Protesting at this stage was useless, so Jake and Lila were scrambling to get ready. I didn't envy him.

"Avery, you know I want you down here permanently. You'd know I was bullshitting you if I pretended otherwise. You're one helluva trial lawyer. Maybe I'm feeling wobbly in my old age, or maybe it's just getting into this one so late in the game. But I need some other eyes and ears, and yours were the best ones I could think of." He grinned his lopsided grin, his stiff, faded-gold bangs falling over his right eyebrow. With his blue eyes and freckles, he looked the quintessential good-time guy, a bit middle-age paunchy but still ready to hoist a few long necks at an oyster roast or dust off the tux for a spin at Hibernian Hall.

"Okay, so I'm a trial observer. I tell you what I think the jury's hearing, where the holes are, how they're leaning."

"Yep." He nodded, his freckled forehead wrinkled. "You know you can't watch everything, when you're the one on stage."

"That's it?"

"Isn't that enough? You can read the depositions, go through the files, see what we've got. But I really just need you in the courtroom, watching my back, making sure I don't miss anything. Until then, enjoy some good Charleston restaurants and get ready for lots of sitting and watching."

Considering what he was paying me, it hardly seemed enough of an assignment. Maybe, since this case was running on such a tight schedule, he just needed a security blanket.

Jake sighed, frustrated. "I don't know, Avery. We haven't got enough. Somebody like this Dr. Demarcos you found might help . . . dammit. This is what it feels like to be flying blind and I've just never let myself get in this kind of fix."

"Jake, every trial is a play, with a story. Right? So what's the story you want the jury to hear?" I needed to hear him explain how he saw this case.

He rared back in his chair, his combative bulldog expression returning. "Story? Ten people died. Their wives, husbands, kids all have a story. One woman is paralyzed for the rest of her life; she can't even hug her grandkids. Two got shot up so bad they may be wearing their own crap in plastic bags for the rest of their lives. Bullets ripped into the sprinkler system. The medics who came in the loading entrance that day still have nightmares about slipping in the sea of bloody water on the floor. My story is getting them some money so they can afford to take care of themselves. Avery, you haven't had a chance to meet these folks, but they would break your heart. All they did was show up for work. Now they got pain and loss for the rest of their natural-born days. If they live that long."

He was hitting his stride. An evangelist's lilt carried his zeal. I wasn't a jury, and this wasn't an act. He really believed in these clients — and in this case.

I pushed back, challenging him. "What's going to make the jury want to give you a happy ending? You got people hurt. But some juror, missing work at his own job to hear this case, he's thinking, hey, stuff has happened to me, nobody gave me millions. This guy went berserk. Go after him. What's Perforce Pharmaceuticals got to do with your sad story?"

He knew I meant to goad him, but it still made his face flush. "Avery, they make millions pushing pills that people probably don't need. They get to thinking they're the saviors of the human race. Imagine that, getting rich while playing God. They get so rich and so godlike, they think their shit don't stink no more. They're making millions every year on this drug, why not make them pay for the problems their drugs cause?"

"That's not going to be enough—"

"Some poor schmuck pays money for a pill that's supposed to help him but, for him and a few others, it doesn't help, it makes things worse. So he's hurt. Really bad. You tellin' me a jury's not going to hold that company responsible? Perforce made money selling it. They knew, playing the odds, that some people would be hurt. They sure as hell can set some money aside to pay for the harm their wonder drug caused. Maybe they didn't mean to make Joe Vincent Wilma crazy, but they did. And they're in a helluva better position to fix things, financially, than the folks who got shot are."

"You saying the drug made him go crazy? Or that it didn't keep him from going crazy?"

That made him think a minute.

"In this case, maybe a little of both."

"In a case like this, that might not be enough."

"I have the guy who wrote the book — literally — on these types of antidepressants. He argues they're

10

over-prescribed and that they actually make some people suicidal, even violent."

"Okay, that's a start. How does he come across on the stand?"

Jake shrugged. "I didn't take his deposition, haven't even met him yet. He's got great credentials. His book is the one that ignited the national debate on these pills."

"So he'll say Uplift made Joe Vincent Wilma start shooting, unequivocally?"

Jake nodded.

"You know as well as I do South Carolina juries aren't fond of 'stuff happens' cases. They want good guys and bad guys. They want to gallop in on a white horse and punish the bad guys. You're going to have trouble if you just say the drug didn't keep him from shooting, didn't keep him from going crazy. You've got to convince them the drug made him crazy. You know that, Jake."

He stretched back in his chair, studying the hunting prints, the mahogany paneling, the deep bookcases, his lips sucking in and out. After a bit, he leaned slowly forward.

"You're right, dammit. That's the difference between bringing a lawsuit and suing somebody, isn't it? I've got a lawsuit, but am I really suing anybody? We can show this drug makes some people jittery or suicidal. But, frankly, did clear evidence develop in time for the company to pull the drug or strengthen the warning label? I just don't know that we can prove that."

Jake was basing his case on strict liability, a no-fault claim, rather than on negligence, a claim based on fault. Under strict liability, a company could have done everything feasible or imaginable to test its product, to try to make it completely safe. Despite that, no product can ever be completely safe. A predictable but unavoidable number of people will be injured using any product. Strict liability allows the unlucky consumers who draw the short straw to recover for their injuries, while the company spreads the cost of the risk to everyone who buys the product. In theory, spreading the risk makes sense. To hardworking South Carolina jurors, strict liability cases smack of unfairness — making a company pay for something it couldn't fix.

"A jury can't get excited about slamming a company that's trying to do its best."

"Dammit." He thumped his acre-sized desk with his fist. "I know that. I'd a helluva lot rather have a negligence case, where I could point the finger and punish somebody for messing up."

He smacked his palms on the padded arms of his chair. "Problem is, I'm not sure we can get evidence that moves this toward a negligence case. That's what I want — I want to prove Perforce was at fault, that they did something wrong, that they could've done something to stop this before Ray Vincent Wilma went berserk and ruined his life and all those others."

He fiddled with the humidor on his desk. When he spoke again, his voice was quiet. "You put your finger on it. That's why I'm not happy with this case. Avery, you know what I want? I want you to make me happy with it."

"I appreciate your faith. But the only thing that ever makes you happy is somebody writing you a big check."

"You cut me, A'vry." Some of the fire returned to his eyes. "It's not just about money."

"Sure."

He leaned forward, earnest now. "You know better than that. Was your paycheck what made you fight so hard for your clients? Watching you, I never believed that for a minute. Money doesn't breed the kind of passion I saw in you. Money makes a great scorecard, but it never inspires passion."

"Nice cars, the most incredible historic mansion in Charleston, and playthings galore. Jake, you love money."

His tone was serious. "I'd be lying, I like my toys. But they came later. Much later. First, I loved the idea I could help somebody, somebody no one else was willing to fight for, somebody who'd been pummeled by the system. Money just tells me whether I'm winning or losing." He cocked his head, grinning. "I admit, it's more fun now that my side of the scorecard looks really good. Especially the Porsche. But

12

having money also means I can gamble on cases somebody else won't take. This is one of those cases."

"Maybe nobody should take this case. Maybe Perforce doesn't deserve to pay for the acts of a sad, crazy man. You've got another problem, if we dare admit it — some of the people he shot practically asked for it."

His reaction surprised me: he nodded in agreement. "That's going to be a tough thing to handle. The whole culture at that plant begged for a shooting spree. Practically every one of them carried guns to work. They ridiculed and sabotaged each other relentlessly. Threw sucker punches in the break room. Even at their friends. Sheesh. The place was out of control, a cauldron."

"How do you think the jury's going to overlook that? They can't. What about Vincent Wilma himself? The man was a walking wreck, long before he ever heard of Uplift. He was violent. He'd attempted suicide. For years, he'd told his buddies he was going to blow the place up. Heck, he was on disability leave for his nerves when he showed up with his guns."

"But look at it. He'd never done anything before. Never. He talked big, like a lot of inadequate losers. But A'vry, he never did anything. Not until he took Uplift. Not until it carried him over the edge." He emphasized the last words with jabs of his finger.

"True," I said, more to placate him than from any conviction. "But I just don't see the science to support it. This looks to me like a sad 'stuff happens' case."

"Not to me, A'vry." He leaned forward. "I truly believe Ray Vincent Wilma wouldn't have ruined his life and the lives of everyone at the plant that day had it not been for Uplift. I believe that. And my gut tells me Perforce Pharmaceutical knew that was a risk, knew more than we've been able to uncover so far. Certainly more than Pete knew when he filed this suit. We're on the train now, though. Out of time and rolling. That's what frustrates me — every instinct I have says there's more. We just don't have it. And I'm afraid we're out of time to find it."

I felt like a psychiatrist sitting beside a couch, purring *um-hms* in a caring tone while the patient discovered for himself what was wrong. No point reinforcing how out of time he was, so I changed the subject. "Have they made any settlement noises?"

"Nah, not really. They might tomorrow or Monday, though. The judge hasn't really twisted any arms, at least not since I've been involved."

"Any way to bluff a settlement offer out of them? You know what a trial like this costs a company. The attorneys' fees aside — and defense lawyers' paychecks don't care if it's win, lose, or draw — think about the salaries their management people are soaking up. While they're preoccupied with this, they sure aren't developing and selling new drugs."

His smile was rueful. "Would you have settled a case like this, Miz Corporate Defense Attorney? You guys can be talked into letting go of some cash when it's an isolated incident, one without much chance of repetition. But Perforce has other Uplift cases lined up. They know this one looks like the weakest of the bunch. That's why they're holding our feet to the fire on this trial date. They're not afraid of bad publicity from a trial. They're afraid of a settlement that makes them look like easy pickin's the next time there's a suicidal spree killer with a prescription for Uplift."

He was right. I wouldn't offer to settle if I were on the other side, at least not until I'd tested the plaintiffs for a few days in court. "Perhaps," my words ran ahead of what I could deliver, "we can still uncover something helpful. I've got some ideas on the medical research end, checking up on Uplift's FDA approval and use history. A long shot, but . . ." I shrugged. "If nothing else, you can just plan on taking you're A-game into court next week. Sometimes David pops the giant in just the right spot."

"That's encouraging, A'vry. Very encouraging." Jake sighed, long and lugubrious, and checked the Waterford crystal clock on his wall. "Lila ought to be here any minute. We're going over the jury pool, see what she's got on those good souls. Did you look the list over? Know anybody?"

"Nope. Not one." I certainly didn't plan to stay around and share Jake's attention with Lila James. Her claws come out and she spends too much energy trying to keep Jake cornered and away from any interloper. Way too much energy. "My time is better spent reading files."

He nodded, studying his notes. "There was something else. Oh, their experts. Do you have a list?" He was back to business, no longer introspective.

"I haven't seen theirs, and I don't have a complete list of your witnesses."

"I thought I'd asked Lila to get you that already." His tone said he thought he'd forgotten something. My experience said he hadn't forgotten — and neither had Lila.

He pushed a sheet of paper across to me. "Our main expert seldom agrees to testify, so he won't come across looking like a hired gun. He's written books deriding psychiatric drugs and medical establishment approaches to mental illness, depression in particular. I'm also planning to use Perforce's own people as my witnesses. Radical, I know . . ."

I tried to read and listen. Then I didn't hear him anymore, transfixed on one name. Dr. Langley Hilliard.

"They're using Langley Hilliard?"

Something in my tone clued him in. I could almost see the pieces trickle into place in his brain.

"Oh, God. Avery."

Langley Hilliard had been my expert witness and the reason I'd left Charleston three months earlier, out of a job and wondering if "want fries with that" was in my future. Now here the SOB was again.

"Is this Lila's idea of a joke?" I knew my face was red, and my eyes burned. The ice in my voice wasn't lost on Jake.

"Avery. I thought you knew he was involved."

"She thinks it's funny to blindside me with that pompous, self-serving asshole? Some warped sense of fun."

"Avery, I swear. I thought you knew. I certainly didn't expect it to still be this raw with you. You really need to get a grip."

"Raw?" The word rolled up out of my throat, my voice husky. If Jake had known me well, he'd have known to be afraid. "Jake, the son of a bitch is a liar. He lies under oath. Anything to win. That's the kind of case you like? Then you shouldn't have bothered calling me." I was out of my chair and pacing.

"Avery." Jake seemed to think repeating my name and patting the air with his hands would somehow cool me off. "I don't know what happened with you and Hilliard last October, but I've been in cases with him before. He's a bit old-fashioned, with a doctors-are-god complex, but I've not had any problem with him."

"You can't trust him, Jake. He's slick and he's believable. And he's a dammed liar." I punched the last word out with venom.

"A'vry." Jake moved back to using a placating drawl. "That's exactly why I needed you. You know this medical mumbo jumbo backwards and forwards. You'll be able to sniff it out, if Hilliard or anybody else stretches anything. They're using Hilliard as an expert on research protocols. If anybody can give me what I need to break him down, it's you."

"So you did set me up. Jake, you sorry son of a bitch."

"You gotta clear your head, honey. I didn't mean to surprise you with this. Why the hell would I do that? That'd be suicide. I thought you knew, figured you'd seen his name on a witness list, read his deposition, that Lila had briefed you. Something."

"Lila—"

He cut me off. "Don't bother goin' there, either. We've both been running like something crazy, trying to get ready for this trial. We've got loose ends flapping around all over the place. Hell, you haven't even had time to read through half the pre-trial discovery. So get off your conspiracy pony and decide whether you can handle being in the same court-room with Hilliard again or whether you're going to slink off with your tail between your legs."

Damn him, his careful aim pricked my righteous indignation in just the right spot — my stubborn refusal to back down from a fight. I slid back into my chair, my jaw muscles still knotted.

"Jake, you're still a son of a bitch." But he was right. Hilliard was on the other side. If he tried some of his slimy slip-and-slide, we'd make sure the jury spotted the slug-trail.

Jake visibly relaxed. "A'vry, we gotta keep some perspective on this. We can't let prejudices or grudges cloud our judgment, can we?"

We?

"You have a copy of his deposition I can take with me? I'd like to read it tonight, before I see Demarcos tomorrow morning."

"Sure. We keep all that in the storage room, next to the file cabinets you've been rummaging through. The depositions are in notebooks, alphabetical by last name."

"Any other surprises before I take my homework assignments and go?"

"Now, how the hell am I supposed to know what's going to set you off the next time?" He gave me an impish smile.

"Just lie to me. That'll do it every time."

"I consider myself warned."

My stomach was giving me that little butterfly-nervous feeling I get when I'm heading into something I should avoid. I hadn't been sure about the wisdom of working on this case. After all, can a defense attorney change her stripes? Even the scant few criminal cases I'd been involved with *pro bono* or while clerking had been on the defense side. Being the pursuer was an unnatural act, maybe a switch I couldn't make. Plaintiffs' lawyers tend to be renegades. I'd seen only a few driven by principle. Most seemed driven by nothing but the next payment on their sports cars.

Jake Baker did a good job talking the passion, but I hadn't been able to watch him close up for long enough to tell what he was made of, how much of it was principle. This trial would tell me. It would also tell me whether moving from one side of the courtroom to the other was an uncrossable divide.

Jake led the way down the hall. My feet sank into the thick carpeting, the gilt-framed artwork closed the halls in on us. The utilitarian workroom was hidden from clients and lined with binder-filled shelves and steel filing cabinets. "Here's Hilliard's deposition. It's a big one. Here's a couple of others that cover some of the same points. These witnesses won't come up until later in the case, so we've got some time to develop — hell, what am I saying? We don't have time for anything." He smoothed the crown of his wiry gold hair.

I couldn't offer any consolation. My own doubts — about his case and my decision to stay involved — battled in my head.

"Can you manage all that?" He indicated the stack of binders I balanced on my hip.

"Sure. It's a short walk back to the inn."

"Your room okay?" He walked me into his lobby, luscious with antiques at whose price tags I could only guess.

"It's the honeymoon suite at Two Meeting Street, one of the most romantic bed chambers in Charleston. How could it be anything but perfect?"

"Well, when you turned down my offer, chaste and proper though it was, to stay at my place, it was the least I could do. Though you don't know, you might have found my place even more romantic."

"Jake, romantic ain't what you're offering." Best to keep it light and playful.

"You cut me, A'vry." He placed his right hand on his heart, pledging allegiance as he held open the massive oak front door for me.

Right on cue, Lila arrived on the sidewalk outside the front entry, glaring daggers at me as she climbed the stone steps toward us.

"I'll leave you two in charge." I smiled in Lila's direction. "I have a little beach reading to get through here."

Lila sailed through the door as Jake held it, claiming possession of the premises without so much as a nod.

CHAPTER THREE

Thursday morning

Clutching three large deposition binders to my chest, I carefully picked my way down the uneven granite blocks that served as Jake Baker's front steps. Like most else in Charleston, the steps were canted, a bit off center. A weathered brass boot scrape stood conveniently beside the steps, though muddy boots had gone the way of horses, highwaymen, and streets paved with ships' ballast. Charleston clings to what past it can.

Along Broad Street, buildings leaned this way and that, a fun-house mirror effect created by time, earthquake, fire, and hurricane. As I approached the massive white church at the corner of Meeting Street, bells began chiming in the countless other churches scattered over the small peninsula that held Charleston.

I always marvel at the sense of history that every breath of air seems to carry here. Charleston is surrounded by wild marshlands, gray beaches, and shanty towns which breed a sense of separateness. And Charlestonians wear that separateness proudly. They fought two wars here over pride and separateness, and a lot of them would secede again, given half a provocation, to maintain their identity and independence. Outsiders miss the point if they only focus on the blot of slavery. You don't have to go back far into the gene pool to find Southerners' war-like border Scots kin, and Southerners will still fight to be left the hell alone.

Bulky tree roots made the narrow, uneven sidewalks difficult to navigate. The notebooks were unwieldy to carry, but the startlingly crisp blue sky made the walk worth the struggle.

Two Meeting Street Inn sat at White Point Garden, right on the Battery, a most prestigious address. The harbor lay on the other side of the sea wall, and live oaks sheltered the park, surrounded by massive mansions built with the riches a centuries-old port brought.

The low-hanging branches in White Point Garden always remind me of what the tour books don't tell. Before the area was reclaimed from the bottom of Charleston Harbor, it had been a stinking, slimy mud flat where the citizenry hung pirates, then buried them in the muck, a reminder to anyone else who would go astray. But stray they did. Genteel Charleston boasted at least two female pirates — I'd been thrilled to learn that in elementary school.

Charleston had been a wide-open seaport town, filled with drunken revelry and debauchery. Even in Prohibition, thanks to an understanding mayor and police force, hidden saloons known as "blind tigers" operated freely. Though Charleston didn't have the party-hearty reputation of its southern sister, Savannah — after all, the Catholics settled Savannah, not dour Huguenots and Presbyterians — it still boasted a lively bar district, thanks to the college students and tourists.

On this tree-shaded street under the blindingly blue sky, those secrets and evils and revelries were far distant in time. Here, I was surrounded by the serene image, the chimera that people believed was Charleston.

I loved believing it, too, even when a dank, musty odor wafted up to street level from underneath a house. The myth was a tantalizing image to maintain.

Balancing the notebooks on one hip, I struggled with the inn's side gate, then took time to savor the smooth perfection of the fluted tulip that supported the second-floor bay window. How many times had I strolled past and thought, what a magical place to stay. And here I was, with Jake Baker footing the bill. Of course, my fantasy had included some dashing prince with whom to share the room. That piece was missing, for sure.

In my room upstairs, I dumped the notebooks on the freshly made counterpane and was mentally running down a list of phone calls I needed to make when my cell phone buzzed in my shoulder bag.

"Avery, doesn't South Carolina have a stalking law?"

"Hi, Mom. Who's stalking you?" With Mom, nothing would be a surprise.

"Not me, goose. Miranda. Miranda Cole. You probably don't know her, she's only fifteen."

"She's being stalked?" The only folks less surprising than my mother are her projects.

"I guess so. I mean, this man is calling her, parking outside her house — her mama's house, anyway — at all hours of the day and night, sending her notes, waiting for her outside the high school. Her mama's scared to death."

"Sounds like stalking, all right. Who is this guy?" I plopped down in one of the wing-back chairs.

"Some goober old enough to be — well, old enough to know better. She met him at the Burger Hut. She's part of that teen after-school employment project. He's about twenty-three and just moved to Camden County a few months ago from somewhere up the mountain. Can you believe it? He insists after only a few weeks that he's got the true love for Miranda." The way she said *true love* gave every indication she either doubted the existence of true love entirely — or entirely doubted the goober's capacity to comprehend abstract terms.

"Of course Miranda's got no daddy in sight. Miranda and her mama live over at the trailer park. Miranda's already developed way past the point where she'll ever be a ballerina."

I never bother to ask any more how my mother finds these people. They can be anybody from white trash to a state senator's son to a hitchhiker she's picked up. She finds them, fixes them, witnesses to them, and — her true gift — knows when to set them on their own. Daddy long ago gave up lecturing her about how she was going to be found dead in a ditch someday. Some folks have a gift for the fringe element, and you just gotta know your gifts.

"—she's been sashaying around like a cat in heat for years now, apparently. Trouble is, this time she's attracted more than she can handle. So. What can we do?"

I stood up to pace. I think better that way. "Call the county solicitor's office." No doubt some assistant solicitor, fresh out of school, would be given the case. "You can also help Miranda's mama swear out a restraining order, unless you think that might make him violent. If he's not completely unhinged, a restraining order should make him back off."

"When you comin' home?" Mom asked.

"I don't know." I checked myself in the mirror, pulling a stray red-gold hair off my lapel. Winter in the mountains would melt away very soon, with spring the harbinger of summering Northerners and tourists. "Soon, Mom. This shouldn't run more than two or three weeks."

She promised to keep me posted about Miranda and the goober. One of these days, one of us should write a book.

I'd just fingered the off button when the phone buzzed again. I always feel a wave of frustration at the intrusion of a phone call, which meant a real love-hate relationship with cell phones. I was glad, though, to hear my younger sister's voice.

"Avery," Lydia drawled.

"What's up?" I checked my watch. "I thought you'd be doing your civic duty somewhere."

"Playin' hooky. Not feeling too well today."

"That cyst acting up again?"

"Afraid so. Nasty little thing really hurts."

Lydia had recently been plagued by ovarian cysts, benign but extremely painful at times.

"What's the doctor say?"

"What do they ever say? My ob-gyn said he'd gotten word about some study they're doing out of Charleston, something new. But I don't know."

Small world. I start reading up on drug testing and suddenly it's everywhere. Like somebody saying, "Look for the color red," and there it is, everywhere you look. Is there a name for that?

"Why don't you give it a try? They're using new drugs and new delivery mechanisms for all kinds of things. This might be the very thing you need."

"I don't know." Her words stretched thoughtfully.

"Almost anything would be better than spending a couple of weeks a month doubled over in pain."

"I asked him about surgical alternatives. You know, with all the publicity about the long-term effects of hormones, that might be best."

"So you're serious about not having any more kids?" I didn't want to talk about the risks of surgery. I've spent too much time reviewing medical records where something went wrong. I sometimes have to bite my tongue.

"Look who's asking, Little Miss Sworn Off Men," she fired back. "You even dating anybody? Valentine's coming, you know."

"Whoa, Nellie. Just asked. I'm perfectly delighted with the niece I already have." *And my love life isn't the topic of this conversation.* "How is that precocious little Emma of mine?"

"Wondering when her Aunt Bree's coming home. We thought you were here to stay. Then we look up and you're gone again."

"You knew my coming back to Dacus was temporary." I sounded defensive, even to my ears. "Just exploring my options. Trial lawyers don't exactly have a rich client list in Dacus."

"But you can do other things. There's lots of other kinds of lawyers here. You could even teach at the university. I'm sure Frank could get you a job. Maybe just part time, to see if you liked it."

"Whoa again." I had to chuckle. "Truce. I won't do your family planning for you and you don't do my career planning, okay?"

She paused. "We just miss you. It was nice having you back. It was like — we had a chance to get to know each other again. You know what I mean? As adults. Then you were gone again. And Emma really misses you."

"I miss her too." An actual lump caught in my throat. I adored that strange little kid, with her uncanny observations on life and her endless questions. "This case is probably going to convince me I'm not cut out to be a plaintiff's lawyer. It's a whole 'nother world, I can tell you that. I should be back in Dacus before the dogwoods bud." I still wasn't quite sure how long I'd stay, though.

A hesitant knock at the door of my room interrupted. "Wait a sec, Lydia." I opened the door.

"Miz Andrews. I'm sorry to bother you, but there's a gentleman downstairs who says he needs to speak with you." The inn doesn't have room phones, which adds greatly to its charm.

"I heard," Lydia said. "Talk to you later."

"He's downstairs on the porch. He phoned earlier, when you were out."

"Thanks."

I followed her down the stairs, then went through the parlor to the wide, shady front porch. A barrel-chested man with close-cropped white-blond hair stood at attention beside one of the porch columns, almost blocking the view of the massive oak in the front yard.

"Avery Andrews." From him, it wasn't a question but a statement expecting confirmation.

I craned my neck to look up, and I must have nodded. He reached inside his jacket, straining the shoulder seams of his polyester suit coat. "I'm Casper Kirkland." He flashed a badge but no smile. "Do you know a young man named Mark Tilman?"

24

CHAPTER FOUR

Thursday afternoon

When Casper Kirkland asked if I knew Mark Tilman, surprise — and then a shot of worry — must have crossed my
face. "Yes, I do. What—"

He motioned to a couple of porch rockers. I kept
watching his face as I accepted his unspoken invitation. The
wooden rocker and floorboards creaked under his weight as
he sat down.

"He had your name, phone number, and this address in
his wallet. His father said you might be able to tell us more
about his movements here in Charleston."

"Y-yes." Suddenly the porch felt chilly, even with the
early afternoon sun coming through the tree branches. "We
were supposed to meet for dinner last night, but he never
came."

"He was in a car accident. At least, we believe it was
Mark Tilman. A wallet with his ID was found a distance
away. With no money. The car was his and the body fits the
description we have, but we'd like confirmation."

I clamped my jaw shut to keep my teeth from chattering. My great-aunt Letha says the deepest grief grows in the

soil of deepest guilt. My anger and frustration at Mark for not showing up for supper choked my memory. Dear Lord.

"Where was — when—" I tried to ask, hating that I must look like any other twitter-headed female faced with bad news. I'd be damned if I'd cry.

He paused a beat too long before answering. "His car ran off the road into a tidal creek across the Ashley River. Toward Folly Beach."

He kindly kept talking, ignoring how I bit my bottom lip.

"We have a few questions about the accident, and we're waiting on a formal identification of the body." He paused again. "Mr. Tilman wondered if you'd be willing to make the ID."

I couldn't trust myself to speak, so I nodded. Mark's brother Gregg had moved to California after college, and it would be hard for Mr. Tilman to leave his invalid wife for the five-hour drive from Dacus for that sad task.

"Can you come now?"

Casper Kirkland's manner was exceptionally polite but matter-of-fact. He had a lot of things to do today, I was sure, and this wasn't his first dead body. I went upstairs to get my purse, buried under the avalanche of binders on my bed.

The air in his car was comfortingly hot from the sun. If anyone asked me to show the way, I couldn't repeat the route that led us from the inn to the dingy viewing room.

They had Mark laid out, visible through a curtained window that struck me incongruously like an aquarium. The sheet was folded back to show only his head. His nose looked swollen and bruised, but it was Mark, even though his resemblance to Gregg was gone.

The grief that enveloped me was partly selfish mourning for my own mortality, mixed with the inevitable guilt Aunt Letha warns against. The questions that gnawed at me were selfish. I wanted to know what had happened to bring this shell of Mark here. I wanted to be able to tell myself I couldn't have done anything to help him while I had sipped she-crab soup and drummed my fingers on the table. Of course I couldn't have done anything. But, for my own peace of mind, I needed somebody to tell me so.

I felt Casper Kirkland staring at me as I signed a form he proffered on a clipboard. I met his gaze. "What happened — to Mark?"

He stared a moment more. "You have time for me to make a little detour on the way back? I wanted to stop by the marsh creek. No harm in you seeing for yourself."

No way this cop could read my mind, but maybe my morbid, guilty curiosity would get some relief. "Certainly."

As we drove across the new bridge, which soared in an arc over the Ashley River, Casper started chatting about Charleston weather, Charleston crooks, and what his ex-wife had thought about him being a cop. He brought her up, so it must still be a fresh wound. Casper — Cas for short, and there was nothing ghost-like and something only mildly friendly about him — didn't look like he carried any scars. It's the ones who carry them deep I'm most wary of.

He kept me distracted until we turned off the main road, the whish of the tires on the sandy road noticeable as the car crept along. We came upon the break in the sea grape suddenly. Once he'd pointed out the crumpled undergrowth, it wasn't hard to see.

"His car left the road there." The road curved slightly, following a tiny wobble in the creek below. The bank of the creek fell away steeply under the roots of the oaks that sheltered the road, probably a ten-foot drop from the road to the water.

"He missed that little curve in the road and ran off here."

Trying to picture it in my mind brought back the flashing lights of emergency vehicles from last night.

I'd driven right by. I bit my lip in the same place where I'd raised a welt on it earlier. I'd driven right by, picking out the track between the overhanging oak trees with my headlights, not wanting to look too closely. Not wanting to be a looky-loo or an ambulance chaser. I'd driven right by.

Cas turned off the engine, parking with the right tires off the road. We hadn't passed a single car, and I didn't know of anything else along this road except the stilt restaurant and endless grassy marsh.

"Up to a closer look?"

Not quite trusting my voice, I shrugged and heaved open the door of the county-issue Ford. We half-slid down the bank to the narrow shoal of sand that sided the creek. Gouges where Mark's car had landed were clearly visible along the sand and into the water. I turned to study the creek bank and the thick undergrowth.

Cas read my mind. "Apparently the car was airborne for a short distance, going fast enough to propel itself into the water. So the bank and the sand didn't slow him down much."

He tucked his shirt into his waistband where it had ridden up during his downhill slide. "He had a bloody nose, probably from hitting the steering wheel. In all likelihood, he was stunned or even unconscious from the impact."

Cas studied me, probably to see how I took the graphic details. I didn't tell him he hadn't seen graphic details until he'd watched C-section videotapes, which is how I'd spent some afternoons in my previous life.

I stared at the tire marks still visible underneath the slow water at the creek's edge. The car must have landed hard.

"But that's not what killed him," I said.

His expression registered no surprise at my stab in the dark. Cas Kirkland wasn't telling me everything. With his hands in his pockets, he seemed falsely relaxed, waiting for me to tell him something. He kept watching my face intently with his practiced manner and his bald-looking lashless blue eyes.

He wanted me to rush in to fill the silence with chatter, but I recognized the technique. I ask questions for a living, too. I waited him out.

Finally he answered. "All I can say at this point is we still have some questions. Looks like we're going to have to wait until the autopsy before we know any more."

I stared across the narrow creek at the shale bank on the other side. The plant growth was thicker there, hanging out over the creek in spots. I pretended not to notice Cas staring at me, but his stare was beginning to bug me.

"How well did you know Mark Tilman?"

I studied the chest-high and impenetrable marsh grass farther down and across the creek. "Not well at all. We're from the same hometown. I knew his brother. Mark found out I was in Charleston and came by my office, said he wanted to talk. Suggested we meet for supper, at the restaurant down the road."

"Who picked the restaurant?"

"He did. He said it was a local favorite, easier to get into than some of the downtown restaurants. And closer to his clinic on the island."

"That where he worked?"

"At least yesterday afternoon. I don't know much about his schedule. I believe medical residents service the clinics on a couple of the islands around here."

"What'd he want to talk about?"

"I don't know that either." I turned to face him.

"Any guess?"

"Nope."

He looked like he was having trouble believing that, but he wasn't ready to make me angry. That might come later.

He paused. "Know anyone who would wish him harm?"

That took me by surprise. "Officer Kirkland, I don't believe you told me what department you're with."

He paused. He had a measured, almost syncopated way of starting his sentences. "It's Detective Kirkland. Crimes Against Persons."

"So routine traffic accidents aren't your usual assignment."

"No." The almost imperceptible crinkle at the corner of his mouth indicated how much he enjoyed playing that ace.

Standing in the sun with the water whispering past, I felt sick at my stomach. "I wish I could help you." I put aside my game-playing attitude. This wasn't a game and it wasn't fun anymore. "I barely knew Mark when he was a kid. The only thing I know about his life now is that he's a medical resident. He also had a Ph.D. in some science field. He didn't show up for dinner last night. And—" I almost said *and I drove right by here last night, past where he was dead.*

"And he wanted to talk to you." Kirkland's tone gave it more meaning than it probably deserved.

"It could have been anything. He might just have been a lonely guy away from home, glad to see a familiar face." This time, I paused. "What makes you think it was something other than an accident?"

He shrugged. "We just have some unanswered questions. That's all." He stared down at the tire marks. The creek's edges were slow-moving, but another tide would carry away all evidence of the car's landing. The sea grape bushes would soon repair the breach. Then no one would be able to spot this place, just driving by.

"Detective Kirkland, something caused you to be called in. I think you owe me at least a little explanation." The frustration in my voice had to do with my anger and guilt, but he couldn't know that.

Cops collect information. They don't give it out, unless it'll help them some way. And unless it won't cost them anything. His eyelids hooded his eyes as he weighed his options, then he said, "He was robbed. His wallet held no cash. The credit cards were tossed beside the creek." The detective studied my face as he dropped his last tidbit: "We don't know if he was dead at the time of the robbery."

I'm sure I looked shocked. I'd heard stories — accident victims in these swamps robbed and left to die, human vultures coming well in advance of any natural scavengers. Buzzards don't try to save their victims, but they usually have decency enough to wait — albeit anxiously — off to the side until their meal is ready. Not so with some of the things that crawl out of these swamps on two legs.

I crossed my arms but said nothing.

He finally said, "Let me take you back to town." He took me by the elbow and heaved me up the embankment to the car.

We drove in silence to the inn at Two Meeting Street. Even though the drive took only twenty minutes, the scenery flashing past — wild marsh, tidal river, fast food, slums, antebellum homes, bustling businesses, tourists — was a world away from that desolate place full of slow water and sawgrass.

Cas dropped me off on the sidewalk and thanked me before pulling off in his dusty sedan.

As I stepped through the opening in the hedge sheltering the stately white house from the street, my cell phone buzzed. I always jump, startled, when that happens, especially when I've wandered off deep in thought.

I didn't recognize the voice. "Avery? Avery Andrews? I — uh — I need to talk to you? About Mark?" His voice rose at the end of each sentence, as if he were asking permission. "This is his father, Martin. Tilman."

"Mr. Tilman." *Oh, Lord. What could I say?* "I'm so sorry about Mark."

"Thank — you."

Please don't let him start crying.

"Did — did you see Mark? Did that policeman . . ."

"Yes, Mr. Tilman. I'm so sorry."

Silence. Then, "Did you talk to Mark? Before?"

"Only briefly, yesterday afternoon. We were to meet for dinner last night, but . . ."

Another awkward pause. If this was awkward for me, think what it must be for him.

"Avery, did he tell you — anything? About—"

"We really didn't talk long."

"He needed to talk to you. To talk to somebody. He didn't tell me much. Just that there was something happening at his work that he was very concerned about and he didn't know who to talk to. I told him your dad said you were in Charleston. I told him it was a sign, that he should talk to you. I told him you'd be just the one, you bein' a lawyer and everything."

And everything, I thought.

"I'm sorry, Mr. Tilman. We never got a chance to talk."

The pause lasted too long. "Avery. I don't know what to do, what to ask." His voice changed. It was quieter, more urgent. "Avery, he was scared. And angry. And — I don't know. I was hoping . . . Can you, is there anything you can do to find out? It doesn't seem right, that he was so worried and upset and now he's dead. Something's just not right. Can you . . . ?"

"Mr. Tilman, you know if there was anything I could do, I'd do it in a minute. I'm just not sure there is anything. I'm so sorry."

"I know. I truly appreciate you going to see — you know. It would've been hard to get down there. Mark's mama's not well, you know. We have to wait the funeral. On the autopsy. It's tearing Mark's mama up."

I tried to make appropriate soothing sounds. Mrs. Tilman was confined to a wheelchair, something degenerative. She'd first been diagnosed when Gregg and I were in high school.

"Avery, something scared him. I thought it sounded odd at the time, but I'm wondering now if he wasn't — if somebody . . ." He couldn't finish the sentence.

I couldn't leap in with any soothing sounds on that one, not after my ride with Casper Kirkland of the Crimes Against Persons division.

"I'm sure Detective Kirkland and the police will cover everything. I've met him and he seems quite competent."

"Avery, I know from my insurance work that cops get busy. Whatever you could do to keep an eye on things, we'd appreciate. This is tearing his mama up."

Apparently Mr. Tilman best expressed grief through his wife.

"Avery, if you could just talk to some folks he knew, find out what was wrong. I'd be happy to pay you. Whatever the charge. I'll sign a contract. You can fax one to the office. Let me give you the number."

I dutifully listened as he gave me the fax number at his insurance office, though I had no intention of sending him a contract.

"Mr. Tilman—"

"His apartment's near Barnard Medical." He gave me the address. "Oh, and Ginnie just reminded me. Mark had a girlfriend, but we have no idea how to get in touch with her, to let her know what's happened. Sanda MacKay. I'm not sure how to spell her last name, but it's Sanda. S-a-n-d-a. We don't know much about her. She's not been here to visit or anything. I think she's an artist."

Denial is a natural part of the grief process. No amount of soothing sounds on my part would make Mr. Tilman admit to himself that Mark had driven off the road and been killed in a car accident. A simple, stupid, lonely car accident.

Telling Mr. Tilman about the gruesome robbery wouldn't help matters. So I wrote down Sanda MacKay's name and promised to stay in touch. His thank-you sounded lighter, as if he felt some relief.

I called directory assistance and got the number for S. MacKay. I'm amazed how well an initial works to hide your identity. I'd once had a nutty client who kept pestering the office for my home phone number. The same nut never once tried to call the A. Andrews listed in the Columbia phone book.

Sanda's answering machine picked up. "This is Sanda. Leave me a message at the tone." Quick and to the point.

"Sanda — um. This is Avery Andrews. I'm an attorney. Mark Tilman's father—" A clicking sound interrupted. Sanda's machine hadn't given me much time to get my act together.

I called back and talked fast. "Avery again. It's about Mark." I left my cell number and hung up.

While Mr. Tilman and I had talked, I had wandered back through the hedge and across the narrow street to White Point Garden. The only other person sharing the too-shady park was a guy trying to teach his dog to fetch a stick. I crunched across the tabby walk to a wooden bench and plopped down facing the old Fort Sumter Hotel. This wasn't really much of a garden — just giant oaks and bleached, crunchy paths through gray-black sand. Live oaks don't lose their leaves, so the shade was dank this time of year.

I sat staring, without really thinking, letting the wind chill my cheeks and hands. I needed to push this business with Mark aside and get busy. Tomorrow was Friday. We had a trial starting and we were flying by the seat of our pants. But my grief — or was it guilt? — numbed my pre-trial anxiety.

One small step at a time. Come on, Avery. Focus. I still held my cell phone, so I dialed Melvin Bertram's number in Dacus.

CHAPTER FIVE

Thursday afternoon

Melvin Bertram's radio announcer voice answered the phone.

"Melvin! It's Avery. How's our soon-to-be abode?"

"Fine." He chuckled. "How nice of you to call and check on your house. Or your office. Whichever."

Melvin was pressuring me to rent the other half of the Victorian where he was setting up his office. He'd made up his mind it was a good move for me, even if I hadn't. "I need a favor."

"Another fine, thoughtful reason for calling."

"Okay, okay. I'm shameless. I admit it. But I call to pay homage to the fount of all knowledge, oh most wise financial guru."

"Uh-oh. What now?"

"Perforce Pharmaceuticals and an antidepressant called Uplift. What can you tell me about them? I mean juicy stuff. Inside poop."

"That's a technical legal term, I presume. Poop. What kind of poop?"

I could picture him sitting at his massive mahogany desk, every silver-tinged sandy hair in place. Probably wearing a light wool sweater and the heat turned down to fridge degrees.

Melvin Bertram had left Dacus fifteen years earlier as an accountant suspected by many of having killed his wife. He'd returned as a successful financial adviser and had decided to stay and run his investment business from Dacus. His clients lived all over the country, so it didn't really matter where he lived, as long as he had internet access and could get to an airport.

"Tell me what makes Perforce and the people who run it tick. Are they vulnerable? If so, where? What do they believe in? Why do they think they're in business? Any whiff of scandal? Personal or corporate. You know, the usual stuff."

"The usual stuff. You realize that's why polite society thinks you trial lawyers are low-lifes, scavenging around for *stuff*."

"Until they need us to fish them out of trouble or fight to protect them. So what do you know? What can you find out?"

"I'm seeing — or, rather, hearing you in a whole new light."

"I doubt you can 'hear' me in a 'new light.' But anyway . . ."

"I've only dabbled on the edges of some biotech venture capital projects, so I don't know how much help I'll be."

Truthfully, I don't understand much of what Melvin does. I just know it involves money, managing it and investing it for himself and for others. He throws the word "venture capital" around a lot, and he'd explained it meant getting people who had money together with people who had good ideas.

"Guess you know all eyes are trained on your trial," he said. "At least all drug company analysts' eyes. Apparently any time a depressed person taking Uplift decided to kill himself or someone else, a lawyer stood ready to explain that Uplift made him do it. Yours is the first case scheduled for trial. The analysts are waiting to see if the great Jake Baker can take down Perforce in this case, because if he can, other lawyers will be on Perforce like ants on picnic potato salad."

"The lawsuit's not that simple, you know." I didn't miss the business-guy disdain for lawyers in his tone.

"To an investment analyst, it's exactly that simple."

I'd known plaintiffs' lawyers with cases lined up or already filed would be watching this case, but hearing Melvin talk about its national scope made it feel more urgent.

"Perforce will give this one all they've got," Melvin said. "They'll have to. They want it to be the last Uplift case, or at least so decisive that all the smart lawyers leave and they can pick the dumb ones off at their leisure."

Perforce losing the suit — or even quietly settling it for some undisclosed amount — would be blood on the waters for lawyers already sharking around a potentially big drug liability lawsuit. So we had a real fight on our hands. A trial is always a fight, but, somehow, I'd never had one play out on a stage with a national audience watching. Or at least I hadn't been aware of it. Maybe that was the difference with medical malpractice cases — one little doctor and one little patient. The doctor always thinks everybody in the world knows he's being sued, but few people really pay any attention or, if he's a good doctor, few change their opinion of him. But a big drug company with millions of dollars at stake — and lawyers with millions in their sights? Different equation.

"I can pull the basic information on Perforce," Melvin said. "How much Perforce is worth, its structure, product lines, distribution. That's encyclopedia entry stuff. Sounds, though, like you want gossip column material."

"I don't know that I'd characterize it like that, but what would you say to me if you introduced me to the CEO or the head research scientist at a cocktail party? Or, better still, what would you whisper in my ear while we stood near the French doors, what juicy bits would you share?"

Melvin laughed out loud. "That, Avery, is what makes you my idea of a truly exquisite trial lawyer. I've got a couple of places I can look, a couple of phone calls I can make. But those will have to wait until tomorrow." "Tomorrow will be great. I'll call you late morning. Or you can call my cell."

"I thought your trial started tomorrow."

"Only the jury selection. Jake and his associate will handle that since I really don't know a soul down here. Meanwhile, I'm playing catch-up, seeing if I can shake loose anything Jake hasn't already found." I sighed. "I really hate feeling this . . . behind on everything."

"You're just anxious because you entered the game late and you don't have everything under control yet. You will — you don't know any other way to attack something." His voice was soothing — and reassuringly sincere.

"Thanks for the vote of confidence. I feel under the gun on this one. Or, more accurately, like I've been shot out the end of a gun, flying fast and out of control."

"We'll see if we can't get you a stack of information to pad your landing."

"Thanks. Made any progress on the house this week?"

"Molasses slow. They came to repair all the screens and broken windowpanes. It took them two days and they didn't do nearly the job you did on your lake cabin."

"You flatter me, hoping I'll be cheap labor for you."

He chuckled. "No, I just want to tell people 'that's my lawyer up there' when they stroll past and ask who's patching my roof." He paused. "On second thought, I'd best not be mentioning lawyers to anyone here in Dacus. That'd lead to one of those awkward silences where they start remembering I was almost charged with murder. Then they start wondering if I know that's what they're thinking, and we just stand there shuffling our feet and clearing our throats."

"Melvin, for Pete's sake. Your imagination runs overtime. If I didn't know better, I'd think you had a guilty conscience."

But I did know better. I'd heard the real murderer confess to killing Melvin's wife. I shivered at the memory and got up from the park bench where I'd taken roost to walk toward the seawall and some sunlight.

"Yeah. Well, I seem to be constantly second-guessing my decision to move back here. Not sure it was a good idea, all things considered."

"Melvin! That's not the song you were singing last week. Then, it was 'Avery, you gotta stay here in Dacus. You gotta open your office next to mine. You should rent the upstairs apartment. You gotta hurry and make up your mind.' Now this?"

"Don't worry. You could still stay here, open your office here. I'd still give you a great price. This place needs to be fixed up and it needs to be used again. Houses can't stay empty. It's not good for them. I'm just getting cold feet. I'm not sure Dacus is a good choice for me, not after all the years of rumor and suspicion. Plenty of people still think I did it, or did something. I'm beginning to think you can't change the spots other people choose to see."

"Don't jump into any decisions. Promise me you'll wait? Okay?"

"I'm not doing anything rash, at least not this afternoon."

"Talk to you tomorrow?"

"Sure thing. Good luck, Avery. I'll see what I can dig up for you."

I clipped the phone back on my belt and leaned against the Battery railing. Winter sun glinted off the gray water. The humid haze that thickens the air most of the year was gone, and Fort Sumter was clear and solid at the mouth of the bay, without its usual surreal haziness.

The folks who watched from their balconies as the first shots of the Civil War were fired on Yankee-held Fort Sumter had lived in these houses directly on the water. It seems odd sometimes that something more than a hundred years' distance in time can still be so real and powerful. Odd, I suppose, until you listen to the Irish talk about the English. Wars fought on your own turf leave deep scars. I haven't met a Northerner yet who understood that.

Why was I trying to talk Melvin out of leaving Dacus? If he decided to leave, it would certainly take the pressure off me. Well, some of the pressure. I'd still have my family urging me to move back permanently. But Melvin's cozy offer of a ready-made office and living quarters in easy walking distance of the courthouse had made me feel trapped. Without that option, it would be easier to make excuses to my family. So why was I lecturing Melvin about staying?

I crunched back across the tabby-paved walk and darted across the street in front of a horse-drawn tour carriage, its passengers with blankets tucked over their knees.

"That's my room, the one with the second-floor bay window," I wanted to tell them as the tour guide pointed out Two Meeting Street.

Back in my room, I decided against sitting at the fragile little writing desk and carried the binders outside to the covered porch. I had it to myself — and for good reason. It felt a bit nippy in the shade.

I read for a while. Hilliard's answers to the defense lawyer's questions prompted questions I wanted to ask Dr. Demarcos tomorrow morning. I was used to immersing myself in a topic, usually medical, and becoming fluent quickly. But I had never had to do it this quickly. I wasn't sure if the slight panic was giving me an edge or whether it would overtake and paralyze me.

I kept reading and jotting notes, trying not to dwell on the difficulties, until my growling stomach overtook me. For good reason. I'd read for several hours and let lunchtime slip into early afternoon.

If I hurried, I could make it to Jestine's, a several-block hike north on Meeting Street. I didn't want to fool with navigating the narrow streets in my Mustang, trying to find a parking place, so I retraced my steps back toward Broad Street and past the now-busy Market Street area. Contrary to tourist — and maybe some tour guide — misinformation, the imposing Public Market with its double-wrap staircase to the second floor had never been a slave market. It had been the nineteenth-century equivalent of what it was now — a place to gather, buy food, drink, and miscellany. The smelly meat stalls were long gone, though, replaced by Ben and Jerry's, specialty spices, and Confederate memorabilia shops.

Walking five blocks more, I found Jestine's open and a table by the window. Thank goodness. I'd had a momentary panic that it might be closed for the afternoon. I'd carried a folder full of deposition pages to read, but I found myself staring out the window watching the occasional couple or family stroll past.

I liked being back in Charleston. I hadn't known whether I would. In my last case here, I'd stepped in when the guy handling the case for our firm left on paternity leave. I'm thirtyish, happily childless, and without many boyfriend possibilities, so I can't get all excited about a family-friendly workplace when it leaves me holding somebody else's bag. The judge in that case had pushed it to trial because of too many previous delays. The parallels to Jake's case were uncomfortably familiar, though the lawyer handling Jake's case had died, not taken time off to play with a baby.

Jake had given me an odd luxury. Lawyers are never asked to be objective. They always have a role to play. In this case, I wasn't an advocate; I was an observer, with the luxury of distance.

Looking at this case, not as an advocate but from a distance, I could envision what would make it the ideal case, but that was a long way from what we had now. Judging from the pre-trial depositions, Jake's case rested on Perforce's failure to warn that Uplift caused agitation and suicidal thoughts in some patients. That premise had two problems. One, in the studies cited by Jake's expert, very few patients became agitated and none committed suicide or went on killing sprees. Second, I wasn't a big fan of defective warning cases.

Everyone around Ray Vincent Wilma knew he was nuts. Warning him he might become agitated would've prevented it? Not a chance. If the doctor who prescribed Uplift didn't know Ray Vincent was on the edge, a warning label wouldn't have helped.

To me, an ideal product liability case would involve a design defect, where every product manufactured had the same defect and I could show the jury how the product should have been redesigned: the Ford Pinto could have protected the gas tank so it wouldn't explode. A defective warning or instruction case was usually a case of last resort; when no design or manufacturing defect presents itself, the attorney claims that warning of the danger would have prevented the injury.

Looking at it objectively, I understood why I wasn't excited about this case. The only way to put together my ideal case here would be to find something in the design or testing process, something that pointed to an error Perforce made or — even better — lied about. Unfortunately, most drug cases aren't my ideal case; most involve warning defects rather than design or manufacturing defects. The drug affects a few people in a bad way, and warnings are the only way — though not a perfect way — to try to prevent harm.

I knew South Carolina juries well enough to be glad Jake was bankrolling this case and not me.

I finished my fried okra with macaroni and cheese and ordered a bowl of banana pudding. It struck me how quiet today had been. Somehow, in Dacus, somebody was always around — my parents, Lydia, Emma, my great-aunts, Melvin, people on the street or in the stores. Always people I knew. Here, other than polite exchanges with a waitress or a phone call or a business meeting, I could be pleasantly anonymous and alone. Maybe that's why I had time to dwell on my doubts. Maybe they were there all the time and I just couldn't hear them for all the distractions.

I downed one last glass of luscious sweet tea and, on the way down Meeting Street, detoured onto Market to get a couple of warm pralines. For a snack, later. Despite having eaten too much lunch, I nibbled one bite, while it was still warm, which led to another. I polished off a whole praline before I'd reached Broad Street and St. Michael's Church. Even walking the length of the historic district back to the inn wouldn't make up for those calories. I was contentedly miserable.

By mid-afternoon, I settled back on the porch, losing myself in my reading and notes. Later, an older couple came out of their room to sit at the far end of the porch, destroying my sense of proprietary solitude. Their murmuring broke my immersion, and I looked around at the lengthening shadows, blinking like a mole come to surface. I'd been motionless for almost three hours.

I shook the mustiness from my brain, that thick, cob-webby sensation from too much concentration, and ambled downstairs for some afternoon tea. I drank two cups of hot cinnamon tea in solitude and wrapped a cheese straw in a napkin for later, to go with my lone remaining praline. I doubted I'd feel like eating supper.

The sky had already turned dark outside by the time I left my china cup on the sideboard and climbed the stairs. I'd finished the depositions I'd brought, so I rummaged in the side pockets of my suitcase, pulling out a battered leather notebook. My grandfather's journal. I'd found this volume — apparently one of several he'd written — tucked in the back of a desk at his cabin. I plumped the pillows on the bed and thumbed the thick pages, planning to rest for a bit.

* * *

The green dial read 11:30 p.m. when I started awake. Dang. I knew from experience that I couldn't turn over and go back to sleep. Usually during trials, something always chews at my brain, waking me up at odd hours.

I didn't have a key to Jake's office, so I couldn't get more reading material or do any online research. I'd done all I could with the materials I had here. No television.

Maybe another walk. That's all I'd done so far — walk and read. But maybe I could wear myself out so I could sleep.

I slipped out the side door — which, in the creaky house, wasn't easy to do quietly — and headed toward Legare

Street. The air felt chilly and damp, and the street lamps were old-fashioned, attractive but dim. I looked for my favorite haunted houses: the incongruous white clapboard where the hunting accident victim appears in the library, the mansion the husband built around the corner from his wife's — allegedly because she'd tricked him into marrying her and he refused to live with her. I didn't hear her carriage rattle past on its way home. The Pineapple Gates next door loomed in the darkness.

I trod quietly block after block, stumbling occasionally on the dim, uneven sidewalks, thoughts bumping about in my head, my hands jammed into my coat pockets. I hoped Charleston's dark streets were as safe as they felt.

As soon as I thought about safety, I noticed the sirens shrieking in the distance.

Then the sound grew, swallowing the silence.

I walked north, drawn toward the sound. At the corner of Montague and Rutledge, over the rooftops to the north and west, I glimpsed what drew the sirens.

A fire.

CHAPTER SIX

Midnight Thursday

I smelled the smoke only after I'd seen the fire, and then the
acrid odor was all I could smell. The sky glowed, then, as
smoke billowed, grew blacker than the night sky had been.
Sparks shot upward. Even though I stood blocks away, I
could see strobing lights dancing off the smoke.

More sirens came, homing in from several directions.

I walked up Rutledge, drawn now to the lights and
noise, smoke and sparks. I jaywalked across an intersection
to get a better view of the burning house, fire-eaten black
and red. Directly in front of me, reflecting the wildly bouncing lights from the emergency vehicles, stood four towering
columns, the only remnants of a fire decades earlier that had
leveled the abandoned Charleston Museum.

Dozens of people stood scattered along the grassy block,
the park left after that old fire, watching this fresh fire.

I climbed the remaining steps to what had once been the
museum's portico. From that vantage, the stark gray-white
columns framed the blistering view across the side street.

Smoke crowded over the flames, so the scene wasn't as
dramatic as movie fires usually are. Thick sparks flew with

the smoke in a spiraling dance from the roof. The firefighters paid more attention to the houses on either side of the three-story fire; they'd already given up on the victim and hoped only to contain the damage.

Smoke grated on the back of my throat. Bystanders stood wrapped in jackets or each other against the cool air and the numbing fear of fire. I studied the huddled groups, their dazed eyes locked on the scene across the street. A red-head in jogging shorts sat on the museum steps with her arms wrapped around her knees, rocking to and fro. Tears streaked silently down her cheeks, leaving her face shiny in the light.

Other groups huddled in clusters among the trees, all watching the fire. Most looked like college students — understandable since the College of Charleston filled several blocks to the east, and many older homes along here had been converted into a rabbit warren of apartments for medical students and college kids. Older faces were also scattered in the crowd, probably homeowners with expensive mort-gages and even more expensive upkeep, and plenty of reason for worry and sadness as they watched.

Clustered near me, under the imaginary shelter of the solitary columns, several cried or fought back tears. Among them, two women, one with the husky build of a swimmer, the other runner-lean, stood like sentries on either side of a woman huddled in an oversized jacket. She wasn't crying, but the emotion on her face was palpable. Older than her two companions, she had thin, high cheekbones, short hand-combed hair, and deep-set eyes.

The runner bent toward her. "Sanda." Then she spoke a little louder. "Sanda." The woman focused on her friends as if from a great distance.

Sanda? I turned toward the fire with more than idle curiosity. The house number had disappeared. As I searched, a portion of the roof collapsed, sending sparks skyward in a daz-zling cloud and ripping startled exclamations from the crowd.

I looked at the house next door, its brass letters shin-ing in the sparks as if someone had picked them out with a flashlight: the odd-numbered house next to Mark Tilman's. I was watching Mark Tilman's house burn.

Sanda wasn't a common name. There couldn't be two here.

I saw no point in waiting and stepped over to the woman. In my most gentle questioning tone, reserved in the courtroom for children and the exceptionally frail, I said, "Excuse me for intruding. Are you Sanda MacKay?"

Her sentries stiffened. She turned her deep-set eyes on me, magnificent in their depth, and blinked once, wearily.

"Yes?"

"I'm so sorry. I had no idea—" I made an ineffectual gesture toward the fire, which had calmed some after the dramatic collapse. "—I really need to talk to you. I understand you're a friend of Mark Tilman?"

Her eyes glistened, the fire reflected in the tears that sprang up. Her bodyguards moved closer, as if to protect her.

"Who — are you?" she asked with a seductively slow voice.

I started to offer my hand, but hers clutched her jacket about her slight frame. "Avery Andrews. I was a friend of Mark's brother. From his hometown."

Her grip on her coat relaxed slightly.

"I hate to bother you. I left a message on your machine earlier. Just now, when I heard your name, I had to speak." I glanced at house.

The stocky swimmer shifted her stance, putting her shoulder between Sanda and me. "Can't you see she's upset? She's—"

"Shirl, it's okay." Sanda made a gentle patting motion with one hand. "You knew Mark — and his family?"

I nodded. In the strobing emergency lights, Sanda MacKay's age surprised me. She looked older than I, late thirties, maybe early forties. Of course, the bad light and the turmoil — and her bereavement over Mark — would've been enough to age anyone, but she was definitely older than Gregg Tilman's kid brother. Was it only yesterday I'd waited

47

for him, frustrated because he didn't come? No, day before yesterday.

Sanda studied me in return. "I didn't know his family."

"Mr. Tilman said you hadn't met. He called me," I explained. "He gave me your name. He wanted to make sure you knew . . ."

It seemed important to tell her Mark's family had known about her. Sorrow shared might not be a lighter burden, but it wasn't such a lonely one.

I hesitated, then blundered on. "Mr. Tilman was naturally upset about Mark — Mark's death. And he, well, he's concerned." I couldn't seem to get to the question. Sanda waited, too shell-shocked to notice my stumbling. "He said Mark called him a few days ago, that Mark had been upset over something at work."

Sanda listened without any reaction.

"Had he — had he said anything to you?"

She sucked her cheeks in, biting the inside, thinking. "He did have more on his mind lately. Something at work — preoccupied him. You know how you can tell, even when they won't say much."

She almost smiled at some remembrance. "But he really didn't say what. It probably had to do with the research project he's working on, rather than anything else. He wasn't one for office politics. Research and patients consumed his time." She finished quietly.

The flames had retreated back into smoke and sparks. The wood framing glowed with red cracks in the charred black wood. The size of the crowd had not diminished. If anything, it had grown.

Sanda stared at the fire. The firefighters still sprayed neighboring houses, trees, and shrubs as the breeze carried sparks away.

"Well . . ." I hated to give up without something I could offer Mr. Tilman, but she looked more peaked, shrinking into the large coat draped around her shoulders. "His dad was wondering, he wanted me to find out what I could."

She nodded. "If you do find anything about Mark, could you — let me know?"

"Sure."

"And tell his family — tell them . . ." Her voice trailed off. I reached out to pat her arm, a gesture my mother would offer. She's a great one for comforting arm pats. Shirl had had enough of my intrusion. She, too, had noticed the blueness of Sanda's lips against the increasing pallor of her skin.

"Sanda, you need to come in." Shirl took her by the arm. "We'll get some hot tea. There's nothing you can do here."

The girl with the runner's build who had been standing with them returned. I hadn't noticed that she'd left. Sanda turned to her. "Any sign of Matisse?"

The girl shook her head, the frizzy burst of hair tied at the crown of her head flicking wildly. "It's so crowded and noisy. He's probably hiding somewhere safe, watching everything. He'll come out when things calm down."

"Matisse?" I asked.

"Her cat," the searcher answered.

"Come on." Shirl tugged again at Sanda's elbow. Sanda moved under the force of that persuasion, but she paused long enough to say, "Let me know if—" Her request died out and she disappeared into the crowd, flanked by her friends, leaving me standing on the columned portico.

The scattered clusters of watchers began to thin as others along the street decided the show was over.

I turned south on Rutledge, I hoped the shortest way back to the inn. I walked quickly past the dark, hulking houses, my soft-soled shoes padding quietly along the uneven sidewalks. No street, no matter what the illusion of safety at other times, felt safe in the dark hours of morning after a scene like the one behind me.

CHAPTER SEVEN

Early Friday morning

My cell phone's buzz jolted me into a defensive mood.

"Yes." I barked into the receiver.

The voice on the other end didn't respond immediately, then asked hesitatingly, "Is this Avery Andrews?"

"Yes."

"Sanda MacKay. I hope I didn't wake you."

I lied. "No. No problem." The clock said 8:00, well past my usual waking time.

"I — I hope you don't mind. I called Mr. Tilman. To find out how to get in touch with you."

"I'm glad you did."

"I — this morning—" She paused. "A package came this morning. I — can you come — see this? I don't know—" Her stumbling didn't sound like the older, strong-featured woman I'd seen last night. After the night she'd had, though, she had a right not to be herself.

"Sure, Sanda. What is it?"

"A notebook. Mark's notebook. He sent it. QuikCourier delivered it this morning."

I held my questions. Since she was staying with a friend — Shirl or the other girl from last night, I supposed — we agreed to meet at the Marina Variety Store, a restaurant near both Barnard Medical and the Medical University of South Carolina. A favorite breakfast hangout for medical students and hospital staff, the Variety Store offered a high cholesterol count and strong coffee. We would both need it.

When I arrived, Sanda was sitting in a booth near the wall of windows, clutching her coffee mug in both hands. She wore an oversized sweatshirt, jeans, and the same jacket she'd worn last night. As I slid into the bench opposite her, I could smell the leftover smoke floating around her like a bad aura.

Strong coffee wasn't going to be anywhere near enough for Sanda. To give her some due, neither of us looked too perky. But I'd only lost part of a night's sleep. She'd lost a lot more.

She pushed a thick manila envelope across the table toward me.

"He sent it to me yesterday, from the island clinic. To be hand-delivered this morning before 10:00 a.m." She attempted a smile. "Before 8:00 is very punctual, wouldn't you say?"

I opened the flap and eased out a thick volume bound in black.

She shrugged. "His notebook. Apparently from his research work. At the hospital."

"Why would he send it to you by next-day courier?" On the front cover, someone had written "Mark Tilman" and an August date, six months earlier, along with some kind of coded letters and numbers.

Again, she shook her head as if on some kind of time delay. "I don't know. I couldn't decipher any of his notes. I — didn't know what else to do with it."

The notes appeared in chronological order, all written in the same hand. Each entry contained initials — maybe patients' names — and other undecipherable scratchings.

"Sanda." I hesitated before asking, since in some circles, my question would be a bit indelicate. "Were you and Mark — um — where did you — were you—?"

"Living together?" She finished for me.

I nodded.

"I have a garage apartment and studio out on Sullivan's Island, but the commute's long. I often stay at Mark's, the place that burned."

"Mark addressed this to you, at his apartment?"

She nodded.

He'd probably planned on being there to get it himself. So why use Sanda's name? The address the courier had for Mark's apartment was now nonexistent. "How'd the courier find you?"

"Sitting on the porch at Shirl's, a couple of houses down. Somebody told him where I was. The guy even asked for a photo ID. A driver's license or something. I didn't have anything."

Slowly my own dim-wittedness dawned on me. "Sanda. You were there last night? In the apartment?"

She nodded. She looked as shocked as I was at the real-ization. "God, it was awful." Her gaze was far away from the booth where we sat.

"Dear Lord, Sanda."

"I'm not sure what woke me up. At first, I thought Matisse had knocked something over and broken it. I heard something break, like glass." She wasn't talking to me. She was remem-bering out loud. "I think I went back to sleep. Then I thought I heard voices. I woke up, called out. You know, sudden-like. For a flash, I thought Mark was home. Then, just as quick, it rolled over me that he couldn't be home. That old house can be noisy, with kids coming and going all night. My place at the island is small and quiet. Too quiet. I just couldn't bear staying out there last night, by myself. After Mark . . ."

She stopped, her gaze tracking around, as if looking for something, but not anything in front of her. "Good thing I did stay at the apartment. Good thing something woke me up. Some of those kids might not have gotten out."

"You spotted the fire?"

She nodded. "I smelled smoke first, then saw the light, on the balcony. The whole thing was on fire. And the draperies in the living room, at the back, were burning and blocking the fire escape. One long interior staircase ran up from floor to floor, on one side of the house. I just ran for that door, screaming. We were on the top floor because Mark didn't like to listen to people walking over his head. Luckily, I made it out the front door to the stairs. I pounded on the other doors. Screaming. Some of the kids came quickly. They knew who the others were, so we got everybody out. The fire was mostly in Mark's apartment, so they hadn't seen it or heard it until I started screaming. I'm so thankful no one . . ." Her voice trailed off.

I didn't want to say anything to Sanda, but too many odd occurrences were gathering, like storm clouds. Something had Mark worried enough to come see me, then he has a car accident and was apparently robbed. Medical residents often have empty wallets. But they don't throw their wallets across the creek, and they don't end up dead with their apartments burned to the ground. Why send what looked like a research journal to his home? Sanda didn't need to be burdened with my musings right now, so I changed the subject.

"Did Matisse make it back home?" I asked gently.

She blinked and looked at me for the first time since she'd mentally revisited the fire. "Yeah." She put one hand over her heart. "Thank goodness. Shirl found him this morning, hiding under a bush next door, eyes as big as saucers."

"Did they say what started it? The firefighters?"

She shook her head. "I haven't heard. It's just too much, all together. You know? Mark. Then the fire."

I nodded. It would be too much, even if it had been dished out in smaller doses. Way too much.

"I'm so sorry, Sanda."

She stared out the window. "I'm just — numb. It was so hot. And smoky. So fast."

To give her some space, I flipped slowly through the pages of Mark's journal, looking for something, some hint about what was so important that he had to see me and had to send the journal. The handwriting varied slightly from entry to entry. Always the same person writing, but with varying moods and different pens.

"Sanda, could I take this with me, to try to make some sense out of it?" The other thing I couldn't bring myself to admit to Sanda was my guilt. I owed Mark something for all my bad thoughts at the restaurant. Maybe his notes would give some hint at what had concerned him. A stretch, but I owed him.

"Sure. Maybe—" She stared at a line of dry-docked sail-boats outside and didn't finish her sentence.

I felt ravenously hungry but didn't order anything. Eating in the face of Sanda's fatigue and grief seemed need-lessly rude. Maybe I should get her to eat something, but I didn't want to be pushy. Her friends had appeared capable of force-feeding her, if necessary. Sanda struck me as someone I would like very much, given the chance to know her. She probably wanted to be alone, but she also needed to have her mind occupied with something other than overwhelming grief, at least until she'd processed part of it.

"You said you have a studio?"

She nodded. "I'm a painter. Among other things. That's how I met Mark." She stopped to add sugar to her newly refilled coffee. The stuff in her cup must already be so sweet she could stand a spoon up in it. "As a medical illustrator. For the hospital."

"That must be interesting. Were you involved with any of the research projects?"

"No. I worked on a journal article with Mark and Blaine Demarcos and several others." She allowed herself a wry smile. "I never understood how six or eight people all write a single article. It mostly looks like the junior guys do the work and the big shots stand in line for the credit."

I'm sure I looked surprised at the mention of Demarcos. "Mark worked with Blaine Demarcos?"

"Occasionally. He was one of the chief physicians on Mark's latest project. Even though Mark was supposed to be a resident, his research Ph.D. and his background always got him involved in extra things."

She warmed to her subject — or to the caffeine and sugar. "I don't know how he managed everything. This latest project involved some of his patients, both at the hospital and at the island clinics, so he could sort of do two things at once."

She stared at her milky brown coffee. "He really loved practicing medicine. He always laughed about that: doctors always practice, they never quite perfect it. He was such a wonderful doctor."

She stated matter-of-fact observations, not hollow adulation. Sanda MacKay was old enough to have had the subjectivity worn off her, but in love enough to have a broken heart. The broken heart looked to be getting the better of her right now.

I thumbed through the notebook, more slowly this time. Toward the end of the entries, one set of initials appeared more frequently than others: TJ. I couldn't, with a cursory reading, decipher much else. TJ looked like someone's initials rather than some obscure medical abbreviation, like *Hx* for *history* or *SOB* for *shortness of breath*. Of course, as a legal term, SOB means something different.

I glanced at Sanda, to see if she'd recovered. She stared out the window. The sky and water had turned from indigo to a watered gray as, somewhere behind the fog, the sun spilled through the clouds.

"Did you know any of his patients?" I asked.

She shook her head. "I don't think so. Mark would've considered it a breach of confidentiality to mention a patient. He was a stickler for privacy and professionalism."

I kept flipping through the pages. The portions I could read easily seemed casual, random thoughts jotted in his own shorthand. This must have been his personal journal, where he talked issues through with himself, rather than a formal research record.

The last entry was dated February 5. Day before yesterday. *Got to find Tunisia Johnson. Hasn't been in office since 1/30.* His emphatic words had embossed the page. I thumbed through the last pages, all blank.

"Even if we'd met someone on the street somewhere, he wouldn't have introduced her as his patient any more than he would've introduced me as . . ." Her voice trailed off behind her fingers as she covered her mouth.

"Who would know about his research, do you think?"

She shrugged. "Somebody at the clinic, I suppose. I don't know. Blaine, you could ask him."

The casual, off-hand way she mentioned Demarcos telegraphed something important. "Do you know him well?"

"We dated for a while. Before Mark. He got me involved in the project where I met Mark."

Her choppy, abrupt sentences returned as soon as she mentioned Mark. She went back to staring out the window and chewing on her bottom lip. During my life as a malpractice attorney, I'd often heard of Demarcos, even used research articles he'd authored. From the gossip around the medical center, I had trouble imagining someone could go from dating him to Mark Tilman. Demarcos was known as a medical hotshot — bold, brilliant, an effective self-promoter. Among female med students, nurses, and legal associates, he rated as an exceptionally good time but an impossible catch. From what I'd seen, Mark Tilman, all-American hometown boy, wouldn't have played in the same league as Blaine Demarcos. But Mark had managed to end up with mature, sensitive, seemingly sensible Sanda MacKay, even though she still spoke of Demarcos with a telltale inflection in her voice, a too-casual aside that tried to downplay their past.

I looked forward to meeting Dr. Demarcos. Real-life soap operas always intrigue me. If I didn't hurry, I would be late for my appointment with him.

"Sanda, thanks for calling me." I slid my hand across the table toward her but stopped short of patting her hand. "I'll call you if I learn anything, okay? You have my number, in case . . ."

Sanda nodded but didn't make a move to leave. Even though no amount of caffeine would jolt her out of her grief, I left her there, pouring more sugar into her cup.

CHAPTER EIGHT

Friday morning

Blaine Demarcos's office wasn't far, so I left my car at the marina and walked. I hoped it would be safe there. Ever since Dad fixed up Granddad's Mustang convertible and handed me the keys, I've been wracked between giddy pride and the fearful burden of stewardship.

Charleston changes dramatically at Calhoun Street around the hospitals. To the south, historical homes crowd together near the harbor; on the other side of Calhoun, the run-down houses are still uniquely Charleston construction but jarringly different from the expensively maintained ones the tourists come to see.

Even farther north and invisible from Charleston proper, though sometimes pungently near, the chemical and heavy industries, shipyards and docks, and suburban developments sprawl around the military bases. Most true Charlestonians limit themselves to their safe nesting ground on the peninsula between the Ashley and Cooper rivers, the confluence of which forms the Atlantic Ocean, or so Charlestonians opine. In their genteel time warp, they can ignore most of the twentieth century — as long as they don't have to cross Calhoun Street.

As I waited at the intersection of Calhoun and Barnard, a medical student, her stethoscope dangling from her lab coat pocket, joined me. On the opposite corner, also waiting to cross toward the hospitals, stood four shabbily dressed men. They looked like street people, but they stood at attention and each wore some element of military dress — a fatigue shirt on one, heavy black boots on another, a vest shiny with badges and medallions on a third. Probably military burnouts who'd settled here near the Veterans Hospital to live on their disability checks.

The walk light blinked green. I should have known better than to stare. Until they started marching in a loose formation, I didn't notice the head gear on the guy leading them: a straw horn-of-plenty, upturned on his head. He saluted a woman pushing a baby carriage as they passed in the intersection. The sights you see.

I had visited the medical complexes often in my medical defense attorney days, talking to experts, using the library, but I'd never learned my way around the maze of passageways that connect the confusion of hospitals and affiliated buildings. I asked directions at the Pink Lady desk, stuck on my paper ID badge, and headed in search of Demarcos's office. She'd said turn left at the elevators, and I found myself heading down, maybe to go under a street.

The smells of stale food and too-strong disinfectant got stronger the farther I walked, and, for some odd reason, that disgusting combination reminded me that I hadn't eaten anything at the Variety Store. I needed to be sharp for this meeting, but I didn't have much time to find something to nibble on.

In frustration, I pushed open an exit door in the corridor, hoping to get my bearings. I found myself well down the block from where I'd entered the hospital. A man wearing green scrubs leaned against the wall near some garbage bins, his back to me.

"Excuse me. Can you tell me the quickest way to the staff physicians' offices?"

It wasn't until he turned to face me that I deciphered what he wore on his head. An upturned horn-of-plenty. A straw one. The guy from the sidewalk. How had he gotten here so quickly? Where were his compatriots?

He looked down at me, his eyes not quite focusing. Then he gallantly removed his headgear, offered me a deep, exaggerated bow, and stood at attention. Then he burped. A loud, luxurious belly belch.

"You're warm, but not hot, dear lady. The next mole hole will take you to your destination." He gestured past the trash bins toward an unlabeled door. "Pop through, up one, to your left. Bid greetings to Gatekeeper Deb."

I left him guarding the green bins, from which issued odd noises, and pushed through the door with a backward glance. Who was I to question his wardrobe or pursuits? His directions magically delivered me to the staff physicians' offices, a few minutes early for my appointment. I made sure I knew exactly where Demarcos's office was and then headed toward some food.

I hate hospital cafeterias. It's not the food so much as the stories I find myself making up about the other patrons — the hollow-eyed family on a death watch, the sleepy intern with mysterious stains on her jacket, the gossipy techs, the old man eating alone. Who needs that much drama on an empty stomach? I bypassed the congealed scrambled eggs, got a gigantic glass of iced tea, and rummaged in my satchel for Mark's journal.

Six by nine inches, bound in stiff black boards, it didn't immediately fall open to reveal the key to its secrets. About half the pages had been used, filled with hurried pen scratches. Each entry was carefully dated and filled with abbreviations.

I flipped to the last page he'd written. Mark had definitely mastered the physician's scrawl. Decoding it would take more concentration than I could muster sitting here in a busy snack bar. I worked backward, looking for TJ. Those initials were dotted through the book on various dates.

I stopped on the December 5 entry, two months earlier. *Referral from Ellin, Jas. Isl. — TJ. Initial prep and consent.*

Could that be Dr. Lazarus Ellin on James Island? I knew him. I'd co-chaired a panel with him at a state-wide medical meeting, where doctors earned continuing medical education credits by learning how not to get sued. Maybe he could help me decode the riddle of Mark's journal. I bent over my cell phone, dialing directory assistance and then Dr. Ellin's office.

His receptionist, in a thick, smooth sea-island sing-song, at first warded me off with expert parries. I carefully explained and asked her to please check with the doctor. When she returned, her voice sounded a bit exasperated — probably with both me and Dr. Ellin. "He can see you at 11:30 this morning. But he really can't spare more than a few minutes."

"Yes, ma'am. I do appreciate it. I know how busy you all are."

A visit to Dr. Ellin wouldn't be too much of a detour from Jake Baker's case. Not too much. I tossed my trash, checked my watch, and found a quiet corner to call Melvin. He was an early riser. Maybe he could give me something helpful for Jake's case, something so my obsession about Mark would not seem so disloyal.

"Melvin. Any news?"

"My dear girl. It's not even been twenty-four hours. How are you?"

"Fine. And you?" Melvin didn't deserve my abruptness. "Sorry, I'm just—"

"I know. In a hurry. What I have so far is the obvious stuff. Perforce Pharmaceuticals has grown from a small family-owned drug company to a multi-billion-dollar research giant. The scientists run the place and always have. The bean counters take a back seat but that's been a good strategy for them over the years. Research scientists want to save the world from horrible diseases and afflictions and, so far, that's been wildly profitable."

I heard papers rustle before he continued. "Uplift is their newest star. Like many drugs, it was twenty years in the making. But its development revolutionized the way we manage brain function. It's an SSRI, a selective serotonin reuptake inhibitor. You need to get one of your neuroscientist experts to explain how it works, but Uplift is the new and improved version. SSRIs are, according to the business press, miracle drugs for depressed patients. None of the side effects of the old dope-'em-outta-their-gourd treatments. Lots of controversy, though, which has sent stock prices dancing over the years since these things went on the market."

None of that was really news. "How do your business sources weigh the controversy?"

"One side cites a handful of folks I'm sure you've already come across, about how drugs can't treat head cases, that they need talk therapy. Others say the drugs have side effects. Others counter that nothing is worse than consigning someone to the depths of depression. Arguments sound familiar?"

"Yep."

"Okay, how about this? Perforce desperately needs Uplift, so Perforce desperately needs to win this lawsuit. Uplift accounts for one-third of its total sales, an incredible percentage for a company its size. Thanks to Uplift's success, Perforce has grown dramatically, so we're talking one-third of a much larger pie than they had ten years ago. At the same time, several Perforce patents are timing out on them; drugs that have been staples for them over the years are going generic."

"They knew that was coming. Patents have a time limit."

"Sure, but for whatever reason, Perforce doesn't have anything else hitting the market that could fill the void. To make things worse, the Nedham Group will hit the market with cheaper generics and huge advertising campaigns as soon as these patents expire. Perforce has already got some competition from that sector on their headache drugs. Nedham is aggressive. There's a rumor they'll try to get a court to speed up the patent expiration."

"They can do that?" News to me and I'm supposed to be the lawyer.

"Can — and have, in other cases. Nedham looks for loopholes in the patent. They spent $10 million to break another company's patent last year."

I leaned against the wall. "Why doesn't Perforce have anything else on the market to replace the patents they're about to lose?"

"Good question, but the answers are only speculation. Maybe they got complacent. Maybe they saw their wonder drug skyrocketing. Six million people a year take Uplift now, so maybe they didn't feel any urgency. Or maybe their scientists just haven't hit any lucky breaks. Sometimes you just hit dry holes in that business. Without the phenomenal growth of Uplift, this wouldn't look like such a dry period. Stock analysts always want more, bigger, better, but it's hard to top a miracle drug. Despite the predictable critics, the market sees Uplift as a bona fide miracle. Unfortunately for its stock prices, Perforce doesn't have a follow-up miracle in the making."

I scrunched against the wall, out of the way of a girl in a tight pink cotton outfit pushing a breakfast cart toward the patient rooms. Jake Baker had probably already hit the courtroom, ready to study the jury pool during *voir dire* questioning, to find twelve who would decide the case. He didn't need an update from me right now. Not this news, anyway.

"I'll make some more calls." Melvin's voice brought me back.

"Thanks. This has been a big help." Demoralizing. Sobering. But helpful.

"When will you be back, Avery?" Something in Melvin's tone changed. Not so crisp and businesslike.

"Don't know. With no hope for a settlement offer, these things can take weeks. But Judge Bream isn't known for dilly-dallying around."

"Folks have been asking about you, wondering if you've decided to set up your office here."

"Maybe word of our impending defeat won't spread that far, so I can still come home after this. Now there's a bright spot." Levity wasn't lightening my mood. "Thanks, Melvin. I owe you." I didn't press Melvin about his own plans. No time for that now.

Damn. I'd lost cases before, but very few — and none this big. Jake Baker probably knew everything I'd just learned. But, for me, having it spelled out hit me right in the gut. I hate losing. More than that, I hate not putting up a good fight. I felt like Alice in Wonderland, with things popping up as they shouldn't and the landscape changing under my feet. Standing still, paralyzed, wasn't going to improve things, though.

I turned back toward Blaine Demarcos's office. I was going to be late after all.

CHAPTER NINE

Midday Friday

Doctors' offices have a look all their own. Lawyers and executives favor dark wood, books, leather upholstery, brass lamps, though a few buck the traditional with sleek art glass, chrome, and miniature spotlights. The goal, though, is to impress, to provide weight and substance and sangfroid.

Most doctors' offices don't impress anybody, and the doctors don't give a flying fiddle. The drug company giveaways — plastic clocks, ball caps, candy jars, and patient teaching aids — are usually spotlighted by institutional fluorescents glaring overhead.

Blaine Demarcos nullified at least part of the stereotype. His office was small and lacked sophisticated artwork, but the furniture and lighting had come out of his own wallet. His mahogany desk, shaded desk lamp, and model Lamborghini paperweight said, *I'm not standard issue.*

His office opened directly off the bright hospital hallway, the door ajar into his subdued, carpeted sanctum. I didn't wait long before a tall, graceful man in a lab coat strode down the hall from the elevators, looking directly at me — the doctor any television medical drama fan hoped would be at her bedside should she awake from a coma.

"Ms. Andrews? I'm Blaine Demarcos."

He offered a firm handshake, complete with long, sincere eye contact. "I hope I haven't kept you waiting."

"Not at all."

"Wonderful. Can I get you some coffee? It's not hospital coffee, so you've no need to fear." He cocked his head, inviting me to take him up on his offer.

"I just came from the snack bar. Thanks. Your time is valuable, and I don't want to waste it."

He indicated the chair in front of his desk for me and settled into his desk chair.

I got right to business. "As I told you when I called, I'm working with Jake Baker on the Perforce Pharmaceutical case. The trial is starting at the courthouse this morning. A friend of mine — Mark Tilman — suggested I talk to you, said you were the expert on human subject testing and new drug development."

"Mark. What a tragic loss," he murmured.

"I'm sorry . . ." I wasn't sure how well he knew Mark. "I apologize if coming so close after his death is awkward."

"Mark and I were colleagues. We're all devastated at his death." His tone sounded clinical, but he leaned forward, his expression showing real concern. "Of course, we were professional colleagues. I'm sure, as his friend, you must truly feel his loss."

I gave a quick nod. I didn't want to trade falsely on a relationship, but I didn't want to say, *Oh, we weren't really that close* and trivialize whatever relationship he had had with Mark. "I spoke with Mark's father yesterday. His family is truly devastated."

Demarcos nodded, his lips pursed in sympathy.

I wanted to move past the awkwardly personal. "Mark said you were the best one to explain drug testing, what's the norm, maybe even give me some insights into how Perforce tested Uplift before bringing it to market."

"Glad to. Uplift is a textbook case, one of the most tested and proven drug launches in recent memory."

Great. It dawned on me Demarcos knew me as a medical defense attorney and might not know which side of this lawsuit I was on. I just needed background, so I didn't interrupt the conversation to explain.

"What makes it textbook?"

He gestured expansively. "It provides the cure or the relief patients need without undue side effects. That's what every physician, everyone in health care, wants — to cure people's problems."

His accent had the sharp, choppy edges of New Jersey or New York. My ear wasn't particularly good at pinpointing someone's hometown from the sound of his voice, but South Carolina hosts enough émigrés from that part of the world that we learn to spot them. His passion for his subject likely sped up his delivery another notch.

"It's not easy, though, finding those cures, getting them approved Some researcher tucked away in a lab somewhere may have a certain disease he wants to attack. Or maybe he's found some compound in some exotic plant or soil or mold, and he wants to see what it might do. They spend years hunkered over microscopes, searching for solutions."

"That's what your research department does here?"

"No, no. The initial discovery phase is usually conducted within pharmaceutical company R&D departments or universities with major Ph.D. research facilities. Pharmaceutical companies and the federal government provide much of the funding. Here, we're strictly patient care. We're not the pioneers, the Lee Standers of the world. He's the one credited with finding the link between manipulating brain levels of certain neurotransmitters and treating depression — the basis for Uplift."

"How exactly does Uplift work? I've read about it, but I must confess, I don't know that I understand it."

"Well," he leaned forward, almost conspiratorial, "frankly, I'm not sure any of us really understand how it works. But neurotransmitters — the mechanism in the brain that carries messages — are affected by levels of certain substances that affect mood. In particular, low levels of serotonin are associated with depression; raising the level of serotonin alleviates depression."

"As I understand it, though, Uplift doesn't add serotonin to the brain. It just keeps the brain from losing what it already has."

"Exactly. It's not like taking vitamins to supply nutrients your body requires. Instead, Uplift helps prevent the body from reabsorbing the neurotransmitters it already has. Hence, the awkward name selective serotonin reuptake inhibitors or SSRI."

"So what made Uplift such a wild success?"

"It works. It's a completely new mechanism for attacking a devastating disease. Too often we use 'depression' as slang for 'I'm blue today' or 'It's raining outside.' But for those who are clinically depressed, it can be a death sentence. In addition, some people are depressed only for short periods of time — maybe through a tough place in their lives. The conventional treatments were often too strong or had side effects that outweighed the benefit. Not so with Uplift.

"Perforce wasn't content with a mere breakthrough discovery. It launched one of the largest, most intensive clinical studies ever done on a new drug. Even the FDA commended them for their thoroughness. That's a major winner in anybody's book."

Great. A freaking FDA commendation. Jake would be so happy to hear that. My dream case, showing Perforce took shortcuts or covered up information about patient agitation, went flying out the window.

"So Uplift doesn't have side effects?"

His TV soap-star mouth made a mild grimace. "I didn't say no side effects. Everything has side effects. Drinking too much water has side effects — it can kill you. But Uplift doesn't suppress all emotion and response to save the patient. If the research is right — and clinical use indicates it is — then

SSRIs help target the organic cause of depression. At least for many people. It doesn't work on everyone, so we haven't fully unlocked the secret. Depression seems to develop along at least two major pathways, so, with older treatments, if one type of anti-depressant didn't work, we just switched to the other. Now, even with the success of Uplift and its cousins, we still have those two older tracks to fall back on, in more intractable cases."

"How do you recognize what's more 'intractable'?" I made little quotation marks with my fingers.

He shrugged. "I'm no psychiatrist, understand. I can only comment from a general medicine standpoint, but the more extreme cases often have more complex psychoses operating. The patients have issues they need to work through that are not solely organic and therefore can't be treated with drugs. Those patients require intensive counseling in addition to drug therapies."

"At what point does your research department here get involved?"

"The pharmaceutical companies often use teaching hospitals, where faculty are trained in research procedures, to conduct the Phase I, II, and III clinical studies. But that's only after animal and other testing has passed excruciating scrutiny by the FDA and within the company itself. After all, they've invested a lot and want to make sure it's a good bet before they sink any more time and money into it."

I knew the FDA's three phases all involved human test subjects. Phase I tests for safety, on twenty or so healthy subjects, often college students. Phases II and III are increasingly broad, often using thousands of test patients, to see if the drug actually works on the disease.

"People complain all the time about the high cost of drugs. What they don't understand — and what the politicians choose to ignore at campaign time — is the high cost of developing those drugs. It may take twenty years to get from the laboratory to the patient, with an average cost of $800 million. Maybe one in fifty drugs moves past the FDA's pre-clinical IND — Investigational New Drug — stage to human testing. Maybe one in four or five of those are ultimately approved for use. Think about all the ideas that don't pan out. Think about all the scientists — and all the microscopes and lab equipment and testing — that may come up with zero instead of a zinger."

"But they make a lot of money when they do hit a zinger."

"Like playing the slots in Atlantic City. Sometimes it's lemons, sometimes it's bells."

It reminded me of dropping a fishhook in Luna Lake instead of a quarter in a slot. Different cultural frames for different folks.

"Who pays for the testing you do here?"

"The pharmaceutical companies, sometimes with federal grants. Occasionally there may be private investors."

"They pay your salary?"

He shifted in his chair.

"Barnard Medical pays my salary, though I may, depending on the terms of a grant, receive additional funds to use for patient recruiting or overhead."

Asking *do you make a lot of money doing that?* would be rude, so I changed the subject.

"So the research you do here is always on something newly discovered and you provide a sort of patient laboratory for them to carry their work to the next level." *Guinea pigs* popped to mind. Human lab rats. But, for a made-for-TV doctor like Demarcos, they probably lined up to help advance medical science.

"No, no, that's not all we do. I didn't mean to create that impression. We don't have researchers bringing new molecules out of the lab to develop; we're not set up for that. But we do generate our own original research here. Frankly, that's what attracted me to Barnard. A facility like this must promote an active research agenda, to attract the best physicians and the funding needed to support cutting-edge work.

"The FDA approves drugs for a particular use, but once those drugs are used by the mass of humanity, with all its quirks, sometimes other benefits are discovered. For instance, an acne cream might help diminish wrinkles, or a diuretic for heart patients might treat androgen-sensitive acne in adult women."

Judging from his passion, Barnard Medical had the right guy in its research department.

"Of course, the drug company can't advertise the new uses unless those uses pass FDA scrutiny much like that given a new drug. Often clinicians — practicing physicians, the ones actually working with patients — are the ones who discover these secondary uses. There's no rule against a physician using a drug for unapproved uses, just rules against the drug company advertising it for that use. Maybe even more important, we also find new ways to help old drugs work better."

"Like what?"

"Like delivering heart medication sublingually — under the tongue — to get it into the blood stream more directly. Or using skin patches for everything from smoking to seasickness. In fact, we're working on something now that—"

A knock at the door interrupted. "Dr. Demarcos." A woman in a hospital-issue smock stuck her head in. "You asked me to remind you of your lecture. You and Dr. Hilliard start in five minutes."

He upped the wattage on his smile. "Thanks, Greta." He waved her away and turned back to me, not making a move to stand up or usher me out.

"You work with Langley Hilliard?" I tried to keep my tone even.

He studied my face. "That's right. He's testified for you before, hasn't he?"

That was a mild way of describing it. I need to remember that the details of my life aren't as fascinating to other people as I think they are. I changed the subject. "You ever testify as an expert witness?"

He shook his head. "I don't have the temperament for that. Or maybe Langley's just such a master at it that I could never hope to compete."

Demarcos took my silence as agreement or encouragement. "Langley is one of those old-liners who came through when God still attended medical school graduations and granted physicians immunity from all mistakes. He's so convincing because he truly believes doctors are infallible. You see that in some older docs. Maybe, back when they were making house calls, all they had to offer was faith." He chuckled. "Me personally? I'd rather be perfecting some more miracle cures. They work better — and pay better."

I didn't respond, but he didn't notice.

"I've enjoyed it, Avery." He stepped around his desk, putting his arm in the small of my back in a courtly gesture as we both turned to the door. "Please let me know if I can be of assistance in the future."

"Thanks again. This has been most interesting. I hope I haven't made you late for your lecture."

"Not at all. You're welcome to join us. We're reviewing some new hip replacement options." He grinned, his teeth startlingly white under the bright fluorescent hallway lights.

"I'll take a raincheck." I absentmindedly watched him stride down the hall as if he owned the place. Guess he didn't need notes for his lecture.

He'd painted, in a few words, a portrait of Langley Hilliard I'd never seen before, but one I could recognize. Hilliard was what, sixty-five years old? Times had changed dramatically over his professional life. Insurance companies second-guessed every move, and doctors were no longer revered. Demarcos was probably right; Hilliard's lies were believable when he defended a doctor because Hilliard really believed what he said — doctors can do no wrong. He didn't have grace enough to get down off his crumbling pedestal and join the rest of us, fallible as we are. A new perspective on Hilliard, but still not one I liked or admired.

I checked my watch. Eleven o'clock. It had been a long day already. I took the nearest exit, which landed me on the sidewalk on the far end from where I'd entered the medical maze — and farthest away from the marina and my car. At midday, just enough sun had appeared to leave a cool tingle in the air. I could walk and check voice mail at the same time.

Mom had left a message.

"Avery? Give me a call, hon. Remember Miranda Cole? That mountain goober boyfriend has gotten seriously scary. You remember Constable Raymond? Got that constable's commission so he can carry a gun and know everybody's business? Well, he told your father — he ran into him at the post office — that someone stole explosives from the highway construction site. You know they're widening Main Street north of town? And one of Constable Raymond's so-called informants, likely somebody he shoots pool with at Tap's, told him this goober is bragging how he was the one who stole it. Miranda's mama's real upset. Your machine just beeped. Maybe you can't hear the rest of this. Call me."

The next message was from Jake, louder and not nearly so breezy. "Dammit! You won't believe what this asshole judge did this morning! Where the hell do these guys get off? Bifurcated my effin' trial. Can you believe it? Bifur-effin-cated it. I'm so freakin' thrilled, I just had to share the news."

I had to hold the phone away from my ear. Good thing I'd gotten outside before I picked up that message. That one would've echoed down the hospital halls. Bifurcated — broken the trial into two parts. As a defense attorney, I'd always fought rabidly for that, especially in cases where the plaintiffs' injuries were gruesome but their case was weak. I hadn't wanted a jury to feel so sympathetic it ignored all the holes in the case and decided to give away some of my client's money. Judges seldom granted my most fervent wish, though. Not unless the injuries were really bad and the plaintiffs' case had enough holes to drive a truck through.

Now I felt split-minded. I knew the logic of what the judge had done and, sitting on the defense side of the courtroom, I would've felt it amply justified. But now that I stood on the other side of the courtroom, well, dang it, we wanted them to hear about those ghastly injuries. We wanted them to know how real the pain and injury and loss were. The judge's decision meant we'd have to convince the jury Perforce was liable before the jury could hear any testimony about the plaintiffs' injuries. The jurors would deliberate twice: first to decide who won and, if and only if we won, then they would hear about the injuries and talk about awarding money.

Jake Baker really didn't want me to leave him a message about my morning's activities. He really didn't want to know.

I walked slowly, enjoying the crisp air. Demarcos was clearly one of the research insiders. Maybe someone with a more objective perspective could tell me something that didn't paint Perforce Pharmaceutical and Uplift in such a glowing light.

Dr. Lazarus Ellin. Mark's journal said Ellin made at least one referral to a research study. If Ellin could give me another perspective on drug research, then stopping by to see him about Tunisia Johnson wouldn't be a frivolity after all.

As I crossed Calhoun Street, was it my imagination or did the breeze carry a whiff of smoke? I was only blocks from what was left of Mark's apartment. Sanda's exhausted face came to mind. Dear Lord.

As I approached the marina, I tried calling Mom but got no answer. I'd have to catch up later on the continuing drama, "As Dacus Turns."

CHAPTER TEN

Midday Friday

At 11:15, I turned left from the Variety Store's parking lot. A modern concrete bridge carries traffic across the Ashley and its bordering marshes to the islands far more efficiently than the old drawbridge had at this time of day, so I'd make my 11:30 appointment.

What had been a modest brick ranch now housed Dr. Lazarus Ellin's office. Over time, road-widening projects, convenience stores, strip shopping centers, and traffic had swallowed up the houses along a once-pleasant neighborhood street. The houses now huddled too close to the road in weedy yards converted into parking spots. Signs advertising phone repair, Madame Ollie's Palm Reading, and Dr. Lazarus Ellin, General Medicine, vied for attention.

My tires bounced over the bumpy break in the curb and crunched to a stop in the graveled yard between a red Ford Escort with a baby seat in the back and a mini truck with faded paint and a bumper sticker that read *Tithe — Any fool can honk*. A gleaming Cadillac, old but well-tended, stood beside the building.

What I took to be a single family crowded the waiting room on the converted front porch. It was hard to tell whether the woman reading a dog-eared magazine actually had a lot of children or whether the children were moving so quickly they only appeared innumerable.

Dr. Ellin's nurse — her tag said *Gladys* — led me straight into his office, which had once been a small back bedroom. Never leave a lawyer lurking about in your waiting room when such can be avoided.

I'd worked with Dr. Ellin, putting together seminars for medical conferences on small practice liability. Even though we'd known each other, with that passing familiarity of occasional colleagues, I'd never been to his office.

Somehow, seeing him at the annual meetings, I'd always assumed he was one of the prosperous, successful Black physicians folks trotted out, just like they trotted me out as a prosperous, successful lady lawyer. Part of the "ones to watch" crowd. His office sent a different message.

The furnishings were cheap, badly battered discards. The linoleum was a violent brown, checked with cracks, ominously discolored in spots, and curling dangerously. Index-coded file folders filled his desk and stood knee-high against the wall. An insurance peer review board would have a hissy fit, seeing how far behind he was with his chart dictation. Or maybe this was his filing system.

The shelves behind his desk held a few books, with framed photographs scattered among them. Most looked like family shots. Out of habit, I studied his books, mostly early editions of medical texts, now outdated. Even the Webster's dictionary was faded and tattered.

Heavy footsteps approached and the flimsy door swung open, creating a flutter of paper on his desk.

"Avery! How good to see you!" He enveloped my hand with a strong, dry grip and settled down in the wooden chair beside me, on the visitor's side of the desk. "It's too early for you to be on the program committee and I doubt you're selling anything. So to what do I owe the pleasure?"

Lazarus Ellin was a tall man, beefy but not overweight. His hair had grayed over the years I'd known him into a gentle silver and his life had arranged the wrinkles over his dark face in a pleasant way.

I chuckled. "No, not selling anything. Asking. For free information. What can you tell me about the wonderful world of pharmaceutical research? And can you tell me how to find Tunisia Johnson?"

From his expression, neither of those questions even faintly resembled what he'd expected. "A little more background, Avery? One topic is very broad. The other may be too personal." He settled back, filling the sturdy wooden chair, his expression reserved.

"Do you know a medical resident named Mark Tilman?"

He pursed his lips, studying a minute. "I don't b'lieve so."

"Did know, I should say. He died in a car accident Wednesday night." I kept talking, bypassing his sympathetic expression. "His research notes indicated you referred Tunisia Johnson to a study. The study prompted my other question, because I'm taking a crash course in new drug development and testing for a case I'm working on. Thought you could help me kill two birds."

"I don't know that I can help you much. I'm at the low end of the research totem pole."

"But you refer patients to studies. How do you know about the studies?"

"Oh, the medical school and the centers here make sure we know. Every now and then, patients come to me, asking questions because they've seen something on TV. But most times, the researchers contact me direct, knowing I have patients they might can help."

"What do you mean, they know?"

"To be blunt, they need Black folks. And poor folks. To make sure their study takes into account all kinds. And I got plenty of people comin' here who aren't rich or white." He shrugged. "Because I do general practice, I got all kinds of ailments coming in, and I get plenty of folks who can use some free medical treatment."

"You learn they're enrolling patients in a particular study, and you have someone with that problem who would qualify. Then what?"

"If I think it's somebody who'll take it seriously and if it looks like it might be some help to them, then I'll refer them. Sometimes I do the follow-up with the patient here, fill out the questionnaires and such. Other times, I don't even know whether they have been enrolled unless they come to see me about something else."

From out in the hall, a penetrating wail cut through his response. The cry rose and fell but never stopped for breath. His nurse pecked at the door and opened it without waiting for a reply.

"Doctor, we've got an emergency just come in."

Her voice was calm but compelling. When she announced an emergency, no one could doubt it was real, even without the wail in the background.

Dr. Ellin didn't waste time excusing himself. I should have stayed put, but the pained cry and the nurse's air of quiet urgency created a vacuum that sucked me along in its path.

Gladys glanced at me as I stood sentry in the hallway across from the examining room door, but she was busy keeping the adults who had crowded into the small room against the wall and out of the way. As Dr. Ellin bent to examine his patient, I could see a small girl, the source of the wailing.

She looked to be six or seven, her wiry hair gathered into several large ponytails, her eyes wide with fright and filled with tears, her mouth a big round O.

Her family members shifted restlessly, unnerved by her plaintive insistent wailing, but none of them spoke.

With gentle words I couldn't quite make out, Dr. Ellin quieted the shriek to a sob. He stepped away from the end of the examining table to flip open some cabinet drawers, gently moving aside two family members — a young man in a Harley T-shirt who might have been her dad and a young woman in her teens.

When Dr. Ellin stepped aside, I saw the girl's hand resting on her knee and almost started wailing myself. Buried deep in the fleshy part of her hand, a fishhook glinted against the blood crusted in her pink palm. A string of fishing line dangled from the hook, curling along her thin leg.

I hoped nothing tugged that line.

Dr. Ellin distracted her with his calm hypnotic words while he expertly snipped the line, letting it fall to the floor. She barely flinched as he gave her a shot.

He talked to her as he waited for the local anesthetic to take effect, then he bent to work. Within seconds, he was cleaning the wound with disinfectant and the nurse was handing him a bandage she'd prepared. He took the little girl's face in his hands and kissed her forehead.

A grandmotherly woman, her flowered dress belted where her waist should have been, looked as though she wanted to kiss Dr. Ellin's feet. Dr. Ellin spoke to each family member in turn, his hand on the little girl's head the whole time and his voice so gentle I couldn't make out more than a word here and there. He gave the mother and grandmother some final instructions before the nurse shepherded the family down the hall to the payment desk. A quiet discussion ended with a dismissing wave of Dr. Ellin's hand and grateful looks from the three adults. A stern but discreet look from the nurse followed, for Dr. Ellin's benefit.

The family left with a large kid in a Panthers T-shirt carrying the little girl, her head on his shoulder.

"Dr. Ellin, you're not the one to set charges for patients," the nurse scolded. Respectful but stern, her voice carried down the hall to where I stood.

"Gladys, you know the Pitkins full well. What good would it do to charge them? They'll pay something when they can." Clearly an oft-rehearsed argument.

"At least charge them enough to pay for the anesthetic you used," Gladys said. "The medical supply won't take chickens and yam bushels and hoodoos in payment the way some folks do."

Dr. Ellin smiled and nodded. I'm sure Gladys was used to him, but it didn't stop her from trying to keep him and his office and her livelihood on an even keel.

I wandered back down the hall to wait in his office. I should let them discuss their business in private.

When he returned, he had two cups of coffee in his hand, one for me.

"Sorry," he said. "Where were we?"

I couldn't compliment the strong, bitter coffee, and he would've been embarrassed if I complimented his bedside manner, so I went back to business. "I was going to ask you about Perforce Pharmaceuticals. Have you ever had a patient participate in one of their studies?"

"Once. One of the best run studies I've seen. Everything was first class."

Great. "What drug was it?"

"For bile reflux. Still not on the market, as far as I know. Worked well for the two patients I referred, though."

Great. Even better.

"Are you doing the follow-up for Tunisia Johnson?"

He hesitated, as if weighing options. "For that study, they needed patients who could come to Barnard Medical for follow-up."

"How can I get in touch with Tunisia?"

His eyes narrowed and his mouth tightened. "I can't tell you." Something in his face shut down.

As usual, an obstacle in my path just made me more determined. The only problem was, I couldn't really explain, even to myself, why I needed to find her. It just felt like something I could fix, unlike Jake's trial, where I felt like we were sinking. "You said Barnard Medical? Would Blaine Demarcos know her?"

He shrugged, his face oddly impassive. "With Tunisia, there's no telling."

To be polite, I swallowed another gulp of coffee and slipped my bag onto my shoulder. No point pushing it any further. "Thanks for letting me interrupt your morning. I know you've got patients who need to see you."

"My pleasure, Avery."

We shook hands matter-of-factly. I couldn't get over the sudden change in his demeanor.

Gladys stepped out of the reception area as I came down the hall, holding out a large Styrofoam cup and plastic spoon. I started to wave it away, thinking it was more of that horrid coffee.

"Here, honey. You take some of this with you. Mizriz Brown brought in a whole mess of bog. We can't possibly eat all this and I just bet you hadn't had lunch."

The thick gray-white stew smelled better than it looked — or sounded. Chicken bog, made with chicken, rice, sausage, and whatever else was handy, cooked into a spicy unrecognizable mush, was a Lowcountry specialty.

"Thanks." I meant it.

I strolled out, scooping spoonfuls of the warm stew and finished the whole cup before I got to my car. The shiny Cadillac had gone, leaving the battered truck and the Escort huddled in the parking lot next to my Mustang.

CHAPTER ELEVEN

Midday Friday

I sat in the parking lot outside Dr. Ellin's brick house, toying with my cell phone, mulling over my options. So far, I'd gathered glowing reviews on Perforce Pharmaceutical and Uplift. Without evidence Perforce knew of a problem and failed to protect patients from it, without some flaw in its FDA approval, Jake's case would be all uphill.

Puzzled by the way Dr. Ellin had shut down on me, I checked online but found no listing for Tunisia Johnson.

I decided to dial the office of Dr. Harold Redfearn in Dacus. Trying to gain perspective through others' eyes wasn't particularly helpful if you didn't know how they saw things, what peculiar color their vision had. You can only judge that if you've known the person for a while. I'd known Dr. Redfearn since he'd begun treating my childhood ills and scrapes, so he qualified.

"Doc, quick question. You ever participate in any drug research studies? Or is that just for guys near teaching hospitals?"

"Hey, Avery. Good to hear from you," he said, subtly chiding me for my abruptness. "And yes, a time or two.

Usually too much hassle for me and the patient, for too little benefit."

Over the phone, his froggy voice conjured up a full picture of his stand-up shock of prematurely white hair and his craggy Frankenstein face.

"When you refer patients, are they treated at a research center?"

"Sometimes. Not always. If the protocol is simple and the follow-up straight forward, we may do it here without them having to go to Greenville or Atlanta. Depends on what protocol the FDA approved. Drug companies want their studies standardized across all test sites, so the protocols are regimented."

"But you don't participate in very many studies?"

"Naw. Too much hassle, if you do it right. I know a couple of guys who've decided it looks like a good revenue stream. What with insurance companies continually cutting what they're willing to pay us for services, I guess some guys look for anything that pays."

"What do they pay you?"

"Usually just enough to cover administrative costs. They can count the income but aren't as good at figuring what it really costs them. Bottom line, I think payments to doctors and patients skew the results sometimes. Say you get a few hundred dollars to sign up patients for a well-funded study and you feel you need the money more than you need your integrity, you might recommend patients who aren't well-suited or for whom something else might be a better alternative."

He murmured instructions to someone in his office before he continued. "Maybe I'm old-fashioned, but I think it's all become too commercial, opened the door too wide for those who like to check their scruples at the door. Too much conflict of interest. At the very least, doctors should tell patients they're getting paid to sign them up, but most don't bother sharing that. They just tell how much the patients will get paid for acting as guinea pigs. It just doesn't feel right to me."

"How much do the patients get paid?"

"Varies. For some, just getting their regular doctor visits paid for is a plus. Any travel expenses or payment for their time is a bonus. Some do it for good-hearted reasons, so they can help find a cure. The problem is, for those living on the margin, money is money. They see only one part of the equation."

"What do you know about the drug Uplift?"

He switched subjects without missing a beat. "Great drug. Effective for those deeply depressed, but also good for mild depression, those who don't want to kill themselves but who might get irritated enough to kill a mother-in-law." He chuckled, probably remembering a particular family. Maybe more than one.

"Kidding aside," he said, "chronic, lifelong depression is a truly horrid disorder. But milder depression can also hit short term, like before menopause or when a spouse dies. Uplift is very effective at getting folks over those rough spots, maybe for a couple, three years. Then they'll be fine."

"How does it stack up against other antidepressants?"

"By far and away, my personal favorite to prescribe. If someone needs something stronger, I recommend intensive counseling along with one of the stronger drugs. Pills don't make all your problems go away. Sometimes folks need help working through their emotions, not just a signed prescription blank."

Which made him one of the golden few among physicians.

"What do you know about Perforce Pharmaceuticals? As a company."

"Can't say I've ever really thought about it. For years, they led the development of new antibiotics. Most of those are generic now, but that's where they made their reputation. Guess what we know about any of these companies comes from the drug reps they send around. Perforce's reps know their stuff, and they offer some of the best drugs in several lines."

More good news. "Thanks for your time, Doc. I know you're busy."

"Saw your dad yesterday. He said you were out of town. See you when you get back? Maybe then you can fill me in on what you're working on."

"Yean. It should be over by then." The way it was shaping up, it probably wouldn't be a story I wanted to tell over lunch at Maylene's. "Thanks again."

Maylene's came to mind because my stomach rumbled faintly. Lunchtime was ticking past, and, with no breakfast, that cup of spicy chicken bog was starting to churn. If I didn't catch Blaine Demarcos now, during lunch, no telling when I could track him down. I drove back over the Ashley River and found a space in a parking deck at the backside of Barnard Medical, near the door where I'd exited earlier. Now that I knew about the secret entrance and could avoid the winding halls, maybe I could get in and out quickly and still catch Jake before court reconvened after lunch.

A doctor, complete with lab coat and ubiquitous stethoscope — why do they carry those things? Don't they have them in the examining rooms? — was coming out the door as I approached. The discreet sign said *Staff Entrance Only*. He kindly held the door for me, rather than force me to use the swipe card I didn't have.

Please, please be there. I needed this to be quick. My wish wasn't immediately granted. Demarcos wasn't in his office, but the duty nurse at the station paged him for me. If I could get all this help wearing a black suit and carrying a notebook, wonder what I could get with a stethoscope strung around my neck?

"Avery. I wasn't expecting to see you again so soon." Demarcos strode toward me.

He didn't say, "What a pleasant surprise," but he smiled as if he meant it.

"I would've asked you this when we met, but I didn't realize you would know. Dr. Lazarus Ellin, out on James Island? He said you might have a current address for Tunisia Johnson."

I hoped mentioning Dr. Ellin would lend credibility to my request.

"Tunisia Johnson?" He said it slowly, as if trying to put a face with the name.

"Dr. Ellin referred her to a study you're conducting. You might have a more current address." Not exactly a lie.

He shook his head. "Sorry. Can't help. She dropped out of the study." He shrugged. "That's a problem we have sometimes, you know."

My expression prompted him to explain.

"For whatever reason — drugs, alcohol, a new boyfriend or abusive husband — sometimes it's hard to keep them involved and compliant with the study guidelines."

I didn't know Tunisia Johnson, but I suddenly felt protective.

My stare must have gone on a bit too long because his gaze shifted. His New Jersey accent became sharp and dismissive. "Sorry I couldn't be of any help."

"Sorry to bother you. Thanks anyway." I managed a quick smile and watched him stride off down the hall.

I hadn't mentioned Mark's research journal at either meeting with Demarcos. I told myself it didn't look like an official medical center document, and I wasn't sure whether it belonged to Mark or the research project. Mark had sent that journal for a reason. No cash-strapped medical resident goes to the expense of sending a notebook by courier to his girlfriend — a girlfriend he expects to see later that day. Last night's fire added to the distant drumbeat I could hear in my head. Until I put some of the puzzle pieces together, the fewer of Mark's colleagues who knew about the journal and its whereabouts, the better.

I knew my next step was a wrong one — but I knew I'd take it anyway. Another question-and-answer session at the nurse's station got me directions to the research department, where the paperwork was managed for the center's pharmaceutical and federal grants.

Demarcos had headed in the opposite direction. Good. Less chance for an awkward encounter. The nurse's directions led me to a tiny cubicle barely big enough for a desk and the large girl who sat behind it. She looked fresh out of high school.

"How may I help you?" She was either new at her job, the product of some new patient-friendly training seminar, or the after-effect of an experimental tranquilizer.

"I'm Avery Andrews." I offered my hand and she shook it, put off her stride momentarily by this unpatient-like initiative.

"I'm an attorney and have worked with several of the doctors here over the years." Not a lie. Technically.

She nodded and beamed. "Yes, ma'am, I recognize your name."

"I understand you handle the research intake interviews for Dr. Demarcos and the other physicians."

Her beaming brightened at my mention of Demarcos. She nodded vigorously. She looked like a chubby puppy, painfully eager to please.

"I need to contact a patient of Dr. Demarcos's who has left a study."

While I talked, I pulled out my notebook, ready to take down the information. Act like you know what you're doing, Aunt Letha always says, and everyone will think you do. I couldn't cite which exact sections of the Code of Professional Conduct I'd just violated, but I preferred to focus on justifiable ends at the moment rather than questionable means.

Her eagerness to help and her obvious respect for Demarcos made my rationalization pinch a bit, but it also moved things along and reduced my chances of getting caught.

She punched up four or five screens on her computer. I could see the screens change but couldn't make out the information as it flashed past.

"Here she is. Tunisia Johnson. She's in Mt. Pleasant." The privacy laws have cost a lot of paper but haven't changed either helpful or malicious human nature. She gave me a street and house number.

"What they're working on is really exciting — a nasal spray contraceptive. Is that phenomenal or what? Easy to use, not messy, and without the pill's side effects." She sounded like an infomercial.

I tried to look appreciatively awed by the concept. "How does it work?"

"Well, I'm no doctor, but a friend of mine — Sarah Jay — works with the study, instructing women how to use the spray. It's supposed to block the pituitary gland from sending messages to the ovaries. It works sort of like the pill but, since the pituitary is close to the sinus passages, the medication doesn't have to float around all over your body before it finds its way to where it's supposed to go."

"That is interesting." A simplistic but, I'm sure, effective description of a complicated process that even the researchers themselves didn't fully understand. With an aging but still fertile female population who'd been on the pill for too long, this could be a significant breakthrough. Even if only a few of the side effects could be avoided, it would open the market to some of the millions of women who had never been able to use the pill.

Demarcos had quite a little pet project here. No wonder he was so close-mouthed and defensive.

"Thank you so much — Deb." I spotted her nametag on her desk. A ceramic dragon held her business cards. *Gatekeeper Deb? Friend of the horn-of-plenty hat man at the garbage dumpster?*

"Oh, you're certainly welcome." She stood to escort me from her cubicle, the perfect hostess.

"What you do must be very interesting, Miz Andrews," she said as she backed me into the hallway. "Being a lawyer, that must be something special. Despite all those awful lawyer jokes." She looked sincerely pained.

How sweet. Nobody had ever worried if bad jokes hurt my feelings. I smiled and thanked her as she squeezed back into her cubicle.

Blaine Demarcos picked that moment to turn the corner at the far end of the hall. I didn't waste any more time saying goodbye.

I scooted into the cross hall, hoping he hadn't recognized me. Did I dare attempt it? I was here. What did I have to lose? A lot, actually. I followed the signs to Medical Records.

Dian, a comfortably padded woman my mother's age, sat behind a counter that ran the length of the records office. I was in luck. Dian's supervisor Jonette, who was immune to my friendly charm and a stickler for detail, was out to lunch.

"Whoops. The lawyer's here. Somebody's lost another patient. How fresh is it? Will I have the record here or do I have to track down the bits and pieces from the different departments?" Dian had pushed back from her desk as I walked in and stood with her hands on her hips, smiling. "Haven't seen you in a while, sweetie."

"Nobody's lost one." I smiled back. "Least not that I know of. But I do need a record. Tunisia Johnson. Here's her Mt. Pleasant address, but I don't have her date of birth with me. You need that?"

Volunteering my lack of information would look less suspicious than if she asked and I couldn't produce it. Apparently word that I was no longer defending doctors — and no longer had a reason to be requesting records — hadn't reached here yet.

I'd once been a regular, though, and I'd learned long ago that too many folks make the mistake of forgetting records clerks are people — often very ignored people who appreciate those who are nice to them.

Dian reappeared from the stacks with a manila folder. "Here she is. Tunisia Johnson. Oops. This one's stuck inside it. Wait a sec."

I froze with my hand out for the file.

"Well, it's another T. Johnson. Tabitha. Ah, same address. Must be her daughter. Yep. Here it is." She plopped both files on the countertop and pulled the patient history sheets.

"Sometimes they accidentally get filed together if they've been in together to see the clinic doctor."

"While I'm at it, maybe I'd better check both." I closed the folders quickly, smiled warmly, and scuttled toward an empty cubicle just as the early lunch crowd, including Jonette, filed in the door. In Jonette's operation, I bet you could set your clock on the lunch returns.

My guilty conscience should have troubled me more, but getting patients' records and maintaining their confidentiality had once been a routine part of my job. So what if it hadn't been a routine part of my job to do that without proper authorization? I wasn't going to share anything with anybody. This Tunisia thing had turned into a puzzle I simply had to solve, just a small detour from Jake's case while I waited for the trial to crank up.

Even when I'd served as the medical center's lawyer, hired to represent them, a certain paranoia accompanied any request for records. I'd learned early on that medical records have a way of disappearing or altering their appearance once an attorney — any attorney — requests copies. I'm not sure of the exact process, but it happens — usually a misguided attempt to cover someone's fanny. So early in my practice, I'd learned to review and copy the original records myself.

I thumbed quickly through Tunisia's records. She'd apparently used the hospital's clinic for her primary medical care. Before that, she'd had no regular physician. Her last recorded visit had been six months ago when she'd seen Mark Tilman for a chronic bronchitis. He'd noted her blood pressure as 142/88 and her temp at 99, both slightly elevated. Nothing else seemed remarkable.

Since both records were slim, I zipped Tunisia's and her daughter's through the collating copier in the back room, dropped the originals in the to-be-filed basket, and waved casually to Dian on my way out. Avoiding the Dragon Lady of the Records Room had probably used up my quotient of good luck for the whole day.

At least I had Tunisia's address. What that got me, I didn't know. But something about Demarcos's casual dismissal and Lazarus Ellin's odd transformation had made me determined to find Tunisia Johnson.

My stomach growled ominously. Mid-afternoon and I still hadn't eaten. With the photocopies tucked safely in my satchel, I headed toward the exit. Contemplating where to grab a late lunch and not paying particular attention to where I was going, I bumped — literally — into Blaine Demarcos.

CHAPTER TWELVE

Friday afternoon

"Three times in one day." Demarcos grabbed my shoulders to steady us both. "The stars must be aligned." His dark eyes focused on my face.

The first thing I registered was not embarrassment at causing the collision, but guilt. I squelched that. No way he knew what I had in my briefcase.

"I'm glad you're here, Avery. Could I buy you a cup of coffee? I wanted to explain, in case I seemed curt earlier."

He took me by the elbow and steered me into the room he'd just left, an employee break room, empty except for ice cream parlor-sized tables, a coffee pot, and a couple of vending machines with loud compressors running. The sterile whiteness of it, as with most hospital areas, was not restful or comfortable. Not really designed to provide much of a break.

"Cream? Sugar?"

"Both. Lots." I might as well get something that resembled food with my coffee, and cream and sugar were the first two of my four basic food groups: sugar, fat, salt, and preservatives. Maybe three of four, since caffeine could count as a preservative.

He doctored up our coffees and delivered them to the table with a flourish. He did move with an astonishing grace. Quick but smooth, like a dancer.

"Avery, I hope I didn't come across as — uncaring when I saw you a few minutes ago. You ever have those conversations where you think back and smack yourself in the head, realizing something didn't come out right? I just wanted to make sure we'd left things on a — pleasant note."

I sipped carefully at my coffee and made an "mm-hm" sound. *Where was this going?* I wondered at his tan. Golf? Skiing? A tanning salon?

He leaned closer to me, elbows on the tiny round table. "I hope I wasn't abrupt about Ms. Johnson. It's just," he looked down at his cup, and then back at me, "you took me by surprise when you asked about her. You see, we'd had some issues with her and Mark Tilman, the resident you mentioned earlier."

"Issues?" I kept my tone even and sipped my coffee.

"I don't want to be indelicate, but, you know — questions about an improper relationship between doctor and patient. You've served as counsel for Barnard Medical. You know what that can mean."

I tried to keep my face composed and didn't respond. Let him fill in the silence.

"Something about you mentioning her, so soon after you'd asked about Mark. You're a lawyer. I guess I had a flashback to that sexual harassment training they give us periodically." He gave an awkward laugh. "You took me by surprise. I guess lawsuit popped into my head, and I came across as defensive."

"I understand. I assure you a lawsuit didn't prompt my questions."

His awkward rambling surprised me a bit. I couldn't get a handle on this guy. "You're saying Dr. Tilman and Ms. Johnson were having an affair?"

He looked uncomfortable. Probably he'd hoped I'd let the subject drop. Guess again.

"That was the implication. Sometimes young doctors get too close . . . "

I sipped more coffee and studied the Italian silk tie peeking from his lab coat collar, but my silence didn't draw out further comment.

"Dr. Demarcos, something I was wondering after our conversation this morning. For a physician, doesn't opting out of private practice mean you've cut your earning potential?"

In the South, religion, politics, even sex are acceptable topics of conversation. But money? How much somebody makes or what something costs? Uncouth. Uncultured. Rude beyond mention. I asked anyway. I'm a lawyer and our societal standards of behavior are commensurately lower.

Demarcos isn't a Southerner, so he replied without batting an eyelash. "Doesn't have to. Depends on how hard you're willing to work. A small but select private practice can augment a pleasantly steady faculty salary. Centers and hospitals want to make sure they attract the brightest and best, so we're allowed to be entrepreneurial. It's all within our contract, counselor." He smiled, no longer running his finger around the rim of his cup.

"The drug companies pay you directly for supervising their projects?"

"Depends on the grant, if the university is providing support, if federal funding is involved, if there are private investors." He shrugged. "At Barnard, we're also allowed to pursue our own projects, depending on whether we can make our business case to the medical center or to private investors."

"Venture capitalists?" I threw out Melvin's phrase.

Demarcos nodded. "This is a good place to get in on the ground floor of some potentially lucrative new drugs and devices."

Passion and a willing audience are a seductive combination, and I'd obviously hit on a topic the professor-physician enjoyed talking about.

"Like reproductive medicine?" I prompted, without mentioning Gatekeeper Deb. "I imagine the world market is very strong, particularly in places like China."

"Indeed." He stared at me a beat too long before he pushed his chair back from the table. "I really need to get back to my rounds. I just wanted to — apologize if I seemed curt this morning."

"Not at all. Thank you for the coffee and the company."

He set our cups in the sink. I wondered what flunky came along behind to wash up. Maybe some nurses manage to give doctors the leveling experience lawyers tend to get from their assistants, but I haven't seen nearly enough of it.

I left the hospital with the Johnsons' medical records in my satchel, hoping belatedly that my mention of contraceptive research didn't get Gatekeeper Deb in any trouble.

The sun had heated the air in my car into shimmering waves. My hunger pangs had subsided into an echoing hollow; but now, fueled by the fiery burn of coffee, the pangs added to the dancing sensation before my eyes. I had to get something — anything — to eat before I got a full-blown migraine. Lydia's always ribbing me about being hungry all the time, but this is what happens when I don't eat.

I pulled into a fast-food drive-through and refrained from ordering everything on the menu board. In a parking slot, I shook salt all over my fries — ah, fresh and hot — and forced myself to chew the hamburger rather than swallow it whole.

Jake hadn't left another message. They must still be seating the jury, so no point in trying to reach him until later.

No company the size of Perforce Pharmaceuticals could be perfect. Somewhere, something had to give me a loose thread I could pull. I just had to keep picking around the edges until I found it. Or until Jake lost his case.

Meanwhile, I'd make a quick detour over to Mt. Pleasant. Demarcos and Ellin hadn't wanted to talk about Tunisia Johnson, which make me even more curious. It wouldn't take long to check her address.

I finished my hamburger and pulled up a map of Mt. Pleasant on my phone. Cooper Street, just off Johnnie Dodds

Boulevard. That shouldn't be hard to find. If Tunisia worked regular hours, she'd be home or getting there soon.

Worth a shot, even though it meant crossing the bridge over the Cooper River in rush hour traffic. I was getting a bit more nostalgic about the old twin bridges, now that they had been replaced, but I'd never much liked crossing those bridges — too rickety-looking and narrow, not solid like a mountain road.

The hamburger filled my stomach, but my brain hadn't gotten the message. In the glare of the oncoming headlights, my eyeballs wobbled in their sockets.

Gray clouds had rolled in from the Atlantic, blotting out the setting sun and closing in the winter evening sooner than usual. I gripped the steering wheel and focused tightly on the taillights of the pick-up truck full of blue crab shells in front of me. I hate high bridges even without maniacs rushing home from work flying past or crowding my rear.

The bridge dumped its load on the sand spit that begins Mt. Pleasant. As I changed lanes, my left signal apparently didn't give the Honda behind me enough warning. He laid on his horn and sped around me while I eased into the double lane of traffic toward Mt. Pleasant.

Streetlights flickered on in the early twilight and the kaleidoscope of headlights and fast-food signs popped and expanded behind my eyes. Great. The aura for a migraine headache. I'd really waited too late to eat.

In the left turn lane, I sat in rush hour traffic through two light changes, massaging my temples and hoping I had packed some of those new pills Dr. Redfearn had given me for these damned headaches. This was a strange one, coming on faster than usual. Tunisia's couldn't be more than a few blocks from here, and the hard part of the trip was already over — I'd made it across the bridge.

The light changed and I turned left. An oncoming car's brakes squalled loudly as I turned too close in front of him. The side street changed abruptly from the melee on multi-laned Johnnie Dodds Boulevard. Within a block, fast food and shopping centers gave way to a desolate tree-shrouded, rough-patched road.

Another turn took me past a church with the face of a fair-skinned Jesus worked into the roof shingles. The street was darker than the boulevard had been, the streetlights scarcer and fainter than the block-lighting halogens. I spotted the sign for Cooper Street and turned.

The houses were a variety of styles and states of repair. I couldn't make out most of the house numbers. My brain throbbed behind my eyes and my hands on the steering wheel were on a delayed reaction timer. My head hadn't gotten the message that I wasn't still hungry. Maybe I should turn around and try again tomorrow.

A turn-around spot didn't immediately present itself. Within half a block of the last house, thick oaks and underbrush swallowed the roadside. Ahead loomed a billboard-sized warning sign, its glow-in-the-dark stripes blazing in my headlights. I told my arms to turn right, but the car didn't obey.

Instead, it missed the sharp turn and plowed straight ahead, barely cutting beside the sign that warned me the road didn't go in this direction.

I felt a neck-jarring bump. The tires lurched off the pavement into the mushy marsh grass. Every jolt played itself out in slow motion, the sharp grass screeching interminably against the driver's door. I desperately hoped it wasn't scratching the paint.

The mud grabbed the front tires and jerked the steering wheel from my hands. The car stopped. My first response was *isn't this interesting*, but a quick panic replaced my lethargy. I remembered — more clearly later than at the time — thinking of Mark Tilman and how I didn't want to die where no one would find me.

Propelled by that thought, I struggled to open the door. The car was stuck in the mud, the front wheels under water at the edge of the lake-sized Cooper River. My car had crossed a wide, seamless sea of grass. The waist-high grass shimmering silver-black in the dusk hid a thick muck of marsh mud.

Could I wade through the thick grass back to the road without sinking out of sight? Where was the road?

I don't know how much time passed before I realized the reason I could see the stars: I was flat of my back. I'd slipped at the river's edge and lay with my feet in the sludgy water, staring upward at the now star-speckled sky.

I reached out for the reassuring cold metal of my Mustang and couldn't find it. It must have moved. Or maybe I had. Then I heard voices.

I tried to call out, but even in the magnitude of my own head, I squeezed out no more than a low croak. God, my head hurt.

I focused on the voices. Maybe they would come without any more effort on my part.

". . . if you hadn't driven halfway to Myrtle Beach lookin' for a place to turn around. Somebody else could'a found her before we got back, long as you took."

"How the hell could somebody find her? Dang car ended up a football field away from the road. You're not careful, you'll end up to your ass in mud."

"Look at that bumper, you shithead. I tol' you, you hit her too hard. No shithead cop's gonna miss that. Jeez."

My Mustang. Oh no, oh no, oh no.

"Shithead yerself. You coulda drove. But no. You had to finish off yer nachos. You got breath like some sewer, all the time eatin' that crap. That bumper coulda been crunched any time. Now shut yer smelly face and get her outta that car."

Grunts and labored breathing came from off to the right. I couldn't tell how far away. The tall grass blocked my view all around and I couldn't convince my head to lift itself, even though the sucking mud was cold and oozing into my ears. I kept staring at the stars through the thick grass waving far overhead.

"Damn door's unlocked but it's stuck. Look out. Stupid car keeps shifting. Help me open it enough to get the inside light on. Damn."

"Where the hell is she?"

I lay quiet and still for what seemed an eternity, listening to rustling sounds and murmurs. Then a splash and a metallic thump followed a piercing shriek.

"Something crawled my leg. Shit, hell and damn. That's it. I've mucked around out here long enough. I'm outta here. Damn snake or somethin'. You're the one rammed her, you find her."

Even though I was having trouble getting my body to respond to anything, the mention of snakes and of *finding her* awakened some primitive alert. An erratic beam of light danced across the grass above me, then the other voice — the shithead rammer — whined, "Hemp, she ain't even in the car. Lookit it. Grass is so deep, you could lose a bird dog in it."

I didn't hear anything for a while but water and mud sounds. I couldn't tell how much time passed. Were they getting closer? Had I passed out again?

Farther away, from the direction slogging footsteps had taken, Hemp's voice came in an angry half-whisper, half-bark. "Find her yerself. Damn, I hate snakes. I hate water in my shoes. I hate you, you dumb shithead. And I hate that mother. I don't care what he promised. Nothing's worth a snake crawlin' up my ass." The voice got farther away, but the vehemence increased.

"She probably fell in the river. She'll wash out to sea with the tide, don't you think?" the whiner's voice asked, closer to me than Hemp's voice.

In the distance, a car door opened, creaking in protest. The whiner screamed in alarm. "Dammit, Hemp. Don'chu leave me here."

Footsteps sucked away fast and heavy. "Hemp! He ain't gonna help Sis," he squeaked. The car engine started. Hemp apparently wasn't listening.

I wasn't sure if I heard another car door open, but I heard one slam. Tires spun in mud, then rattled on graveled pavement. The tire noises whined off into silence, leaving only the shushing of the grass and the slurp of slow, rhythmic water around my legs and waist and the deafening chorus of frogs reclaiming the night.

CHAPTER THIRTEEN

Friday night/Saturday morning

Staring without blinking at the stars, I thought I'd lain there for only seconds. But it might have been hours, because the moon had moved into view over my water-logged toes and the tide rose so that the marsh creek tickled me under the chin.

As I unstuck myself from my marsh mud tomb, I began shivering uncontrollably in the night air.

I cautiously peered over the tall grass. My poor car sat fifteen or twenty feet to my right, the trunk reflecting the moonlight above the thick, sharp grass. The front end must have continued to settle after I'd gotten out, squelching itself into the riverbank. The rear end poked awkwardly into the air. I gave a couple of dry, tearless sobs.

I hoped the door had closed before any mud got inside. And I hoped Mustangs were watertight, since I was discovering, as my mud-caked self dried in the chill air, that marsh mud stinks. My poor car.

My legs moved with the agility of a foam rubber Gumby, but the slick mud grew firmer as I moved away from the river. I waded through the sharp grass, hoping I'd picked the shortest distance to the road. No streetlights to guide me. How had the car come so far?

Somehow I wobbled the distance to the road and collapsed against the road sign that had vainly tried to warn me of danger. How long ago? The moon didn't supply enough light to read my watch, which had probably stopped ticking under its slimy coat of mud. I was shaking so hard my teeth chattered.

Like a simple-minded imbecile, I leaned on the sign, head bowed, studying a watch I couldn't see. The headlights of an approaching car picked me out.

At first, I was bewildered, then hopeful. Then panic-stricken. But my brain, my muscles, my emotions moved too slowly to do me much good.

The fear that Hemp and the shithead whiner had returned for another look-see jolted me. I pushed myself away from the comfort of the warning sign. I would run back in the marsh grass to hide.

Instead, I toppled over like an ankle-bound loser in a three-legged race.

The headlights stopped, reflecting off the luminescent orange of the sign over my head. A door opened. It sounded heavy, like a pick-up truck. A voice, slightly slurry, called, "Hey, you all right?"

The ludicrousness of the scene struck me. I giggled. I'd fallen over like a hundred-pound sack of dog food and lay stretched beneath the carnival orange glow of a road sign, and some half-potted reveler — what night was this, anyway? — wanted to know if I was all right.

He must have been reassured by my hilarity, taking it as a sign that my blood alcohol level matched his. Shoe leather scuffed across the asphalt, onto the roadside gravel. Snakeskin boots came to a halt in front of my face.

"Lordy, what happened to you?" His beery breath enhanced his drawl, but I wasn't about to question the providence or the proclivities of my Good Samaritan.

"Car accident." I managed through clenched teeth. I was shaking again, more violently now. No wonder patients fall in love with doctors who save their lives. I would've kissed him then and married him immediately — if a peroxide vision wearing tight jeans and a scowl hadn't appeared over his shoulder as he hunkered next to me.

"Eddie, you gonna get us killed. First you gotta drive through shanty town in the middle of the night and then you gotta stop for who knows what. I swear—" Drinking obviously made her bitchy. Least, I hoped she'd been drinking. Sober, that screech of hers would be hard to take.

"Shut up, Deely. She's hurt bad." He turned to wipe his mouth against his shoulder. My marsh mud stench must be getting to him. "We gotta git her to a doctor. Do-you-want-to-go-to-a-doctor?"

He talked to me as though to a half-wit. I didn't really want to go to a doctor. I just wanted to get away from here and get warm. In that order. Through my vicious, freezing fatigue, I muttered, "Uh-huh."

"Jeez, Eddie. She stinks to high heaven. Why don't we go call somebody to come get her. If you think I'm—"

"Shut up, Deely" was the last thing I heard. I only faintly remember the trip, my head bouncing against the bottom of the pick-up bed, the smell of tire rubber and old bait, street-lights flashing past overhead.

I came to when Eddie and a guy in a lab coat, a limp stump of a cigar sticking out of his mouth, let down the tailgate. They studied me as if I were a beached porpoise, then grabbed either corner of the flowered bedspread I lay on and pulled me out where they could maneuver me onto the wheeled stretcher.

A red sign overhead read *Emergency Med*. Great. A doc-in-a-box. Eddie chose not to stick around for lengthy explanations. He told the gray-haired cigar chomper where my wrecked car was sitting, butt-end skyward, and climbed into his truck.

As he fumbled for his keys, his truck door hung open just long enough for me to catch Deely's petulant proclamation. "If you think I'm doing anything back there after she's stunk it up, you got another think coming. I don't care what you found in the condom machine at—"

The door slammed shut before the inevitable "shut up, Deely." The gurney wheels bounced my aching skull over the rough parking lot and into the fluorescent-lit hallway. I zoned out for another little while but came to when a woman with dandelion hair began scrubbing the mud off my feet and legs. She and my feet seemed far away, and she didn't look too disgusted by the task. I couldn't talk around my swollen tongue well enough to answer any of her questions. I floated away again into a cold dream.

When I woke up, I knew for sure I'd been asleep because I was clean and warm, wearing a paper dress and wrapped in a cotton blanket. A police officer stood over me. The nurse gently called "Miss? Miss?"

I tried to sit up. Talking to a guy with a starched uniform and the requisite Dick Tracy jawline intimidated me enough without doing it flat of my back. The nurse tried to dissuade me, but I fought her as well as my own lethargy.

As soon as I sat upright on the narrow table, I wished I hadn't won that fight. My body seemed made of gelatin and string, and my stomach churned violently. But this beachhead had been hard fought; I decided to stay upright if it killed me.

"Ma'am, if I could ask you a few questions." A statement, not a question. What is it about cops? Do they all come that way? Or do they become looming and stern after they become cops? Another imponderable.

"We've had your car towed from the creek. Here's the address of the garage. You'll need to call them in the morning and let them know what you'd like to do. Do you understand?"

I nodded. He wasn't being rude. Just observant, since I was staring at the business card as if I'd never seen one before. The card sported a cute little color picture of a wrecker.

"Can you tell me what happened?"

"Not sure." I shook my head and wished I hadn't. "These two men . . . I was getting a headache. I think they might have run me off the road." Even I knew how disjointed that sounded, and I was the one talking.

"Ma'am?"

I tried again, willing my tongue to work. "There were two men. It's — I think they bumped my car. As I started into that turn. They ran me off the road."

"When did this happen? How do you know there were two men?"

"It was getting dark. They came over to my car."

"Did they help you out of the car? Can you describe these men?"

He held a flip-top black notebook, small in his large knotty hand. He looked too young to be a cop, but most of them do, until one day they look too old.

"No. No, I was out of the car. They didn't find me." Mark Tilman flashed into my mind. "I must have crawled out myself, before it settled into the riverbank. They didn't find me."

"Why not? Were you far from the car?" He looked skeptical.

"They must have taken a while to get across the marsh grass. I got out and fell in the grass. They didn't see me."

"Did they bring you to the doctor's office?"

My brain and my tongue were slowly beginning to work. "No. I said they didn't find me."

The creases around his mouth conveyed his cynicism, or his loss of patience with me. I felt strangely distanced, numb.

I hesitated, not wanting to sound silly and melodramatic. "I just kept quiet."

I hadn't admitted it, even to myself. Those men planned to kill me. I clutched the sides of the examining table, my paper dress rustling as I started to shake. My teeth chattered. I clenched them shut.

My obvious shock seemed to convince him I wasn't lying, but he asked, "What did you have to drink this evening before the accident?"

"Nothing." No point in getting indignant. Even I knew I sounded drunk. The look he shot the doctor, with one eyebrow raised, and the doctor's quick nod told me they'd already taken blood samples to test for themselves.

"Two men, you say?"

I didn't know why. Those flashing ambulance lights in the swamp last night — no, night before last — kept strobing through my thoughts. And Mark's body. "Things they said. I don't know. I just know they — scared me. I stayed hidden in the grass. Until they left."

He stared at me longer than necessary, apparently hoping I would add something. I didn't. I was still trying to remember past the fear I'd felt to what they'd actually said.

"Who brought you here?"

"I don't know. Some kid and his girlfriend. In a pick-up truck. They found me at the side of the road. At the warning sign in the curve."

For a moment, I wondered why the doctor hadn't tried to make Eddie and Deely stay. The doc, his damp cigar still clamped in the corner of his mouth, didn't offer anything about Eddie.

"And you say you can't describe these two men?"

I shook my head, but only once. The movement upset the jelly in my head and started the room slopping around. "I never saw them. I only heard them. I was hidden in the grass."

"Would you recognize their voices if you heard them again?"

I thought about it. The whiny shithead's voice pulsed memorably. "Ye-es," I said. "I believe I could."

"Any reason why someone would wish you harm?"

"No." I hesitated. "You might want to talk to Casper Kirkland. He's a Charleston cop."

"About what?" He wrote down the name but didn't look particularly excited about it.

"He's investigating another car accident. In a swamp, last night. No, night before last. Wednesday. On James Island."

His partially raised eyebrow said *So?*

"I don't know why, I keep thinking about that accident. Probably nothing. A friend's car wrecked in a marsh creek out on the island. He died."

While I talked, I convinced myself that I saw boogiemen where there weren't any. The cop, his heavy knuckles wrapped stiffly around his Bic pen, scratched something in his notebook.

Then he looked at me. My hands still clutched the sides of the examining table, but my teeth had stopped chattering. "You're sure you've had nothing to drink. Taken any medication?"

I shook my head, only once for each question, but firmly.

"You understand we can check?"

"I'm a lawyer. I know."

His right eyebrow — the most mobile one — crooked upward a notch, but he said nothing. He just stared, then asked, "Are your pupils usually so dilated?"

I stared back. "I'm sure I don't know. Maybe you should ask the doctor here what he thinks." I'd managed to sit up this long without toppling over or throwing up, so some of my spunk was returning.

The doctor surprised us both by speaking, his unlit cigar drooping dangerously. "Have you taken any prescription medication this afternoon, like a muscle relaxant?"

"No."

He shrugged. "You seem groggy. And your muscle tonicity and reflexes are suppressed."

"I told you. I haven't taken anything. I skipped lunch and ate too late, which gives me a headache. I was dizzy right before the accident. But I didn't take anything."

Under the buzzing glare of the fluorescent lights, their stares were questioning, even accusatory. I wasn't taking any more of this.

"I'd like to get home now, if you don't mind." I wobbled and nearly fell as I got off the table, weakening the effect of my exit.

Just as I wondered how I would pay my way out of this brightly lit inquisitor's chamber, the cop — his badge said *Brewton* — produced my satchel. "Your keys are inside," he said. "I can give you a lift home, if you like."

While settling my bill and listening to instructions to call them if I had any questions or problems, which the receptionist had obviously repeated often, I tried to think of some other way across the Cooper River to my room. But whom could I call at 2:00 a.m. on Saturday morning? Anyone I knew acting his age would've fallen asleep in front of the TV hours before. Anyone still awake was having more fun than I was and wouldn't appreciate the interruption.

After checking my wallet and realizing I didn't have enough money for cab fare, I graciously accepted Officer Brewton's offer. The receptionist begrudgingly loaned me a thin cloth robe to wear home over my paper dress.

My clothes were decomposing in a plastic garbage bag, sealed tight. I'd have to throw them away, but I carried the bag anyway. I loved that deep-purple suit and matching silk blouse. Damn. And my Mustang — my grandfather's Mustang. My stomach roiled at the thought of it wrecked and smelling of marsh mud. Best not throw up in the nice officer's car.

Officer Brewton and I didn't talk. He dropped me at the side door of the inn. Light from the decorative street-lamps shone dim and shadowy. A passing car slowed, gawk-ing at the police car, maybe hoping to see some action. Or maybe my asylum-escapee wardrobe merited the longer look. Officer Brewton waited until I slipped through both the gate and the side doorway. I gave a goodbye wave and pushed the door shut until it clicked solidly.

Exhausted, I took a long soapy hot shower to boil off the lingering smell of dead fish and disinfectant lotion, scrubbed myself with the thick Egyptian cotton towel, and crawled stiffly into bed.

I set the alarm, knowing I wouldn't want to get up in the morning. My body was beginning what I knew would be a full-scale protest. My head felt stuffed and numb.

I was determined to find Tunisia Johnson or her family. They might not be able to tell me anything about Mark Tilman or his notes about her. Or why he'd mailed his journal to Sanda before he died. Maybe it wasn't important, but I had to try to get some answers, and the only direction I knew to take was back over the Cooper River bridge.

CHAPTER FOURTEEN

Saturday morning

I might as well have slept late because I couldn't rouse any-body at a car rental place until after 8:30. The first two I tried wouldn't deliver a car and a third couldn't deliver until noon.

The bruises where the seat belt caught my breast and shoulder were already amazing. I could hardly wait for the Technicolor versions. The rest of the damage seemed limited: soreness that would get worse before it eased off, scratches, bug bites, some swamp mud under my fingernails — and probably places I hadn't discovered yet.

I studied my eyes in the mirror. Last night, the pupils had, despite my denials, been dilated. They now appeared normal. The headache that had crashed in like a hurricane tidal surge trickled as a memory.

Warm sunlight beamed through the bay window. Below, a few dog-walkers and joggers drifted by. Bathed in that sunlight, the memory of last night grew surreal. At the doc-in-a-box, I had denied the oddity of what happened, but today, aching and awake, I was forced to wonder what had caused my odd lethargy last night.

A low-blood-sugar migraine explained part of it. The accident itself could have dazed me, but it had been more than that. Something I'd eaten? That had been the problem, I hadn't eaten anything. Just ice tea, some coffee with Demarcos, more coffee with Ellin. The chicken bog Gladys gave me — uh-oh, maybe I'd gotten something that disagreed with me; no telling how that stuff was fixed.

Maybe I'd call the cigar-chomping doc-in-a-box later and talk to him. If I could remember his name. Or where his office was. I couldn't return the cloth robe he'd loaned me because I'd wrapped it in a plastic bag and limped across the street to toss it in a street-side trash can, along with my gorgeous purple suit. The paperwork from the doctor's office was probably in the robe pocket.

The car-rental delivery guy met me just outside the inn's wrought iron gate to get my signature and present me with the keys to a boxy, nondescript toy car. The kind no one would weep over if it landed in a swamp.

I checked my messages. Jake had called about 10:00 last night. "Av'ry? Didn't finish seating a jury. Don't know what we have yet, but I'm not feelin' too good about a couple of them. Hope to hell you've thought of something useful. Let's get together at the office. Judge Bream's decided to reconvene court tomorrow. Saturday, no less. He wants to get this jury empaneled. He usually breaks at noon, so maybe we can touch base then." He sounded tired.

I faintly remembered the business card with the color picture of the wrecker and found it in my satchel. No answer, so I left a message.

I would wait to call Mom and Dad. After all the work Dad had put into fixing up that car, I dreaded seeing it in the daylight or telling him about it.

Traffic over the bridge ran lighter but only slightly less frantic than rush hour the night before. The added challenge today was the tourists and day-trippers — mostly in minivans and bulky SUVs — racing across the Cooper, headed

110

for Sullivan's Island beaches or the ship museum at Patriot's Point. They would have a nice day, not too cold.

I retraced my route from last night, realizing how little of the trip I remembered. I'd had migraines before, but that headache was a new dimension.

The fair-haired Jesus stared from the church's shingles. That hadn't been a hallucination, though it looked odd on what had to be a Black church, given the neighborhood.

The warning sign stood big as a billboard but not as orange as I remembered it reflected in my headlights last night. The expanse of marsh grass carpeted the tidal creek with a wide border. Faint tracks where my car had been pulled out were evident.

I navigated the ninety-degree turn at the warning sign and easily found Tunisia's address in a clump of houses a half mile farther down the road. The street number was painted in bright blue letters on a cement block at the edge of the drive.

A young Black woman answered the door, a baby with a crusty green pea-stained mouth balanced on her hip. "Tunisia itn't here."

I studied her closely, wondering if she could be Tunisia, afraid I was Child Services or a bill collector or other undesirable. But she didn't look more than fifteen or sixteen years old, and she didn't look like she was lying. I hoped that baby wasn't hers.

An older woman appeared behind her, her expression more cautious, more questioning. A little girl about three clung to her skirt, one of those angelically attractive little girls who make even child-phobic lady lawyers take pause.

The little girl wore an electric pink play jumper and matching canvas shoes, and she worked thoughtfully on a Tootsie Pop. Through the screen, I caught a whiff of grape.

The young teenager with the crusty-faced baby stepped aside as the older woman took her place at the screen door, but she continued to lurk in the background. Apparently I

111

held a bit more interest than the flickering blue light of the television.

The matronly woman wasn't softened by my smiley faces at the little girl. "What egg-zactly is your business with Tunisia?"

"Well—" I had prepared a plausible opening statement, but I'd expected a more cordial greeting. And I'd planned to be talking to Tunisia Johnson. "Are you — would you be her mother?"

She hesitated, as if weighing how much trouble an admission could mean. She then nodded, almost imperceptibly, putting her hand on the little girl's head and drawing her closer. For protection or assurance, I wasn't sure which.

She was more likely Tunisia's grandmother, but at least she admitted kinship.

"I'm a lawyer."

Her fingertips tightened on the wooden frame of the screen door.

"I'm — uh — following up on a request by Dr. Mark Tilman. I believe Tunisia is a patient of his."

I chose my words carefully. Neither Mark nor his dad had given me any kind of retainer, and technically I had no right to dig around in the files or lives of Mark's patients, which left me free-floating in ethical limbo-land.

The woman hesitated, then came to some decision about me. Probably the wrong one, since she unlatched the screen door and pushed it toward me. I followed her into the dimly lit living room where she flicked off the TV and motioned me toward a seat.

To the teenager with the baby on her hip and the little girl crunching softly on the chewy center of her sucker, she said, "Layla, Tabitha, you all go on in the kitchen and start setting the table for dinner."

I got the sense there were others in the house, in the shadows down the hallway and in what looked to be the kitchen. The rustlings were quiet and the house dim.

"Tunisia mentioned Dr. Tilman," she said as she edged herself into a puffy corduroy chair that matched the sofa where she'd seated me. She waited for me to explain my visit.

"I wondered if I could talk to Tunisia. I had a few questions I thought she could help me with. About a project Dr. Tilman was working on."

I spoke of Mark in the past tense, but I hesitated to tell her he was dead. I didn't want to distract her before I got a lead on Tunisia.

"She's not here."

"Well, when might she be home?"

She just shook her head, her lips pressed firmly together.

"Does she still live here? This was the address in her medical file."

She didn't answer.

I crawled farther out on my limb. "I need to follow up on a research project Tunisia is involved in. It's very important that I find her."

She stared silently a few seconds more. Another woman marched through the doorway from the kitchen; she was about the grandmother's age, but rail thin and more certain in her movements.

"Tunisia ain't here. She's been gone. Runned off like her mama did. Probably with that no-account T-Bone or whatever fool name he had."

My heart didn't have time to sink. The woman in the corduroy chair weighed in with surprising force. "She did not, Bessie. And you know it. Tunisia itn't like her mama. She didn't leave Tabbi, especially not for that crazy piece of trash."

Bessie settled onto the other end of the sofa, dislodging a slide of supermarket magazines between us, which she immediately straightened. "Believe what you want, Linnie Ann. She's gone. Been gone. And Tabbi's here. You explain it."

Linnie Ann shook her head and kept shaking it.

I intervened in what appeared a well-worn argument. "When did she leave? Do you have any idea where she is or when she'll be back?"

Linnie Ann crossed her arms tightly over her ample bosoms, still shaking her head.

"There's no telling," Bessie said. "Her mama used to take off regular. Go to New York or wherever some man with money would take her. Tunisia turned out no better'n she ought."

"Bessie, you got an evil mind. Tunisia wouldn't leave Tabbi any more'n she'd cut out her own heart. Something's gone wrong. She wouldn't." Tears welled in Linnie Ann's eyes and she started rocking slightly, to and fro. "She wouldn't."

At her obvious distress, Bessie eased off, her voice more gentle. "Linnie Ann, she's gone. You know she was acting funny. Now she's gone. She'll likely be back, but that don' change things. She's done gone."

"Acting funny?" I tried to use my most soothing, clinical voice. I needed an opening.

"Oh, crazy. She wadn't sleeping good, and she was moody. Had bad headaches. Headaches likely what made her crazy. She said sometime it'd hurt so bad, it was like a curtain of blood come down over her eyes. Blood black was all she could see. Just crazy."

"Have you — have you called anyone? Are you sure she's not in a hospital or something?" *Would they have thought to call around?*

Neither replied. Not even the talkative Bessie. Then Linnie Ann said, in a quiet voice, "She'll be back soon. She loves her little girl. She done good by her, changed everything for her. She'll be back."

Bessie fought not to look smug or to disagree. These two must be sisters, despite their differences in appearance. Was Linnie Ann Tunisia's grandmother and Bessie her great-aunt? I didn't ask.

I tried another tack. "Was she getting any help for her headaches?"

Linnie Ann didn't answer. Bessie said, "I don't know, but I think she seen that Dr. Tilman. She took Tabitha to the clinic for her check-up last week. Maybe Thursday?" She looked at Linnie Ann, who nodded.

"She had a bad one. Said she was having trouble catchin' her breath. Thought she might be getting sick. So she probably talked to him then. You can check with him about that. Last week, she went. With Tabitha."

I should have told them about Mark's death then, but I didn't. I'd have to carefully read those records from the hospital, including Tabitha's clinic records.

I'd intruded on these women long enough. "Thank you so much for your time. When Tunisia gets home," I emphasized the word *when* as I handed Linnie Ann my business card, "please have her call me. My cell number's on the back."

Linnie Ann slipped the card into the pocket of her housedress.

"Would T-Bone or any friends, at a job or school or somewhere, know where she is?"

Neither woman said anything. Neither one of them wanted to talk about T-Bone, and they'd already played out their long-running battle. More questions were pointless.

"Thank you very much for your time. I'd appreciate it if you'd let me know if you hear from Tunisia. It's very important." I tried to broadcast confidence that she would be home soon. I couldn't broadcast far enough to reach them.

Before crossing the river to Charleston, I found the wrecker service that had towed my car. Steve, the guy with his wrecker pictured on his business card, said he saw no structural damage — just a lot of mud to be cleaned from underneath. He gently patted the front fender, promised to clean, wash and wax the car, and deliver it to Jake Baker's office lot later that morning. I could have hugged him.

On the high-arcing bridge back to Charleston, I tried to steal glances off to the right. I could see the rooftops of the more opulent houses that crowded parts of the Cooper River, but Linnie Ann's modest neighborhood was completely hidden by treetops, separated from the river-front mansions by some invisible line.

I parked the rental car in Jake's lot. My satchel, rescued last night by Officer Brewton, still had Tunisia's and

Tabitha's medical records inside. Before Jake came for our noon get-together, I could read their records in more detail while I waited on hold with the local hospitals, checking whether an unidentified young Black woman had been admitted.

Bessie said Tunisia had left last week. No, that she'd taken Tabitha to see Mark Tilman last week. They'd never said when she'd left. Tabitha's record would narrow the time. While I was at it, maybe I could decipher some of Mark's journal.

No one at the area hospitals kept me on hold very long. Apparently unidentified patients are not a daily — or even yearly — occurrence. I even tried the smaller hospitals in outlying areas like Summerville and Kiawah. No mysterious unidentified patients.

I called the coroner's office to see if any unidentified Black females had been found. And I called Monck's Corner, in the only neighboring county with a coroner's number listed. Nothing.

Maybe Tunisia was in New York after all, and I'd fallen for Linnie Ann's hopeless optimism.

I spread the medical records on the table, arranging the charts in chronological order. On Tunisia's record, the Mt. Pleasant address was written in pen, beside a crossed-out Charleston address. I jotted down the old address: DeBard Street. I didn't recognize the name, but it might help me find Tunisia.

Tabitha's chart was slender, without many entries. To be thorough, I read the entire record from beginning to end, which didn't take long since Tabitha was, according to the file, only three years and two months old.

Tabitha's chart listed Tunisia as her mother. No father's name. Tunisia's grandmother, Linnie Ann Johnson of Mt. Pleasant, was given as the emergency next of kin.

Tabitha had visited routinely for her shots and the usual childhood ear infections, colds, and scrapes. Her growth was duly noted. Different doctors had seen her, as would be usual in a clinic staffed by residents and interns. Most recently, though, she'd seen only Mark Tilman.

The note for her last office visit was one of the longest in the record. Mark kept detailed office notes. Like most fledgling doctors, he wrote down everything and tried out all the obscure abbreviations and observations he'd learned in medical school.

Apparently Tabitha fought a running battle with ear infections. She'd taken a round of antibiotic but was still sick. Mark noted that he prescribed cefaclor and that they'd discussed allergy tests and maybe a specialist referral to see about tubes in her ears. *Cost is a consideration*, he wrote.

In the next paragraph, he'd written:

Mother, Tunisia, presenting with severe HA. Questioned about her fatigued appearance, replied not feeling well lately. Episodes of severe SOB, blurred vision. BP 164/110. Pt. still participating in project at B.Med. Insisted that she contact Hilliard about her sympts. Discont. research protocol.

Hilliard? What the — why did Mark want her to contact him? My jaw muscles clenched. I kept reading.

Patient concerned that sympts. may be side effects of res. protocol. Pt. talked to Hilliard and he didn't think so. Commented "money I'm getting to see this through sure comes in handy paying Tabbi's bills." Make note to see Hilliard re payments.

Mark's records were chatty, but I found myself frustrated that he hadn't written more.

Hunched over the records in Jake Baker's conference room, the lucid part of me recognized Hilliard's only research role was likely as a paper-pushing administrator. But the vengeful part of me, the part my mother says is Granddad reincarnated, wasn't rational. Wasn't there a Bible verse? "Let not the root of bitterness . . ."

Hilliard was a liar. He'd sell out anybody, particularly if it served the double benefit of protecting a doctor from the consequences of his actions and feathering Hilliard's own nest. If he'd lie on a witness stand to protect a doctor, he'd lie about anything.

I opened Tunisia's file. She had visited the clinic for about six years, including the time of her pregnancy and Tabbi's birth. Early on, she had seen different physicians each time. On two occasions, the last one two months before she came in to confirm an at-home pregnancy test, she was given metronidazole. Treated for STD — sexually transmitted disease — twice within two years. Add that to a pregnancy with no father in sight. Dear Lord.

Her aunt — or great-aunt — Bessie seemed so sure she'd taken off, just like her mother had. Apparently her background made that plausible. But Linnie Ann had been equally sure that she hadn't. After all, Tunisia had left Charleston, moved back to Mt. Pleasant to raise her daughter. She hadn't aborted her, which would have taken less time than getting rid of her sexually transmitted trichomonas infection. But she hadn't.

So where was she? Was she really the reason Mark sent his research journal by courier? Had I missed something?

In early December, Mark noted that Dr. Ellin had suggested Tunisia ask about a research project — the Rabb project, he called it. Headed by Hilliard. A contraceptive project. Did that signal a new boyfriend? Or a return to her old life?

I dug through the shower of papers on the conference table until I found Cas Kirkland's number. I should've thought to ask him earlier. When he didn't answer, I left a quick message: "Mark Tilman was trying to find a missing patient. Tunisia Johnson, a young Black woman from Mt. Pleasant. Do you know her?"

I turned back to the charts. Tunisia's chart showed no recent visits, and Mark hadn't noted the visit she'd made with Tabbi in her chart, the visit when he'd been so concerned about Tunisia's condition. Apparently she didn't come to the clinic for herself very often, but combined with visits she made with Tabbi, she had seen Mark regularly over the last few months. I pushed aside Demarcos's insinuation of a relationship between the two. The records were purely clinical.

Mark could have also seen her at Barnard Medical, as part of the research group. Maybe he'd recorded Tunisia's follow-up in his research journal. Or was there a separate research file? If so, those must be stored separately from the hospital's medical records.

I stacked the loose pages of Tunisia's clinic chart and stretched. Jake must have been delayed at the courthouse. I got a Coke from the refrigerator and flopped down on the sofa with Mark's half-sized black notebook. Abbreviations and references I couldn't decipher complicated Mark's chatty style. I'd read plenty of medical records, but a Ph.D.'s research notes presented virgin terrain.

Impatient, I thumbed through jottings about the progress of different patients, notes to himself about things to compare with other patients' files. *LM* (someone's initals?) *reports severe HA* (headache). *Hx* (history) *of migraine. Include in intake questions* was a typical note — or at least typical of the few I could understand.

Mark meticulously dated each entry. He wrote more legibly than most physicians, but mood or fatigue or haste varied his handwriting from day to day. He wrote with strong, sure strokes, usually in black ink.

The initials TJ began appearing in the research notes on December 27. The TJ notations appeared at regular intervals and read much the same as the other entries. LM and her headaches reappeared, along with a note dated January 31: *c/w TJ.*

January 31 was one of the last entries, the day after Tunisia's and Tabbi's visit to the clinic, when Mark had urged her to report her problems to Hilliard. Mark had also noted Tunisia's symptoms in his journal, underlining *Fam Hx stroke unknown. TJ's mother not available. See LH. C/w LM and others.*

"C/w" meant "compare with." LM was likely another patient. His notes were beginning to make some sense.

I shut the notebook and stroked its smooth cover. Mark apparently spotted something wrong with Tunisia, something to do with the Rabb project. Did Mark know Tunisia planned to run away? Had his journal been sent to tell someone she was leaving, to stop her for her own good? Was he worried because having her drop out of sight would compromise the research? Or did something else prompt his concern?

I listened to traffic shush past on Broad Street outside. I was wasting my time. Tunisia Johnson had hit the road again for her own reasons. That stupid notebook, the traffic accident, those men at the river, the fire, all stupid coincidences.

My cell phone buzz startled me.

"Avery? Cas Kirkland. I got your call. Can you come down to the station? Something I think you'll be interested in. In the Tilman case."

Tilman case? Cas Kirkland still had some agenda he wasn't sharing. How could I resist such a charming invitation?

Lunchtime had passed with no word from Jake, so I left him a phone message. Outside, Steve had delivered my car as promised. I checked it over carefully. The dent was small, thanks to the old-fashioned metal bumper. Steve the wrecker guy had meticulously cleaned all the mud, even from the wheel wells and underneath, with the same reverence and concern I had for this car. Bless him. I probably needed to park this car back in my parent's garage. I obviously couldn't handle the responsibility or strain of stewardship.

I cranked it and turned toward the police station.

CHAPTER FIFTEEN

My midnight exploits had left my muscles in tangles, and I craved a nap. Jake Baker might call me back to his office at any moment, but I wasn't about to pass up Cas Kirkland's invitation. As I cut through the back way, I spotted a familiar street name: DeBard Street. Surprised, I cut a quick right. On my way, I could check Tunisia's old address, the one crossed out in her medical chart.

I circled the block twice before I was sure I'd found it. Only a few blocks north of Calhoun Street, the apartment house was a world away from Linnie Ann's Mt. Pleasant home. Trash littered the gutter. Graffiti — the only paint on the canted wood-frame buildings — showed little artistic talent.

Guys perched on the curbs and steps and leaning against each other showed little sign of talent for anything but drinking and staring. The few women I saw — probably a lot for this time of day — were the only residents who appeared gainfully employed.

One girl showed particular interest in my car, strutting out in the street as I slowly cruised toward her. When she saw me behind the wheel, though, she spun on her stilt heel and sashayed back to the sidewalk, angrily shaking her long curly wig.

The only pale face in the neighborhood besides mine was a guy in a Cadillac parked on a cross street. I glimpsed him through the crack in his tinted window while he negotiated with a girl who couldn't have been more than fifteen. He sported a rat-brown toupee and the Grand Canyon wrinkles of heavy drink.

Even in mid-afternoon, a white girl in a red vintage convertible shouldn't drive too slowly through here. Tunisia had done good to get back to Mt. Pleasant. I didn't think it smart to stop and ask whether she'd returned here. Nobody would answer truthfully anyway.

I turned onto Liasset and into some semblance of a world I knew, with fast-food chicken places and buildings that had paint.

What had Tunisia been doing, living in a place like that? I doubted she'd been flipping burgers at a North Charleston McDonald's. And what about her light-skinned daughter with the liquid brown eyes and the grape Tootsie Pop? Damn. Was Tunisia, despite her picket fence and porch swing surroundings in Mt. Pleasant, back on the streets? The thought of old Cadillacs, cheap toupees, and hopelessness made me queasy.

A cop behind a glass window buzzed me through a security door to the administrative offices and directed me to one of those observations rooms just like on TV. On a table in the middle of the room, a cop sat watching the drama play out in the interrogation room next door.

Through the one-way glass, I could see Cas Kirkland and another officer in a small room dominated by a scarred metal table and four chairs. Three of the chairs were occupied — two by cops and the third by a wizened, sun-browned raisin of a man.

He had few, if any, of his own teeth. His eyes sank into the wrinkles in his unhealthy red-brown face, and he reminded me of those animated clay raisins on the television commercials. He didn't sound as though he could sing as well.

"Dauber, come on, man." The cop across from Cas wheedled. "Dave, over at the pawnshop, already dropped the dime on you. This watch was your prize, along with some worthless old liquor bottles you dug outta the creek. You've wasted enough time. You were there. What's the harm in telling us? 'Less, a'course, you did him yourself."

Dauber had been twitching in his seat like a beetle on a string. At that comment, he really got agitated. "I didn't do nobody. You lyin'. You lyin'. I don't know nothing. I just dig bottles."

Cas sighed deeply. Even a slight movement from a man his size draws all the attention in a room that small. "Joey, why don't you go out and get us some coffee?"

Joey made an exasperated sound and bounced his chair off the wall as he stood to leave.

Cas leaned back and spoke conversationally to Dauber. "Find any of those South Carolina Dispensary bottles out there lately? Those are a real find."

Joey stepped into our darkened room, nodded at me, and joined the silent cop perched on the edge of the table to watch the conversation in the other room.

"Shore nuff." The excitable little raisin danced in his seat. "Can't get 'em much anymore, seems. Too many folks digging, I reckon. Some college kids come out places, now. Some a'them Cit'del boys." He looked crestfallen.

"Yep.' Cas matched Dauber's disappointment. "I wouldn't mind having one of those Dispensary bottles myself. I hear one can bring a good month's wage."

"Let me tell you, that'd keep a fella like me for quite some time, what with my disability check. But nope, they's hard to find."

Cas nodded sympathetically. He casually reached for the watch the other officer had flung on the table in front of Dauber.

"Mr. Dothan, I'd appreciate knowing something about this watch. A nice young fella, a doctor, died out in the marsh Wednesday night. You show up with this watch and some creek bank bottles at a pawn shop on Friday morning. I can't help but think you could help us out." He paused, turning the gold link watch in his hand.

"That kid didn't deserve what happened to him. I'm sure you want to help. His family, they're wondering, you know."

Cas should have taken to the stage. He wrung every last ounce of pathos from his plea. I thought little Dauber Dothan, hunkered in Cas's shadow, was going to cry.

He started shaking his head, biting his bottom lip. "They flung the watch away. And his wallet. Just flung 'em away." Dauber Dothan sounded sad, disappointed by the flinging of the watch.

I didn't know what Cas had expected to hear, but that wasn't what I was listening for.

"Who, Mr. Dothan?"

"Two fellas. They come after he wrecked. I heard this loud noise. Then next thing I know'd, there's car lights underwater, shinin' right under water. Damnedest thing ever." He shook his head in wonderment. "I thought they'd come to he'p him." His voice clearly said they hadn't.

What two men? I wanted to tap on the window and ask.

"Where'd they come from?" Cas asked.

"The road, I reckon. I didn't hear a car, but then I'uz a ways away. That road's right soft there, not paved or nothing. They'uz there on the bank." He shivered and crossed his wiry brown arms over his chest, covering his faded Spoleto Festival T-shirt.

"The two men came down to the car?"

Dauber nodded and chewed his bottom lip with his thick yellow teeth. He nodded again, as if watching something play out in his head, something he didn't want to see again.

"Did they try to help him?"

124

Dauber took a breath. "That's what I thought at first. One of 'em opened the door. I couldn't see too clear. They'uz on the far side. But the inside light come on, and he's slumped over the wheel."

He fell silent again. I held my breath, afraid his reluctance to relive it would win out and he'd clam up.

"Then, I just don't know. Somethin' happened. I slipped in the water. Scared me bad and I fell and filled my waders. He was over him. Had his head. Then one of 'em flung somethin' across the creek, and they left."

His voice was sad. "The car lights went out." He was silent a minute, watching the picture fade.

Dauber wasn't squirming any more, but he uncrossed his arms and fidgeted with his fingers.

Cas let him sit quiet before asking, "You found the wallet and the watch on the opposite bank?"

Dauber looked up at Cas. I couldn't tell what was in his eyes. Alarm? Shame? Fear? All those reactions at once?

"Had to go that way to get to my scooter. I left it on that bank. Had to go that way. But I knew there wadn't anything I could do for him. I looked. But there wadn't. And I just picked up the watch. Didn't think he'd mind. I left the wallet. So somebody'd know him. And I called. To tell 'em about the accident."

At that, the two cops watching with me stirred and exchanged glances. Dauber must have explained an anonymous 911 call for them.

"That's helpful, Mr. Dothan. And no, there wasn't anything you could have done to help that young fellow. You shouldn't have removed the watch, though."

"Or the money," muttered Joey, the cop who'd been in the room with them earlier.

The other cop, a young guy who barely looked old enough to shave, shook his head. "Think he's telling the truth?"

Joey shrugged and slid his butt off the table. "They're always lyin' about something, thieving old rummy." Joey left and reappeared almost instantly in the room next door.

Cas was winding down the interview and asked Dauber if he'd repeat his statement for Officer Joey Bayler. No one mentioned that Joey hadn't brought any coffee.

Cas joined me. "Want a Co'Cola or something?"

I must have held every muscle tense during the interview because I had a hard time loosening up to follow him down the hall. After last night, my body kept warning me it was tired of abuse.

We parked ourselves at a wobbly little table in the break room. Cas still carried the gold watch in his hand. He laid it on the table and popped the top on his soft drink can. "What did you think?" He eyed me as he took a loud gulp.

I picked up the watch, gently turning it over. The engraving read: *To Mark, with love, Mom and Dad.*

I looked at him and shrugged. "You think he was telling the truth?"

"I asked first."

I fingered the heavy metal watchband. The watch kept good time. Finally, I nodded. "I think he was. He seemed — I don't know, embarrassed, maybe. About taking the watch. Or scared, for some reason, about what he saw. But I think he was telling the truth."

Cas rolled his Coke can between his palms and nodded thoughtfully.

"What happened out there? What did he see?"

Cas looked at me, studying my expression in an odd way. Then he said calmly, "Someone broke Mark Tilman's neck."

CHAPTER SIXTEEN

Saturday afternoon

My stomach lurched at Cas's words. Good thing I don't vomit easily.

Broke his neck echoed in my head, but I couldn't get a sound out.

"The autopsy prelim indicates he died of a broken neck. His nose was bloodied and broken, probably when his car crashed. We questioned whether hitting his nose on the steering wheel could have snapped his neck. The medical examiner thought it possible, but unlikely. He won't say more until everything's complete. That could be weeks."

"But from what Mr. — Dothan said, you think—" Bile ate at the back of my throat.

"Sure sounds suspicious. His account was a bit disjointed, but something went wrong out there. Something's got him rattled."

I nodded, solemn. That's what had struck me about Dauber Dothan's story. He'd chatted easily until he got to what happened after the car crash. The mental pictures he replayed frightened him: his own actions, letting his greed overcome his common decency — and what he'd witnessed, what the men who'd appeared had done.

"So you think Mark was — murdered." I said it aloud to see if the word, said and heard, would make it easier to accept.

"It fits what we know so far."

I crossed my arms tightly. "But who would — why?"

Cas shrugged. "Sometimes we never know for sure. Something usually turns up." He looked at me with his flat blue eyes. "We thought you could help."

Now we came to the real reason he'd invited me to hear Dauber Dothan. I rocked back and forth in my chair, as if to keep warm in a room cool enough for cops in wool pants. Too much information crowded into my brain, trying to reprocess itself. The most important bits had to do with last night and what to tell Cas and how to tell him without sounding melodramatic.

My story started spilling out before things sorted themselves for me. Maybe I just needed to hear the story out loud before I could begin to believe its absurdities myself.

I told him about my drive last night looking for Tunisia, my headache, the accident. And, finally, about the two men I'd only heard but not seen.

"Would you recognize either of them again? Can you describe them?"

I shook my head, clutching either elbow in a death grip, remembering how desperately I'd wanted to sink into the cold mud, to disappear, to keep from seeing or being seen.

"I'd recognize their voices." I strained to remember the voices, knowing that time and fickle memory would take the voices farther away. I also knew it would take more time and distance to forget the fear that washed over me again, fresh and sharp as the saw grass.

"Do you — you don't think it could be the same guys, do you?" I had to ask.

An expression moved across his face. It didn't stay. "Seems a bit too much of a coincidence. Did you see what they were driving?"

"No. But I think they bumped me from behind."

He clicked the tab on his drink can several times before he spoke. "You said you had a headache last night. The blood work showed you weren't drinking. Do you think you could have been drugged?"

"Huh?"

He looked up from his can and let out a deep breath. "I have a confession to make. Officer Brewton from over in Mt. Pleasant called me this morning. Checking up on you." He gave a half-smile. "Frankly, you're lucky the Highway Patrol didn't work that accident. They'd have hauled your ass to jail."

I would've spluttered with indignation, but he'd hit too close to home. "They asked plenty of questions about that last night. Worst thing I did yesterday was have coffee with a couple of doctors. I get hungry and get a headache. Maybe I ate something I'm allergic to in some chicken bog — the food additive MSG can give me a headache. I always get headaches." I tried to gather my self-righteous indignation about me, but had trouble holding it tight. I changed the subject. "So who were the guys Dauber saw at Mark's car? Did they kill him?"

Cas studied me. "You have any ideas? After all, the way some might look at it, your invitation lured him out there, knowing he would have to drive out over the dike."

He was trying to needle me, but I didn't need to hear that. This was the part that hadn't completely reordered itself in my head. "The only things Mark and I might have in common are our hometown and whatever he wanted to talk to me about. Nothing ever happens in Dacus." I shrugged. "So it has to be something here."

"You don't know what that was."

"Well—" I drawled it out. He wasn't going to like any of it — probably wouldn't believe any of it, so what did it matter? "I've got a bit more idea than I had the first time we talked. He mailed his girlfriend a notebook."

Cas latched onto the wrong thing. "You've talked to the girlfriend?"

I nodded and tried to push the conversation back where I thought it should be. "A research journal of some sort. I think he wanted to talk about something involving research he was doing at Barnard Medical."

"Is this girlfriend here in town?" Cas pulled out his little flip-top notebook. "Any indication they were having any problems?"

"No. For Pete's sake."

His eyebrows lifted at my tone, but he kept scribbling.

"It's the hospital, Cas. Not anything to do with his girlfriend. It's something at the hospital, with his research."

"Sure it is. Those were two neurosurgeons Dauber Dothan saw in the tidal creek, operating on Mark Tilman's neck. And a couple of orthopods came looking for you in the swamp last night. I'm surprised Dauber didn't notice their nice white lab coats and their Mercedes. Funny he didn't mention that."

Exasperated, I spelled Sanda MacKay's name for him. "I have Mark's research journal, the one she called me about. I've deciphered most of the abbreviations and scribbles; if you're interested, I can finish translating for you." He nodded absently as he made notes beside Sanda's name.

I changed the subject. "Do you know somebody named T-Bone who—"

His head snapped up. "You need to back away from him. He's serious trouble." His sharp tone said that was an order, not a request.

"Who is T-Bone?"

"None of your business, if you are smart. He's a — pimp, to put it politely. A very dangerous little psycho. How'd you run across him?"

I shrugged. "Someone just mentioned him—"

"Cas." The kid cop from the interrogation room came to the door and jerked his head, indicating he needed Cas down the hall.

"Can you wait here a minute?"

I nodded and Cas swung around the corner, moving quickly for such a large man.

T-Bone, a pimp. Sadly, Tunisia Johnson looked like a dead end in more than one way. As to Mark, I had to admit to myself, now I wasn't looking at Cas Kirkland's questioning smirk, that the vision of lab-coated thugs with MD license plates was a bit ludicrous. But, then, Detective Kirkland didn't know some of the doctors I knew.

What could Mark have wanted to talk to me about? Why had we both had such oddly similar accidents? Thanks to a snake, mine had a better ending than Mark's. The two men last night hadn't really threatened me. The whiner speculated maybe I'd float out to sea — not exactly a Good Samaritan, but not a threat, either. Were they the same men Dauber had seen? Did the rear bumper of Mark's car have a dent from a rear end nudge, like mine did?

I've seen enough simple mistakes, serious shenanigans, and overblown egos around Barnard Medical that I could believe just about anything. But Cas was right; no doctor or administrator would be hip-deep in water moccasins and leeches, breaking some medical resident's neck. Sure, plenty of them might want to snap a lawyer's neck, but they never follow through on the urge.

Even though doctors have the disposable income to hire their dirty work done, good hit men are hard to find. In a state where Pee Wee Gaskins is our most famous mass murderer, what caliber of hit man could anybody expect to find? Assume you find a hit man. How do you get rid of him? Anybody with enough money to pay a hit man has enough money to pay blackmail. I had to agree, reluctantly, with Cas. A hospital could certainly supply the motive for murder, but could it supply the means?

Maybe Mark had walked in on some high-level mob confab in a patient's room. Right. South Carolina overrun with hit men and mobsters. And Carl Hiaasen writes for the *Frogmore Daily Gazette*. The most likely explanation was robbery. Mark's wallet was empty and Dauber Dothan hadn't admitted taking the money. Maybe that's why they tried to get into my car — to rob me.

Cas returned, his face solemn. His stare, with his lashless eyes, was too direct. He looked like he was trying to make up his mind about something.

"What?"

"Just got a call. A body turned up. A young black female."

I could tell from his expression he knew who it was.

"What happened?" My question was almost a whisper.

"They're still working the scene. In an abandoned building, not far from here. It's — odd. The detective who picked it up called. He recognized her. I'm heading over there."

"Can I come?" I stood, gathering my satchel, too intent on my search for Tunisia to doubt that he'd take me along.

"No." He shook his head. "This isn't—"

"I'll stay out of the way. I just need — to see. I met her family this morning. Her little girl. It's — personal. I'll be quiet. Invisible." I stood next to him in the doorway, my satchel over my arm.

"No. You wouldn't be allowed into the scene anyway."

The disappointment on my face must have softened his response, but it didn't change his mind. "I'll call you later. Okay?"

I nodded, reluctantly. Of course they wouldn't let me on an active crime scene, and what could I hope to accomplish?

That didn't stop me from waiting in the parking lot and discreetly following Cas's unmarked car the few blocks to the scene.

My tailing job wasn't discreet enough. He parked behind a line of official vehicles and waited on the sidewalk for me to pass, giving me a "scram" sign. I waved and nodded, slowly driving on down the narrow street crowded with cop cars and gawkers.

Dear Lord. This area looked worse than the shambles I'd seen on DeBard Street. The only improvement here was no hookers or clientele. If they operated as openly — which I doubted, given the backwater desolation of the place — they were long gone. Not good for business, cop cars and gawkers.

Crime scene tape roped off a three-story standard Charleston single house, added onto over the years. The paint had peeled off years ago, and the dry, gray structure seemed to lean in upon itself, hopeless and tired.

I turned around down the block and eased back by, but couldn't really see anything except several cops, including Cas, gathered outside the crime scene tape on the backside of the house. Cas's arms were crossed over his barrel chest, his white hair glowing almost pink in the sun. He concentrated on the ground at his feet, oblivious to my drive-by as he listened to a younger uniformed officer.

I drove toward Jake's. That grape-flavored little girl. Dear Lord, Turisia had made it out. Why go back? I wanted to sob.

As I crept down upscale King Street, crowded with shops and shoppers, my cell phone buzzed.

"Avery, dammit. Where the hell are you? This case is going down the shitter and my so-called staff is blown to the four effin' winds."

I sat with my mouth hanging open for a second. Rather than come out fighting — my initial response — I just said, "I'm a few blocks from the office, Jake. I'll be there—"

"I said twelve effin' noon. It's now—"

I punched the off button. In a few seconds, the phone buzzed again. I dropped it in my bag. It stopped, then started again as I walked into Jake's office a few minutes later.

He saw me, slammed down the receiver he was holding, and spun to confront me. I got to him first.

"Don't you cuss me, you sonofabitch."

Something in my face made him back up a step.

"Is that clear?"

"Avery." He held his hands up in surrender, looking as if somebody had let the air out of his balloon. "I'm sorry, Avery. Dammit. My dick's in a ringer." His tone was apologetic. I gave him points for that, but he wasn't going to take his frustration out on me.

I thumped my satchel on the edge of his desk, wincing from soreness, and stood facing him. "How's the jury look?"

My mouth was tight with anger, but I was ready to move past his temper tantrum.

A twitching muscle at the corner of his mouth telegraphed that he'd like to blow up again, but he squelched it.

"'Bout as useful as an egg-sucking dog in a hen house." He plopped into his oversized desk chair. "The judge — who incidentally hates personal injury lawsuits and personal injury lawyers — is sharpening his knife on a strop under his bench, waiting for a chance to carve my balls off and string 'em up like Christmas lights. How the hell you get a state court judge that hates personal injury? Thought all those unimaginative, uncaring twits ended up on the federal bench."

He leaned his chair way back. "Tell me something, A'vry." His voice was plaintive.

"Jake, you don't want to hear it. Perforce has a great reputation. Uplift is a very helpful drug. It saves lives, restores people to some level of normalcy. Doctors love it." I sank into the chair and shrugged. "What can I say?"

"In two, three days . . ." His voice trailed off. He wanted to pick a fight with someone, but now he had sense enough not to pick me. "I'll need you in court Monday. Opening statements, first thing."

"You're kidding. So soon?" No wonder he was boiling over.

"Judge is moving this like a freight train on full throttle. Doesn't believe in wasting a jury's time, he says. To hell with fairly representing the folks who've been injured. He's not even doing the usual arm-twisting to get Perforce to consider offering a settlement."

He didn't have to explain what that meant. The judge had already made up his mind that it should be a defendant's verdict. He didn't intend to wheedle even a token nuisance settlement out of Perforce to cut the trial short.

No need to reinforce for Jake why there wouldn't be a settlement offer. If he asked, I could give him the word on Perforce's weak patent research and development strategy, but he wasn't going to ask. Not today.

We sat in silence. I rationalized I'd followed up all the leads I had for Jake, even though that didn't help Jake. He had a bunch of injured folks, thousands of his own dollars sunk into trial preparation, and a deck stacked against him.

"I got one more peremptory challenge left. One effin' more. I had to let them seat a woman who's a secretary for the defense attorneys' association in order to hold onto that one strike. I got a judge who wouldn't strike her as prejudiced."

That was bad. Attorneys on both sides get a limited number of challenges or strikes they can use to excuse a potential juror. The judge, though, has unlimited strikes. He can set aside anybody who may be unduly biased. Hard to imagine somebody more biased against plaintiffs than someone working for defense lawyers, but not much to do about it if the judge disagrees.

I didn't bother telling Jake about my car accident or anything else. He was in trial mode. A nuclear disaster wouldn't easily penetrate his focus.

"Avery. We haven't found the magic key to this case." He thumped his feet to the floor and swiveled his chair to face me. "That means we're left with trying the hell out of the case we have. We got to try this like we've never tried a case before. I'll need you there, watching my backside."

I nodded. Jake was going to have to fight his way out of his wallow pit. Too bad I couldn't give him a hand up. I was too sore.

"What's scheduled this afternoon?"

"We'll seat the last three jurors and hear the pretrial motions." He played with a pewter shark paperweight on his desk, swimming it back and forth on his blotter.

"You'll get all that done today?"

He shrugged. "Judge Bream had his way, we'd proceed directly to the flogging and hanging part."

On the corner of his desk, my satchel buzzed, startling us both.

He smacked his palms lightly on his blotter. "Gotta go. Oh, and would you look at the stuff we have on Tixtill

135

— one of Perforce's other drugs. I want to see what you think about getting the problems they had with Tixtill admitted in this case. Talk to you later."

I grabbed my bag and headed for the hallway to answer my phone.

"Avery. I been calling you for days and all last night, but I couldn't get through. Where have you been?"

Mom. I'd forgotten to call her. Even worse, I hadn't told her about my car accident. Now wouldn't be a good time.

"Um. I've been working, Mom. Sorry. I got your message, but it absolutely slipped my mind."

"You okay? You sound — preoccupied."

"I was expecting another call, but I can talk. It's too early for that other call."

"Well." She didn't sound too vexed at me for not calling her. Or too convinced that all was well. She changed the subject. "You got my message about the dynamite?"

"Um-hmm."

"That county prosecutor — actually it's some new kid, not from around here. Josiah's off at a meeting in Hilton Head and no use to anybody as a prosecutor. This kid just says there's nothing he can do with the — and these are his words — 'tenuous word-of-mouth hearsay evidence you've brought forth.' Kid's got a rod up his butt, if you ask me."

Mom occasionally hangs around her aunt Letha and picks up bad language.

"Now I ask you, if a county constable is not a good source of information, I don't know who is. I got Miranda and her mama to stay over here until Josiah gets backs from Hilton Head—"

"Mom—" The targets of a crazed, love-struck hillbilly dynamite thief as house guests. Not a good plan.

"—seemed the best solution. Constable Lester is helping keep an eye on things, and your father has a gun or two."

A .22, probably loaded with birdshot, and a .38 Police Special that likely hadn't been fired since I last took it out to shoot cans, so long ago the soft-nosed bullets would have disintegrated by now.

An armed and dangerous constable who only had three teeth to call his own and my father with a .22 — provided, of course, someone alerted my father to the need for a .22. He has developed an admirable capacity for blocking out most of what my mother gets up to. It's the only way to survive in the maelstrom.

Now certainly was no time to distract her with my trial, with Tunisia, or my car accident. I had survived, and some mud in my wheel wells could hardly compete with stolen dynamite for dramatic effect. The rest, I'd have to save for a real conversation.

"You don't think it would do any good to call Josiah in Hilton Head, do you?" she asked.

"No, probably not." Considering he'd likely met a Bambi or a Tawni and considering how much he'd have been drinking by this late on a Saturday afternoon, I really didn't think calling him would do any good. "You called the sheriff's office, didn't you?"

"They said they'd alert the patrols, but you know how seldom they drive by out here. No, I expect we'll be fine. We'll just wait until Monday. Josiah's supposed to be back from his meeting by then."

Tanned, rested, and ready to take on Miranda Cole's dynamite-thieving mountain goober.

"You all be careful, Mama."

"Of course we will, honey. Good luck with your trial. When you gonna be home?"

Soon I assured her as I said goodbye.

Now, on top of everything else, I could worry about Mom and Dad. No point in telling Mom how many times innocent rescuers get caught in the crossfire of domestic disputes. This sounded like a doozy, but no point in lecturing. She wouldn't pay any attention. Dad couldn't do anything with her. Prayer was likely the only option.

I had wandered to the parking lot while we talked, planning to look over my notes and map my next steps. First, lunch needed to be in the mix. Jake seemed to operate on adrenaline and late-night, large-size bourbons. Not me. It was officially late afternoon, and I wasn't going to repeat yesterday's killer migraine. If that's what I'd had. I doubted the doc-in-a-box had tested for anything but alcohol. Doctors often hate to even test for that because a positive result may mean the doc gets dragged into court to testify. If the accident is minor and the cops aren't pushing for a criminal charge, it's just easier to turn a blind eye. I'd best eat lunch.

My phone buzzed. This time, it was Cas Kirkland.

CHAPTER SEVENTEEN

Saturday afternoon

Cas Kirkland tends to bark, the short, staccato delivery of someone used to giving orders. Ex-military? Probably. But now, his tone was subdued and solicitous. Probably as close as he gets to a tender moment.

"She's been there a while, but one of the guys who used to work Vice recognized her. It's Tunisia Johnson."

I didn't quite trust my voice. "What happened?"

"Looks like something kinky went wrong." He wasn't going to bother being sensitive.

"Where?"

"Upstairs. In that abandoned store building."

I didn't say anything so he could fill in the blanks.

"The place is a regular Grand Central for scum. Folks looking for privacy, a place to hide, shoot up, get laid, take a crap. They pried the boards loose on a back window and used that as the secret entrance."

"What happened?" I repeated.

He took so long to answer, I thought our connection had broken. "Apparently she'd learned some new tricks. Or she found a john into something new. Seen guys do this to themselves, but never seen anyone do it to a woman. She sure didn't do this to herself." His tone was clinical. I didn't think he intended the undercurrent of anger for me. "You heard of autoerotic asphyxiation?"

"Yeah." In law school, one of the peripheral benefits of a forensic medicine class. "A guy puts a noose around his neck while — stimulating himself. The brain panics at the loss of oxygen and the panic intensifies his sexual pleasure." I wanted Cas to know I too could be clinical.

"Sometimes the jerk ends up dead. Great way for your mom or wife to find you, trussed to a chair with your dick in your hand and your eyes and tongue bulging out."

Whoever walks in on such a scene often thinks the guy has been tortured and murdered. City cops aren't usually fooled, especially if they've seen it before. Or they've at least heard about it; apparently investigating one is so memorable that it's a favorite topic with forensics guys, hence my law school education.

"So what's this? An accident?" My stomach lurched as I pictured this woman I'd never met but about whom I knew too many intimate details. Now the cops and crime scene guys and the medical examiner knew even more intimate details. The thought embarrassed me. And made me sad.

Cas hesitated before answering. "Something's funny about this one. She was spread on a mattress on the floor, the rope around her neck, arms, and feet. The way the thing was rigged, any — activity — would have slowly strangled her."

He talked more to himself than to me. "But something's not right. Hard to tell on black skin, though she's light-skinned, but my guess is someone moved her after she was dead. Lividity looks like the scene might have been staged. We'll know more when the ME finishes."

I swallowed to keep from gagging; glad we were talking by phone. "After she was dead?"

Cas didn't say anything for a while. "The rope left no visible bruising. Hard to be sure until the autopsy, but I'm not believing this was an accident."

We were both quiet, playing our own mental pictures. His, I'm sure, were more vivid than mine, and mine were sickening.

"When did she die?"

For some reason, knowing when someone died always seems so important. As if, when we know the exact moment, we could remember where we were and we would remember having noticed. Surely something as significant as death leaves its mark on the fabric of our shared universe. Getting philosophical keeps me from crying.

"Don't know. The heat's gotten to her a bit. Whoever stuffed her there hadn't counted on how much heat builds up, even in February. The smell attracted attention. That's why she was discovered, or at least why someone finally reported it."

"Dear Lord." I thought of Tabbi, the little grape-smelling girl with the wide, intelligent eyes. And Linnie Ann and Bessie and the neat little bungalow in Mt. Pleasant, and that sad fright-scene on DeBard Street where Tunisia used to live and work.

"When will the medical examiner know something?" Charleston was one of the few counties in South Carolina with a medical examiner. Most of the other counties still had part-time coroners, some of whom had day jobs as funeral directors or farmers.

"Late today or tomorrow."

"Thanks for letting me know." I paused. "Do you have to — are you the one who has to tell her grandmother?"

"A patrol officer has already gone over to do that."

Makes sense to train the young ones in — and give the old ones some relief, before they turn completely to stone.

"Thanks for calling, Cas."

"Avery, I don't have to tell you again to stay away from T-Bone, do I?" His voice was a stern order.

"You think he—?"

"He's not your concern. He's very dangerous. Do you understand?"

141

"Yessir. I'm a lot of things, but stupid isn't one of them."
I had to hang up before I started crying. I hadn't even known
Tunisia Johnson, but the thought of her, trussed up and on
display left me sick.

Just when she seemed to be pulling her life out. Or had
she. Had her old life come full circle, caught up with her?
Why did this woman I'd never met disturb me so? Because
Mark Tilman had said find her. Before he was murdered.
Was there a connection? Were their deaths something omi-
nous, or just a sad coincidence?

Looking at it logically, someone likely followed Mark
home, thinking he carried drugs or syringes or something
with street value to and from the hospital. Or someone witnessed the accident and took advantage of the situation.
Dauber Dothan could be lying to protect himself.

Tunisia was easy to figure. Somewhere out there, a scary
guy named T-Bone lurked. Her lifestyle led almost predictably to a bad end. Too many possibilities. I needed to stop
distracting myself with this drama and focus on Jake's case.

I sat slumped in my car. I needed to eat, but I certainly
had no appetite. My muscles ached with even small movements, especially where the seatbelt had caught me. Hungry
and mourning Tunisia and the trial and everything else, I
didn't quite trust myself to drive.

I locked the car and grabbed a pack of peanuts from
the snack machine in Jake's building, then went to my temporary lair in the corner of the conference room where he'd
set up a computer and phone for me. My brain — and my
ire — were still chewing on Langley Hilliard's involvement
with Tunisia's research project. I plugged Hilliard's name
into an online search and got an unexpected hit in a business
"insider" news column, dated yesterday.

*RABB RUMORED TO LICENSE NEW
CONTRACEPTIVE*

*Rabb & Company, the new drug start-up headed by
Pendleton Rabb, is rumored ready to sign a license agreement*

for an intranasal contraceptive developed by Dr. Langley
Hilliard at Barnard Medical in Charleston, SC.

Neither party would comment on the deal, but inside
sources say the contraceptive has proven at least as effective
as the birth control pill without many of the side effects that
concern women as they age. The market is strong as increas-
ing numbers of older women look for safer alternatives with
ease of use comparable to the pill.

Insiders say the agreement should be penned in a few
weeks following certification of a final testing stage.

I'll be damned. Langley Hilliard with a lucrative little drug
deal for himself — and two people associated with the Rabb
project were dead. Pendleton Rabb wouldn't like hearing
about that, as he hands Langley Hilliard a big check for a
license agreement.

Next I pulled up the Tixtill information Jake had mentioned. Easy to see why this was on Jake's radar screen. Three
years earlier, Perforce Pharmaceutical and its chief medical
officer had pled guilty to thirteen misdemeanor counts in
a criminal administrative hearing involving an ulcer drug
called Tixtill. The government had charged the company
with falsifying test results and failing to report adverse events
to the FDA. After a series of smoking-gun internal memos
appeared, Perforce stopped fighting, pled guilty, and paid
substantial fines.

This was exactly what I had hoped to find — about
Uplift. Juries love nothing better than to learn that a company has lied, cheated, and tried to cover up. Cover-ups
always give juries a wonderful excuse for awarding damages
— often with punitive damages added on to punish the mis-
creants who tried to get sneaky. But I couldn't get excited
about this. The Tixtill guilty plea was three years ago, and I
hadn't found any reference to wrongdoing involving Uplift
or its development. Did mistakes made with Tixtill have anything do to with Uplift? Probably not. Would a jury believe
that, if Perforce lied and finagled in one case, they would do

it in another? Maybe. Were past sins admissible? Probably not. I'd have to mull on this a bit.

I tried another keyword: Pendleton Rabb. Several articles — mostly *Atlanta Journal-Constitution* news pieces — scrolled on the screen.

How I love clicking and scrolling. No more dusty basements full of allergy attacks. No more lugging bound periodicals to carts, then rolling them to a photocopy machine hidden away in a subterranean cavern. Point. Click. Printer whirrs. More stuff than I could've found in a week, right at the end of my index finger. Sometimes checking the legitimacy of sources or the authenticity of information was difficult, and it came out of context, in bits and pieces. But, ah, the ease. With no sneezing.

Pendleton Rabb's life unrolled before me: a phone number and address for the company's Atlanta headquarters, a website showing his political contributions — mostly local, all Republican, and surprise, his home phone number. Even *Forbes* and *People* had run articles about him and his family.

A relatively young family-owned firm, Rabb & Company manufactured a variety of consumer products, including children's aspirin, foot fungal sprays, and herbal shampoos. The Rabbs, relatively new to Atlanta, had become society page fixtures — and judging from a small mention of a domestic disturbance call and a couple of society page pictures of Pendleton with women who weren't his wife — gossip column favorites as well. When did this guy have time to run his company?

Forbes hinted at some new drug development ventures Pendleton planned to pursue aggressively, including some joint ventures. "We're a small company, so of course I'm intimately involved in everything we do."

I crab-walked the heavy armchair over to the credenza and dialed the Atlanta number for Rabb & Company. A pleasant recorded voice informed me that the offices were closed, so I tried the home number for Pendleton Rabb.

The woman who answered had been hired for her talent at screening out nut cases. I explained that I was a lawyer

— which impressed her not at all — and that I was calling about the research project at Barnard Medical — which got me transferred, after a long wait, to a fellow named Ed.

Ed didn't seem inclined to chitchat.

"Mr. Rabb is not in at the moment. If this is a business matter, I suggest you try to reach him at the office on Monday." Ed should get a job recording unctuous phone messages about pre-planned funerals.

"I have critical information about one of his research projects. If—"

"Mr. Rabb doesn't conduct business on weekends. He's quite adamant about that. Call him Monday."

"For Pete's sake, you mean to tell me if I called to report his company was burning to the ground, you'd want me to wait until Monday morning?" I was riled by his cool, clipped tones — and the fact that I had no leverage.

"No," he replied. "I would expect you to call the fire department. Good afternoon."

The dial tone buzzed loudly.

What did I expect, especially on Saturday? And what was I going to ask Pendleton Rabb? Maybe I could open with "Did you know people involved in your research project keep dying?"

I'd channeled my pretrial energy into searching for Tunisia. Now that she'd been found, I felt at loose ends, all fidgety with nowhere to go. Mark was dead, in a mysterious car accident with two men in a swamp. I'd had my own encounter in another swamp, frighteningly similar, though I refused to get all melodramatic about it. Tunisia shows up in a scene out of some sicko sex movie, and the contraceptive research project she enrolled in now led right to Hilliard.

I paced back and forth the length of the conference room. Was I reading too much into it? I had plenty of reason to despise him. Had I lost my objectivity? Vendettas aren't pretty — and can be pretty stupid. But Hilliard was the linchpin. Mark's colleague. Tunisia's research chief. Expert witness in Jake's trial. Hilliard.

Who could give me some more information on Hilliard's little deal? I'd probably tapped out Demarcos — I didn't know what his involvement might be with this project. Dr. Ellin, maybe? He'd really shut down when I mentioned Tunisia's name. Was something going on there?

My cell phone buzzed. "Hey, Lydia. What's up?"

"I got a wild-hare favor to ask. I know you probably can't do it, but I thought I'd ask, just in case." Her voice sounded odd.

"Spit it out."

"Do you get Sunday off? Is there — anyway you could meet me in Atlanta tomorrow? Go shopping? Is that too far?"

That wasn't what I'd expected to hear. "Shopping?"

"I've got that doctor's appointment early Monday, so I'm driving over tomorrow. Frank can't come with me and — well — I just didn't want to — I thought it would be fun. Only if you have time, though."

Atlanta was a two- or three-hour interstate drive from Dacus, but no roads led there from Charleston.

"That'd be fun. I've got to be back early Monday morning, but I'm just marking time until then. Let's see—" I started clicking through a travel website. "The best option is for me to fly in tonight. I can meet you tomorrow at the hotel?"

We agreed to stay near Lenox Square — restaurants and shopping galore.

"Avery, are you sure you've got time for this?"

"Absolutely."

"Great. Now I'm excited." Her voice sounded lighter.

"Me, too. See you tomorrow."

My brain raced through all the loose ends I needed to batten down: plane ticket, packing, contacting Jake. This was lunacy, but at least I was moving. Lydia never asks for anything, but she'd dreaded this doctor's appointment more than she would admit, even to herself.

I booked a ridiculously expensive non-stop ticket and shuffled through the stacks of papers, deciding what to carry with me.

I picked up my web-search printouts. Atlanta. Ed at Rabb & Company was in Atlanta. Ed had ticked me off. I hate being told no. Langley Hilliard was scheduled to testify on behalf of Perforce next week, and Jake could use details about Hilliard's little drug development deal when he cross-examined him. In addition, Rabb would likely appreciate a warning about two mysterious deaths before he signed a contract with Hilliard. Thank you, Lydia.

On the way to the airport, I called Mom.

"Atlanta? Don't know why that would surprise me. You never can sit still right before a trial."

"What do you mean?"

Mom just pshawed. That's actually a sound she makes, and it's quite rich in meaning. "You always skitter around like a water bug just before a trial. Why don't you just come home for the weekend? You could rest up, go hiking."

"I'm going to meet Lydia. Keep her company before her doctor's visit on Monday." I say, skittering around. I didn't mention Lydia's anxiety and neither did Mom. Lydia must have known Mom wouldn't have time to ride to Atlanta with her and didn't want to share her worry with her just yet.

"That's nice." I could hear an unspoken *pshaw*. "Just don't push yourself too hard. I'm certainly glad Lydia's finally getting that checked. Did I tell you Olivia Sterling and Harrison Garnet have started keeping company?"

"You are kidding!"

A little girl rolling a tiny multicolored suitcase plowed into the back of my knees, almost knocking us both into a heap.

"They've been coming to church, and he brought her to the spring Men's Club dance."

"What happened to his wheelchair?" Last time I'd seen Harrison Garnet was a few days after Thanksgiving, when we'd solved an arson and murder at his manufacturing plant.

"Once he got rid of that wife of his, Harrison's whole life seemed to brighten up. 'Bout time he and Olivia got together. They should've married forty years ago."

Long time to wait for true love. Olivia had never married, after Harrison got lured away by someone else. I realized I was standing in the middle of the airport, grinning like a fool.

"Everything else okay there?"

"Seems to be," she said, without elaboration on any of her special projects. "Just wish you could come home."

"This trial won't last forever." I didn't elaborate beyond that.

We signed off, I checked in, cleared security, then called Jake's number. No answer.

"Jake, it's late Saturday. I'm flying to Atlanta, following up on an idea. I'll be back tomorrow night. Think it might help you handle one of their witnesses. You have my cell phone number."

In the back of my brain, I'd mused all afternoon on Tixtill and Perforce's criminal guilty plea. Jake wanted the jury to know Perforce had been bad in the past so Perforce would be suspect again. Realistically, though, Judge Bream wasn't about to let Jake waltz in and introduce that old case, particularly since, try as I might, I'd found no hint of similar wrongdoing in the development of Uplift. True, my search had been cursory and my evidence anecdotal, but the endorsements were consistent and glowing.

One way to get it admitted was as reputation evidence, but that was a long shot. Reputation evidence was used most often in criminal trials to discredit a defendant who claims he has a spotless past. Prosecutors wait with bated breath hoping a defendant will open the reputation evidence door just a crack, so the crook's rap sheet can come back to haunt him. If Perforce said it was a sterling company with a spotless reputation, maybe Jake could use Tixtill to create doubt in the jurors' minds.

I'd once faced a plaintiff's attorney trying to use reputation evidence in a medical malpractice trial after my witnesses talked about the doctor's excellent reputation among his colleagues and patients. The attorney claimed he should be allowed to introduce evidence about the number of times the doctor had been sued to show his reputation wasn't that good — evidence that's not usually admitted because past lawsuits, like past crimes, usually don't have anything to do with the current case and, in fact, would unfairly prejudice the jury.

The judge had agreed with me — the reputation evidence wasn't admitted. Judge Bream was unlikely to allow it in this case, either; but I pulled out my laptop and emailed Jake a lengthy message, including a couple of citations Lila could use in preparing a trial brief. Just in case he found an opening where Tixtill would fit.

I kept my suspicions about Hilliard and his development deal to myself; no need to cloud Jake's thoughts with a half-baked idea.

CHAPTER EIGHTEEN

Early Saturday evening

Charleston's tiny "international" airport stays busy mostly with military families from the nearby bases, coming and going from overseas. So few people waited to board the afternoon flight to Atlanta, I feared they would cancel it. But fly we did.

En route, I studied an Atlanta map I'd found in the gift shop and located the streets for Rabb & Company and Pendleton Rabb's home address. In *People* magazine, the picture of Pendleton's house was distinctive and the street name was well known and didn't include Atlanta's ubiquitous "Peachtree," so I could probably find it.

I opened my notebook to talk to myself about Tixtill. I usually think better on paper, but I couldn't make myself focus on the words, dancing from topic to topic. Day after tomorrow, the bailiff would be announcing, "All rise." Maybe I could replace my much-lamented purple suit in Atlanta. I'd wear my gray suit on Monday, with the pearl blouse. I kept thinking about Tabbi Johnson and her grape Tootsie-Pop.

No way to spot when we flew over the line between South Carolina and Georgia, states separated their entire length by water, and not much to distinguish the two states until the sprawling suburbs began to spread out from the gloom.

Atlanta has character. Everything from left-over hippies and street people in yuppie-built shanties to Coca-Cola, Ted Turner, the Olympics, and the street corner where Margaret Mitchell was struck dead by a car. Atlanta is a schizophrenic sprawling urban Southern eccentric, with lights spreading forever.

Fortunately, Saturday evening wasn't the airport's busiest time, and I lucked into what had to be one of the few Georgia cracker cabbies in the city.

"Whur to?" he asked into the rearview mirror, his buck-toothed grin, his chin, and his Adam's apple all competing to see which could get closest to the windshield.

"You sound like you would know Atlanta well." My Carolina drawl got broader and flatter along the vowels, just being close to this thatch-head named Rowly. That's how his nameplate announced him, anyway: Rowly Edward.

Rowly whirled around to face me, afraid I'm sure that the rearview mirror didn't reflect his deep hurt. The fact we were barreling out the airport exit toward I-85 North wasn't reason enough for him to keep his eyes on the road. I grabbed the edge of the seat.

"A'course I do. What do you think?"

"Good. Because I have several places I need to find and I really need your help." Now I had a Southern man with something to prove. Might as well make use of my Saturday evening.

"Just tell me where to. You'll get there."

Company headquarters was close to the airport; seeing it would give me time to get used to his driving. I hadn't ridden with anyone else since my mishap in the swamp and I was surprised at my own skittishness at not being in control.

"Do you know Rabb & Company headquarters? Just off I-85?"

"A'course I do." He hit the accelerator, rocketing into downtown-bound traffic which would've done most other cities proud during rush hour. Dusk had long passed and headlights shone in a steady stream.

Rabb headquarters would be deserted, but I wanted to see it for myself. Though I tried to squelch my own frankness, this whole enterprise was beginning to feel like idiocy.

Rowly Edward did know his way around. Rabb & Company's white gothic headquarters, a Tara cliché gleaming into a broad reflecting pool, was visible from the interstate.

"You wanna go in?" Rowly Edward asked, whipping out of traffic and onto the exit ramp. A guard gate loomed ahead. A woman in a security uniform stepped out to meet us, her belly straining unbecomingly at her pants.

Rowly assumed a chauffeur's pose, eyes straight ahead, as I rolled down my window. "I wonder if Mr. Pendleton Rabb is in tonight?" Might as well carry the idiot act all the way. I really just wanted a chance to study Rabb's unbelievable building.

"No, ma'am. He's not. Not on Saturday. Perhaps you would like to call for an appointment Monday morning." With her hands behind her back, she bowed solicitously toward the taxi, genteel and polite. She seemed to take this late-night cabbie visit in stride, more used to functioning as a uniformed greeter than a guard.

"Thank you. I will."

Rowly turned the cab around as I gawked out the back window at the mocked-up Southern plantation house, more Las Vegas than Atlanta.

"Where to now?" Rowly's puppyish good spirits didn't seem the least bit dampened by our peculiar mission. He had his foot on the brake and his gaze on me in his rearview mirror, awaiting instructions. I fumbled with my notes and map, looking for the address.

"Do you know where Paces Ferry Lane is?"

"Who-ee," he whistled through his orthodontically challenged overbite. "Nice neighborhood. That where this Rabb fellow lives?"

"That's the street. How hard will it be to find the house, do you think? I've got a picture, but no number."

Rowly flicked on the dome light and studied the black-and-white print of the magazine photo. I realized it looked almost exactly like the corporate headquarters building behind us.

"No problem at all. Hell, ever'body in Atlanta knows that house. The parties they got there, ever' cabbie in town has drunks to carry home after those."

"Drive on, Rowly." I settled back in the worn and slightly greasy upholstery.

Back on the interstate, we flashed past the towers of downtown Atlanta, decorated with glistening lights for the evening. The speedometer read seventy-five, but we were moving with traffic.

"Rowly, you from Atlanta?"

"No, ma'am. From a little town near Columbus, near where Lewis Grizzard was from. Loss of a great American. You know, him and me been married the same number'a times. Lucky none of mine ever wrote a book about our double-wide, like one'a his did. Must be something with us Georgia boys, reckon?" Rowly grinned, a buck-toothed preen.

"You been in Atlanta long? You sound a lot like Lewis Grizzard. And — what's that other guy's name? Jerry Clower?"

"Well, he's from Mississippi."

Like that was a long way from Georgia.

"Been here quite a few years now. First come to try to get a part on *Matlock,* but they didn't really film much'a that here. Working to get my country singin' career started. I'm only cabbin' until I can attract the right kind of attention."

Pointing toward Nashville or even Myrtle Beach as better choices might be rude. What did I know about the country music business?

"You write your own music?"

"Some. Been told I sound just like Hank Williams. That's Senior, not Junior. You know, Junior's just a little too — I don't know — long-haired for me. Don't you think?"

"You ever get nervous, on stage in front of all those people?"

"Naw. I just think about how good I sound. And how much ever'body's enjoying listening to me."

This guy kept leaving me with nothing to say.

We'd exited the interstate and wound our way along a maze of residential streets among rolling hills. Rowly handled the wheel with self-assurance.

The homes became more elegant and farther apart, and somewhere we crossed a line that guaranteed a burglar alarm sign in every yard and at least one German car in every circular drive. After Charleston, with its crowded streets and walled European gardens, Atlanta looked land-rich and sprawling.

It came into view around a slight bend, glowing at the end of the narrow residential street. Pendleton Rabb's Atlanta home. A small affair, probably no more than ten thousand square feet, discreetly protected but not hidden behind wrought iron gates and sheltering oaks.

Rowly stopped where the road dead-ended at Rabb's gate. A generous oval drive in front of the gate provided the curious but uninvited plenty of turn-around space.

Rowly didn't maneuver into a turn but sat with his headlights shining brazenly into the return glare of the estate's floodlights. He pointed. "There's a call box. You wanna see if he's home?"

"Heck. Why not. Pull on up." The worst they could do is tell us to leave.

A voice crackled almost immediately after I pressed the button. "Yes."

"May I speak with Mr. Pendleton Rabb? I'm an attorney from—"

"I'm sorry. Mr. Rabb is not receiving guests this evening. Perhaps you could try his office on Monday morning for an appointment."

The call box gave an audible click of dismissal.

"Too bad there's not a party tonight. You could get in then, for sure. Particularly late, when bunches of 'em would be losing their lunch on the lawn or their underwear upstairs."

That too left me speechless, since it seemed a little more worldly than I expected of Rowly.

"What now?" Rowly asked, patiently willing to run up the meter for me. The house loomed beyond my cab window.

I sighed. "I don't know, Rowly. I just don't know."

"He owe you money or something?"

"No Nothing like that," I assured him. "He's about to invest in a new drug, which means crawling into bed with a doctor I don't trust. I didn't have time for phone calls and appointments, so I decided to risk the direct approach."

"I hope you don't mind my saying this, but you ain't walking up on this too smart."

Actually I did mind him saying it, since it was true.

"I suppose you have a suggestion." My tone was only mildly flippant because he sounded as if he did.

"You know anything about this guy?"

"You mean," I thumbed through my papers, "other than the fact that he's worth an estimated hundred million dollars — estimated because all his company stock is closely held; that he often has his picture taken with leggy blondes even though he's married to a short, dark-haired socialite; and that he's an elder in his Presbyterian church."

Rowly took it in stride that anyone flying into town on Saturday night to track down some guy would do her homework.

He cut the taxi's headlights but kept the motor running. Staring at the house, he chewed the inside of his cheek. "How much time you got?"

"Not much," I admitted. "Got to be on a plane tomorrow night."

"That don't leave us enough time to try the long-legged blonde. Not you, ma'am," he hastened to add. Apparently I'd acted startled. "Lord, you're too short and nowhere near blonde enough for him. Naw, I know somebody." He nodded sagely. "But you ain't got enough time."

That was an intriguing comment on Rowly's range of skills and contacts — or on Atlanta's availability of talent. I was destined never to know which.

"Nope. Ain't enough time to set up something like that. So we'll just catch him tomorrow. He's bound to go to church, don'cha reckon?"

Rowly turned to face me, solemn as a bucktoothed man with a wobbly Adam's apple can be.

"Rowly, you're a genius." I asked him to take me to the J.W. Marriott at Lenox Square and settled back, suddenly exhausted.

"So, ma'am. What is it you do, if you don't mind my asking?" He talked to his rearview mirror while slicing through the dark streets toward where the posh people shop.

"I'm a lawyer."

He nodded but didn't press me for more. I had the feeling his reaction would have been the same if I'd been a Mafia hit moll or a member of an FBI sting operation. Rowly, for all his rednecky-ness, had the air of a man who'd seen it all and done most of it. "I'll see you at seven o'clock sharp," he promised.

I didn't ask how he knew he wouldn't be on a cab run or question his enthusiasm for my quest. I was too tired to worry about it. I paid him, wondering if the tip was too much — or not enough to bring him back tomorrow. Might as well take another stab at seeing Pendleton Rabb in the morning before Lydia arrived.

CHAPTER NINETEEN

Saturday night and Sunday morning

I paced about my hotel room, from bathroom to window and back; still moving long after I'd arranged and rearranged my meager belongings. My mother frequently points out that I wrongly equate action with accomplishment. "They also serve who only stand and wait," she says. Someone told me she stole that from Milton. In any case, here I was, have credit card, will fly.

I checked my voice mail. Nothing from Jake Baker. No point in leaving him another message. On a fluke, I tried Pendleton Rabb's numbers one more time.

The recorded voice at Rabb & Company, sexy but efficient, informed me that the offices were closed until regular business hours on Monday. She didn't give a number to call or buttons to push in case of emergency, or even a beep to leave a message.

Too het up to sleep and tired of pacing, I thumbed through my notes on Tixtill, but I couldn't actually focus on any of the words.

Spread out on the table was the real reason I'd come to Atlanta. Not to help Tunisia Johnson or Mark Tilman or get dirt on Langley Hilliard, but to run away from the Uplift case. I didn't have to be a psychologist — or my mother — to recognize avoidance when I saw it. What had I been thinking, going back to Charleston? I felt anxious, at loose ends. No, at the losing end.

I shoved the papers back in my satchel. Staring mindlessly at those files wasn't doing any good.

Stretched out on the white bedspread, I thumbed through Mark's journal, backward from the last entry.

Why had Mark sent this to Sanda? By courier, the same day he was supposed to meet me. I still couldn't get over a cash-strapped resident popping for the cost of a courier to deliver it. Maybe if he'd stuck an engagement ring inside . . . Was the note to find Tunisia a note to himself? To Sanda? Or someone else?

Had something happened that afternoon to frighten him? He couldn't have been too concerned or he wouldn't have mailed it to his own apartment, and he would've included more instructions. Maybe he simply wanted to keep someone at the clinic from asking to see his notes.

Too many questions.

I thumbed backwards through the journal, searching for sleep more than anything else. But the word *Rabb* caught my eye.

January 26. Called Rabb HQ today. J.B. oversees project. Warned re sensitivity reactions. More widespread in population than earlier #'s. Will upset L.H. J.B. to notify P. Rabb personally.

Warned about sensitivity reactions? Sensitivity reactions to the drug. That would make a lively conversation starter when I caught up with Pendleton Rabb. I kept reading.

January 29. Called Rabb & Co. J.B. assured me P.R. aware. Would respond. Talk to L.H. re reassessing all subjects enrolled in project.

L.H. — Langley Hilliard? Mark's news would've upset him. J.B. must be somebody at Rabb & Company. Maybe I could find him. Or her. Or maybe I should just go shopping.

* * *

I discovered the second morning after a car accident is even more painful than the first morning after one. The alarm clock buzzed me out of a shadowy dream where I ran up and down darkened flights of stairs in a ramshackle building built over the water. When I woke, my arm refused to turn off the clock radio. Slowly, I found none of my major muscle groups were happy with me.

In the wall-sized bathroom mirror, I studied the seatbelt bruise that had eaten my right breast and crept up my neck. Thank goodness I'd packed a turtleneck.

A hot shower and some stretching loosened me enough to creep downstairs with my overnight bag.

Rowly waited, checking his watch in an obvious way. He was lucky I'd made it at all. He graciously popped out to lift my bag into the trunk, more from an anxiousness to get started than from cabbie courtesy.

We parked ourselves at a discreet distance, facing away from the gates of Pendleton Rabb's Southern gothic home. And we waited.

"Rowly, just out of curiosity, how much is it costing me to sit here?" The meter wasn't running.

"Aah. I don't have to charge you anything unless we're rolling. Then I gotta account for that." He kept his eyes on his side mirror, watching the gates behind us.

A low entertainment threshold. I'd dug my worn leather notepad from my bag, thinking I'd use the time to brainstorm on the Uplift case — or to plan what I was going to say to Pendleton Rabb when I finally got close to him. But instead of doing anything useful, I stretched my legs across the seat and stared out the back window. And fidgeted.

By this time tomorrow morning, we'd be in court. I pushed the thought aside.

Lydia had called earlier, saying she'd be at the Marriott at twelve o'clock — which meant she wouldn't be there until after one. I hadn't eaten breakfast, so I was hungry, and I'd drunk too much coffee, so I needed a bathroom. I didn't think borrowing a neighbor's bush would pass Paces Ferry Lane muster. So I squirmed, snoozed, and tried to decide why I was here.

We'd been parked over an hour. Rowly slumped in the front seat, his head bobbing to the Sunday morning gospel tunes on a country station. I half-expected the Atlanta cops or a private security service to roust us, but no one did. A couple of guys jogged past. Neither of them paid us any attention.

Somehow, the Rabb research project was connected to two deaths. Mark Tilman and Tunisia Johnson didn't have anything else in common. I hadn't found a personal relationship, despite Demarcos's rumor. Maybe somebody at Rabb could shed light on what had worried Mark, why he had called them. Most important, I wanted to understand Hilliard's financial interest in the contraceptive project, something Jake could use on cross-examination to rattle him. I knew from experience that, when rattled, Hilliard could be volatile. A rational part of my brain knew my animosity toward Hilliard was irrational. Still, he deserved to be brought down.

I almost dozed off. When the iron gates began to move, I thought my bloodshot eyes were playing a trick. The gates jerked in response to some remote signal and a large dark Mercedes with tinted windows barreled down the winding drive.

Rowly sprang to life, hitting the ignition and almost shouting, "That's him!" He restrained himself until the Mercedes cleared a couple of driveways past us, then he pulled out to follow.

He kept enough distance to see but not be noticed. "You've done this before," I commented.

"Well, studying PI stuff and fren-six books is a hobby of mine. Sure wouldn't want to be a PI in South Carolina — you can't pack heat there."

I didn't ask about Georgia law or whether he was currently armed and dangerous. I didn't want to know. Lucky me. I'd found Atlanta's only redneck Philip Marlowe wannabe country music singing cab driver.

We followed Pendleton Rabb's Mercedes to the Peach Way Presbyterian Church, where Pendleton emerged from the back seat waving and greeting the severely clad parishioners, most of whom had driven themselves to church and parked in the back lot. Pendleton looked enough like his *People* photo that I recognized him, though he was pudgier and balding. Hard to believe he had a party-boy reputation, but money will buy a lot of things.

Pendleton helped his wife out. She adjusted a brocade suit that would have funded my entire wardrobe.

"That must be him," Rowly said. Leaned forward, clutching the steering wheel, he was scarcely able to contain himself. "You gonna try to catch him now?"

I hesitated. Rowly eased our cab in where church-goers' cars turned the tree-lined lane into a parking lot.

"Naw. We'll wait. The service is starting in a few minutes. No need to make a scene here." I didn't want to admit it, but I was chickening out.

Rowly looked crestfallen. Through the open cab windows, we could hear the organ prelude begin. The baroque music and the elegantly attired church-goers made me homesick for the worn wooden pews, "Are You Washed in the Blood," and the old blue hymnals at the Dacus First Baptist.

"How about we go get some breakfast and come back?" I suggested.

Rowly rolled his eyes, but he drove me several blocks to an intersection loaded with fast-food choices. I opted for a lard-laden biscuit, ice tea, and a restroom visit. Rowly got himself a cup of coffee and tried not to look too anxious to get back to the stakeout.

Of course, I failed to appreciate how much distance would separate fast food from the Peach Way Presbyterians. I'd also not counted on the Peach Way Presbyterians being in such a rush to adjourn for lunch. When we returned, the parking lot was emptying and it wasn't yet noon.

With a series of non-verbal grunts and squirms, Rowly reprimanded me for what my hunger pangs had wrought, but he settled down as soon as we spotted the Rabbs folding themselves into the shiny black Mercedes.

Rowly smacked his palm on the steering wheel and cut off a gray-haired couple crossing the street. "Missed him. Don't you worry, though. He won't get back behind those gates without seein' you."

See us, he would, if he bothered to look out his back window. I thought Rowly would drive up the Mercedes' tail-pipe. Apparently, though, tailgating is common in Atlanta traffic, and after only a few hours here, I understood the etymology of the phrase "Driving like a bat out of Georgia."

Rowly correctly predicted that Rabb wouldn't disappear behind his estate gates. Instead, he was going to disappear behind the gates of the Peach Way Country Club.

"Whoo-ee," Rowly said. "This is some more country club." The guard, who almost saluted as the Rabbs drove in, flagged us down.

"We're with the Rabbs," Rowly yelled out the window. He hit the accelerator as the guard glanced after the disap-pearing Mercedes.

I didn't risk a look back to see if he gave chase or called for help. When we pulled up under the porte-cochere, I let out the breath I'd been holding as we'd wound around to the elegant gray stone clubhouse.

The Rabbs were already mincing through the front door as Rowly squeaked the cab to a stop. Not the usual coach of choice for coming to the Peach Way Club, but in Atlanta, eccentrics are thick on the ground. I hoped that would stand me in good stead for the next few minutes.

I pictured Hilliard to psych myself into bulldog mode as I trotted into the grand hallway. "Mr. Rabb! Excuse me. Sir!" The clink of dishes and hubbub of voices signaled the direction of the dining room. Damn, he was in a hurry — he must have skipped breakfast.

I caught up with him just inside the dining room door. The maitre d' greeted him and studied me with grave suspicion. The missus disappeared toward the powder room.

"I wondered if I might have a quick word with you."

Judging from Rabb's expression, this interview wasn't starting well. The look he gave me could've deboned chicken.

"I'm Avery Andrews. I'm a lawyer. From South Carolina. You received a call last week from Dr. Mark Tilman. I understand—"

"What are you doing here? This is a private club." His eyes shifted quickly from me to the tables seated closest to us.

The maitre d' wasn't going to haul me out himself; he was on the house phone calling someone to do it for him. I didn't have time to win friends here.

"Mr. Rabb, I understand your company is funding research on a new contraceptive, and I understand the project is of personal interest to you. That it's your first significant pharmaceutical initiative since you became CEO."

Eyeing me as he might an escaped lunatic, Rabb took a step backward and bumped up against the decorative balustrade at the dining room entrance. He was probably wondering whether it was safer — and less embarrassing — to humor me or to make a run for it into the dining room.

"I understand Dr. Mark Tilman reported problems that developed during some drug testing in Charleston, at Barnard Medical."

At the mention of Mark Tilman, the tip of Rabb's tongue darted out to wet his lips.

"I understand he contacted someone at your company with the initials J.B."

He kept looking around, as if waiting for someone to rescue him. It struck me he didn't look or act like a corporate CEO.

"Pendleton." In a booming drawl, a short, well-padded man in an expensive suit announced himself. He gave Rabb a

163

familiar thump on the arm, but his assessing gaze was for me alone. The movement positioned him so he could, in part, block me from Rabb.

"A problem, Pendleton?" he asked, his voice friendly, his green eyes wary and fixed on me.

"Avery Andrews, Mr.—?" I offered my hand and tried to reclaim some control.

"John Barden. Mr. Rabb's attorney." We struggled briefly, with him gripping my hand and watching my eyes to see if I'd wince, before a flicker of amusement at the corner of his mouth heralded a truce in the handshake battle.

"I'm an attorney. I've come from Charleston, investigating what may be a double murder." I threw the last word at Pendleton. I was being overly dramatic, but I had only one chance to get Rabb's attention before I got hauled out the door.

"Miz Andrews," Barden drawled seductively, a Southern charmer, honeyed and smooth. "I serve as Mr. Rabb's corporate counsel. I'm sure any questions you have would best come through formal channels. This doesn't sound like something that need interrupt Sunday dinner."

In my most resonant courtroom voice, my mention of murder carried well into the dining room. We were drawing more than polite glances, particularly from a guy who'd come in behind Mr. Corporate Counsel.

The new guy didn't speak. He didn't have to. His buzz haircut and the strain his shoulders inflicted on his suit coat announced that he wasn't just an ugly briefcase carrier for Rabb's lawyer. He watched the lawyer with dog-like devotion and only glanced in my direction as if to have my location marked when the order to attack was given.

"Miz Andrews." The lawyer took my arm and turned me away from the eavesdropping diners and toward the front door. He dropped his voice to a quiet threat meant only for my ears. "Now is not the time. If you don't leave, I can assure you Mr. Wix here can make your visit to Atlanta memorable indeed, starting with a visit to police headquarters."

Wix, the junkyard dog in the muscle-stressed suit, stood at attention behind us.

John Barden seemed to enjoy his role as anti-tourism director. "This talk of murder is nonsense. Why would we know anything of that?"

"I thought Rabb would want to know about a potential public relations nightmare before you all sign any agreements with Langley Hilliard. And I'd appreciate understanding Hilliard's relationship on this end. A lot rides on a trial he is set to testify in. My timing isn't the best, but I've come a long way for those answers and I don't have much time."

With impeccable timing, Rowly made his entrance at the end of the hallway. His prominent Adam's apple, buck teeth, lumpy cotton pants, and scarecrow straw hair were clearly out of place in the Peach Way Club. He didn't look much of a match for Wix, who could bench-press Rowly and me at the same time. But Rowly's appearance disconcerted Barden long enough for me to turn back to Rabb.

I tried a gentler tone. Threatening him wouldn't work — he had adequate coverage for that event. I decided to appeal to something more basic. When one tactic isn't playing to a jury, try another one. Quick.

"Mr. Rabb, I know your company's reputation. You would want to know if anything threatened your company's reputation or your customers." I talked to Pendleton, but for the first time, I included Mrs. Rabb in the conversation. She had just joined us, coming from the powder room. Judging from her carefully colored hair and swollen feet jammed into luminescent pearl pumps, she knew the fragility of appearances.

"Two people — a physician and a patient — have died. I think it's related to the contraceptive project Hilliard is working on. I wanted you to be warned."

"That's ridiculous. How could birth control kill anyone?" Pendleton Rabb found his voice but not his sense of irony.

"I don't know that it did, but someone didn't want Tilman raising questions about the project and stopped him. Permanently."

165

"Miz Andrews," Barden said, "if you are alleging that Mr. Rabb or anyone at Rabb & Company knew anything about these deaths, that's absurd, my dear."

"It's not absurd that Mark Tilman made two phone calls to Rabb headquarters warning that some research subjects developed an allergic sensitivity to the drug. I need to know if Hilliard also reported those occurrences, through official channels. If Rabb & Company has invested in this project, I do hope you had the research subjects sign some extraordinarily well-written disclaimers of liability." Offering to help wasn't working, so I took off the gloves.

As corporate counsel Barden shifted from one foot to another, his expression told me we were finally sight-singing from the same sheet of music.

Mrs. Rabb spoke for the first time, her accent a deep Georgia drawl but her tone sharp. "What is she talking about?"

"That new contraceptive, Adrienne," Pendleton answered, ignoring her and staring at me.

"That nose drops idea? That whole thing is crazy anyway."

"Spray, Adrienne. A nasal spray." To Wix, he said, "Tell her to go away."

"Pendleton, they're waiting our table." Mrs. Rabb wanted to get on with the important business of the day. John Barden side-stepped Wix and took my arm, leading me toward the exit.

Rowly followed at a respectful distance, looking a little forlorn that the party was ending.

"Miz Andrews." The counselor leaned close, talking in a low, insistent tone. "You are correct. Dr. Tilman called the corporate offices. I took his call a week ago Thursday. Tilman's call prompted us to delay our final contract with Hilliard and his colleague, pending our audit of their research protocols and results."

"What kind of contract?"

His expression said I was pushing his beneficence.

"Customarily, when external researchers develop products that interest us, we compensate them either with consulting fees or stock options in the future development of the drug or product."

"Doesn't that create a conflict of interest?"

"Do your homework, Miz Andrews. It's quite common, when anyone has a potentially lucrative idea and needs financial help to make it marketable. Dr. Hilliard has performed clinical research for several drug and biomedical firms, so we rely on his reputation, both in his field and as a research team head. Our dealings with him were standard."

"What did Mark Tilman say that caused you to delay?"

Barden hesitated. Over his shoulder, I saw Pendleton and Adrienne disappear into the dining room. Wix stood guard near the door. Closer to us, Rowly leaned against the richly paneled wall.

"He reported the incidents you mentioned. We decided closer audits of the early stages of the research project were in order." He looked me right in the eye.

"So you're suspicious enough to doubt Hilliard's results?"

"That's all I can tell you, Miz Andrews. Whatever wild scenario you've invented is just that, an invention." He rocked forward on the balls of his feet, both hands in his jacket pockets. "The death of Dr. Tilman and the death of that patient are, as far as we would know, simply unfortunate. I trust that answers your questions."

"One more, please. Will you still contract with Hilliard after you examine his research records?"

He smiled with only one corner of his mouth. "That will depend on our audit, now, won't it? Good day, Miz Andrews. Have a safe trip back to Charleston."

He turned toward the dining room, but I called to him. "When was the contract supposed to be signed?"

He turned, looking exasperated. "The preliminary agreement was to be faxed last Monday."

He spun around and padded down the thickly carpeted hallway. Wix kept his post.

Rowly stepped to my side. "Get what you needed?" He spoke too loudly for the hushed setting of the Peach Way Club.

I really wasn't sure.

CHAPTER TWENTY

Sunday afternoon and Monday morning

Shopping malls overwhelm me into a stupor. To shopping maven Lydia, though, the loss of my purple suit gave her a mission. I got to admire the expert in her element as she led me through store after store, and we both allowed ourselves to ignore what Monday would bring.

For supper, we talked and laughed over salads at the hotel before I left to catch my late-night flight.

From the airport, I called Cas Kirkland's office and left a message: "Tell the medical examiner Tunisia was enrolled in a medical experiment studying a hormone-based intranasal contraceptive." When I had to tell the kid cop on the phone that intranasal meant "up your nose," I knew I'd better call Cas again tomorrow with more details.

Tomorrow. Damn. The trial. Even though I wasn't trying this case, I still had a touch of the stage fright that normally sets in the night before a trial. Maybe everybody gets it — actors, ballplayers, country music singers. I once sat in the Charlotte Coliseum watching the Hornets play, wondering if those guys got stomach aches or hives before trotting out wearing skimpy clothes in front of twenty thousand people.

I just needed to be more like Rowly, thinking about how good Jake's case was and how much everybody would enjoy listening to him.

For most of the flight back to Charleston, I flipped aimlessly through my Uplift notes, unable to focus for all the stray thoughts darting about in my brain. Looking back, I felt a tad embarrassed about my brazen idiocy with Pendleton Rabb, but polite phone calls wouldn't have shaken loose the admission that Hilliard's lucrative little deal was now on hold. Now to figure out how Jake could make use of that.

On the other line of attack, I was still convinced no company the size of Perforce Pharmaceuticals could be perfect, despite all the praise it garnered. Somewhere, something had to give me a thread I could pull. I just had to keep picking around the edge until I found it — or until Jake lost his case.

Traffic on I-26 into downtown Charleston was light. I fell in bed without brushing my teeth and had to get up to brush them because I couldn't sleep without doing it. Finally, I slept.

* * *

The next morning, I slipped into one of the theater seats in the fourth-floor courtroom. The judge's bench sat empty, but a couple of bailiffs and the court reporter milled around down front, indicating the judge might reappear at any moment. Jake, Lila, and the defense counsel were also *in absentia*, their tables littered with papers, and Jake's laptop screen discreetly folded over. The defense table didn't display such sophisticated toys.

I looked around the elegant courtroom, trying to put the attendees into appropriate categories — regular court watchers, press, lawyers or clerks with motions pending in other cases. A faded, matronly woman halfway down the aisle stared at me, and I turned to smile at her, just being polite.

She leaned over. "Are you a lawyer?" she asked in an exaggerated whisper.

One never knows how to answer that question, though it's usually safer to admit it in a courtroom than it is out in polite society. "Yes, ma'am."

She slid down until she was two seats from me. "Can you tell me how long this case will last? The one against the drug company?"

I took a wild guess. "Are you one of the plaintiffs? One of the people suing?"

She hesitated, then nodded.

Best to know who you're talking to, especially in South Carolina, where attorneys — or their representatives — risk censure or worse for talking to anyone related to the other side in litigation. I doubted she was the CEO's mom in court for the day, but better safe.

"I'm Avery Andrews. I'm helping Mr. Baker with the case." I offered her my hand, then regretted it. That business reflex felt inappropriate with folks older than my mother. Her hand rested in mine like a fragile-boned bird.

"It's difficult to say how long it will take. This judge likes to move things along, I'm told. But it could still be several weeks."

She adjusted her purse in her lap and sighed, studying the judge's bench.

"Your name is . . . ?"

She blinked out of her reverie, her upbringing kicking in as a reflex. "Ada. Ada Jones." She nodded politely.

What was the protocol here? I was allegedly helping represent her, but I had no idea who she was or whether she or someone in her family had been hurt. I felt as though I'd shown up at a funeral for someone I didn't know and for whom, at any moment, I might be asked to say a few words.

She kneaded the handle of her black pocketbook, but her angst had nothing to do with what to say to me. From the look on her face, her thoughts were all far away and very much at home in her head.

"I never dreamed I'd be in a place like this."

The courtroom looked like a well-to-do church social hall, but I doubted that's what she meant. Her bewilderment had nothing to do with her physical location.

She sighed, shaky at the end. "James would've known whether this was worthwhile. Or whether to just leave it alone. Part of me says if they made that man crazy, they should be made to pay. That I ought to fight for James, because he's not here to do it. But another part of me hears him saying, Go home, Ada. This is none of yours."

James Jonathan Jones. One of the names listed as plaintiff on the court filings.

"Your husband was killed."

Her head tilted, like a bird who has heard a sound. "Yes." She blinked rapidly, to see past the tears that crowded her lower lashes.

"I'm so sorry, Mrs. Jones."

A quick nod. Another sigh, as if gasping for air. "It's the first time he ever went anywhere without me." She continued looking toward the judge's bench. "He'd known Ray Vincent Wilma as long as he'd worked there. Fifteen, sixteen years. They was friends, much as anybody is with folks they work with. How could he . . ."

Another deep breath. "I heard he walked up to James. They heard him shooting, off in the plant. I guess you just get confused. Don't know what to do, what to make of it. Then Ray Vincent come around the corner. This other guy, Milt, Ray Vincent come to him first. 'Get outta here, Milt. Now,' he said."

Her voice growled the command, as if she'd heard it firsthand. She probably had, replayed endlessly in her head.

"Then he come to James. 'Sorry, man.' And he shot him." Her voice carried the same hushed surprise as if she'd said *and Jesus came out of the spaceship*. "Shot him five times."

She was silent for several seconds, staring ahead. Her hands gripped the handle of her purse, but the kneading had stopped. "Why would he do a thing like that?"

She didn't expect a reply. She just needed to say it out loud one more time.

I reached over and put my hand on top of hers. "I don't know."

With moist blue eyes, she stared, as if gauging me, and asked, "Did that medicine make him do it?"

She asked in a way that said she wanted the truth. But I couldn't comfortably tell what I believed. "It's — complicated, Mrs. Jones. There are studies . . ."

She stared at me a moment more, then turned back to the front. "Seems to me folks have choices in life, to do what they do. Seems to me Ray Vincent Wilma decided to shoot some folks and shoot himself. Make a name for himself. Get on the news. Couldn't be big any other way. He made a choice. He made a choice to shoot James and not shoot Milt." A small sigh. "Don't quite see how a pill could make him do that."

She looked down at her hands, then back at me, waiting for a response.

"No, ma'am. Things don't always make sense, do they." A statement, not a question. I waited a polite interval and said, "It was nice meeting you, Mrs. Jones."

She nodded.

I slipped out of the courtroom. I didn't know where I was headed. I just knew I didn't want to face any more difficult questions.

This case finally had a face. A bewildered, pained face. Some couples get to a place where they just tolerate each other. Not Ada Jones; she really missed her husband. *It's the first time he ever went anywhere without me.*

I wandered down the thickly carpeted courthouse hallway, the floor-to-ceiling windows gathering what light they could from the overcast sky outside. When I pushed through the heavy door to the plaza downstairs, the harbor breeze blowing up the street felt cool and damp, but I didn't need anything heavier than my suit jacket.

Avoiding the congregated smokers, I shuffled toward an empty bench, planning to wait a few minutes for the recess to end before I returned to the courtroom.

As I started to dial my voice mail, my phone buzzed.

"Avery. Dammit. Where the hell are you?"

Jake's voice hissed from the phone as if he were trying to whisper.

"Outside the court—"

"More to the point. Where the hell were you this weekend?"

"I told y—"

"Why the hell are you trying to wreck my case? I knew you could be a loose cannon, but dammit, Avery, why you got it aimed right for my balls?"

"Jake." I barked to get his attention. "Jake. I'm outside the front door. Maybe we could talk better—"

The phone beeped. He'd cut me off. The smokers stayed in their circle, ignoring me. I didn't know where to look for Jake, so I waited until he appeared through the oversized glass doors.

I rose to meet him as he steamed toward me, his tailored jacket tails flapping behind him. His face was almost purple and his jaw muscles bulged. He came at me with such force, I took a step back.

"Do you not know the rules about lawyer-witness contact? Do you want to be disbarred? Do you want *me* disbarred? Are you demon-possessed? What? What is it?" He screamed his last words, giving a Rumpelstiltskin-like hop.

"Whoa. Jake. Whoa. Back up. What are you talking about?"

"I just got a severe ass-chewing from that lisping idiot Judge Bream, and you don't know what I'm talking about."

At least his voice had come down an octave, though the smokers could probably still hear every word.

"You don't know what it means for an attorney — that would be you — to approach an opposing party in litigation

— that would be Pendleton Rabb — without counsel present?"

"Wha-at?" *Omigosh.* "Party? Pendleton Rabb? How?" I reached for the bench and sat down. *Omigosh.*

Jake stood there, blinking. "So you did talk to him. Or rather, you did 'violate the sanctity of his home and club with threats and innuendo.' I believe that's how Arthur Vendue put it to the judge."

"Pendleton Rabb is a party to the litigation?" My stomach churned. My breakfast bagel might end up in the potted shrubs.

"Avery. Dammit." He grabbed my arms and shook me. He was in my face, but I was too stunned to object. "Rabb's the CEO of Perforce Pharmaceutical. Sure he's a figurehead, but he's still treated as a freakin' party to the litigation. What the hell were you doing stalking him around Atlanta?"

I shrugged myself out of his grip. "As God is my witness, Jake, I didn't know."

He stared at me, slack-mouthed; his shoulders slumped, looking like a banty rooster who'd just discovered he wasn't six feet tall. "Shit." He kicked the bench and spun away, then paced back. "How'd you miss that?"

I really felt like throwing up, but I wasn't going to let Jake see that. "How would I have known, Jake? I just joined this case. I couldn't possibly have covered it all. He's not named personally in the suit, he's just a corporate officer. How the hell was I supposed to know the head honcho at Rabb & Company also headed Perforce? How? None of my research mentioned that relationship."

In the back of my head, my guilt complex taunted me. *If you'd done your homework, A-ver-ee.*

Jake slumped onto the bench. "Rabb & Company is Junior's personal undertaking. His father didn't quite trust him to run Perforce, so they named their new CEO from outside when dad stepped down. That still doesn't explain why the hell you're chasing Rabb around Atlanta."

Both of us had quieted down, which was good. More folks were dribbling out the door of the courthouse, and the smokers had enjoyed enough of our street theater.

"Hilliard is working on a research project that involved Rabb & Company, a project that's gone seriously wrong. I wanted to learn more about it. I thought maybe you could use it to discredit Hilliard on the stand."

Jake stared at me, his arms limp at his side.

"I thought it would help. I wasn't finding anything that directly attacked Perforce or Uplift." I shrugged. "I thought it would help."

"Crap. So the best thing we got so far gets us a possible contempt-of-court charge and maybe even a professional reprimand. Great."

I let the silence settle before I asked, "Now what?"

He stood and paced a narrow area in front of me. "We can prepare an affidavit, or maybe you can present your version before the judge in chambers. But we're going to have to nip this one in the bud pretty damn quick. We got a case to try. Dammit." He stomped his foot. "Something's gotta fall our way in this freakin' case sooner or later."

CHAPTER TWENTY-ONE

Monday afternoon

The judge had, in chambers, scolded me and Jake soundly for my misbegotten midnight excursion, but he'd apparently been convinced of its innocence. After all, no lawyer would be that stupid on purpose.

Now, on my first real day in court on this case, I sat in the observer's gallery, just behind the railing where Jake and Lila sat with a couple of the key plaintiffs. Other plaintiffs and family members sat around me. I'd smiled and nodded at Ada Jones when I'd entered. She sat farthest back in the sizeable crowd.

The judge sat at his bench high above everyone. The court reporter pressed her talking tube around her mouth and repeated the proceedings into it, unheard by any of us. The jurors were spending the morning back in the jury room probably whiling away time with bored chitchat as Jake led the defense attorneys on a merry chase around Tixtill and the issue of reputation evidence. I couldn't believe he'd tried to get it in — and not a half-hearted attempt. He was going to the mat on this one. Judge Bream, though, was reaching the end of his patience.

"Counselor. The point you've raised has been duly noted in the record. Again, I fail to see that a nexus has been drawn between the earlier conviction involving Tixtill and any issues raised in this case. I am therefore holding that evidence concerning the drug Tixtill or the FDA proceedings against Perforce is inadmissible. Now . . ."

"Your Honor." Jake's exasperation was evident — as was the judge's.

"Counselor. I have ruled on the matter. If you choose to pursue it further at this time, I hope you brought your toothbrush with you, because you'll be spending the night courtesy of the county on a contempt charge. Do I make myself clear?" Judge Bream peered over his reading glasses, gavel in hand.

"Yessir," Jake said, suddenly meek and respectful.

"If there are no further motions? Bailiff, please bring in the jury. Plaintiff, you may call your first witness."

Jake shuffled and reshuffled the papers in front of him. I knew where his mind was — the exchange with the judge was over for him; he was focused on the next step. Funny, as I watched it play out, having the Tixtill testimony blocked probably felt more like a personal affront to me than it did to Jake. Odd how much difference a little distance made. Jake already had something else to command his attention, while I sat safely back with nothing to do but watch it unfold. I couldn't do anything except feel frustrated.

The jurors filed in and took their seats, waiting to watch the next scene in the play. They looked like an ordinary jury — men, women, Black, white, Hispanic, very old, very young, in between. They appeared interested. What wasn't visible was what they brought into the jury box with them: prejudice, misinformation, irrationality, poor education, sleep deprivation, a bad divorce, really good wake-up sex, morbid curiosity, an ulcer. Whatever. Jake and the defense attorneys would have stricken from the jury anyone who knew one of the plaintiffs, worked for a drug company, or took Uplift. But each juror brought baggage, knew things, liked or hated things that the attorneys couldn't divine — and both the defendants and the plaintiffs were at their mercy.

Jake's first witness was Susan Chee, the receptionist for Bradt Industries, the scene of the shootings. She struggled a bit as she climbed into the witness box.

Jake asked her to introduce herself. In a subdued voice, he used her answers to begin unveiling the story.

"Ms. Chee, you were at work on October 11, two years ago?"

"Yes, sir." She leaned into the microphone.

"Tell us about that morning."

She blinked, as if surprised at being given the reins. "We-ell." She pulled the microphone closer to her mouth. "Brenda and I got to work at the usual time. About eight o'clock."

"And Brenda is . . . ?"

"She did the billing and accounts receivable."

"You two worked together?"

"Well, yeah. In the office there."

Jake nodded. She took a quavery breath and continued. "Like any day, we got some coffee. She always started the pot. We caught up on stuff. You know, at home and all."

Jake prompted her when she paused too long. "What happened next, Ms. Chee? Just describe the morning in your own words."

"Well, the door opened — from the manufacturing floor — and Ray Vincent Wilma was there."

"Was it normal for him to come into the office area?"

"No, sir. The plant guys don't really come into the staff offices. Unless something's wrong or they need something. Like they have to see Human Resources or something."

"So you weren't expecting him that morning?"

"No, sir." She shook her head. "But there he was. At first, though, I didn't know it was him."

"What do you mean?" Jake stood over to the side, so she would be turned toward the jury as she talked to him.

Susan Chee shrugged. "He just looked funny. He didn't look like himself. I remember thinking, all at once, you know, who is that — oh, it's Ray Vincent — he looks so strange."

"Then what happened?"

"Well, before we—" Her lower lip quivered. "We didn't have time — Brenda and I — to say hello to him. He had a gun. He raised it. And shot—" Her voice broke. A tear rolled down one cheek.

"He shot Brenda Smalls?" Jake said, soft and matter of fact.

She nodded, then remembered to speak aloud. "Yes."

Jake waited.

"And — he shot me. I didn't really know what was happening. The noise was so loud. Very loud. It was hard to know what was going on. I don't remember falling. I just remember lying on the floor next to Brenda. I watched his boots as they walked down the hall toward Human Resources, and I heard more shots. Brenda jumped at the noise, I remember. Her hand was close to mine. I took it. We just laid there, real quiet. Kind of under the edge of the desk. The boots came back. Brenda made a noise. She — whimpered."

Susan Chee stopped talking and looked at the ceiling, trying to stop her tears. The watchers in the courtroom held their breath.

"He . . ." Her voice was hoarse. "He stood over her. He-shot-her." She mewed the words in a whisper and paused. "Her hand went limp."

Jake stood still as a statue and let the silence grow, let the picture develop in the minds of everyone listening.

Susan Chee didn't sniffle into a handkerchief. She just stared forward, tears streaming down her face, her lips pressed in a sharp line.

After an almost unbearable silence, Jake asked, "And then?"

She turned to Jake. Her voice stronger, she said, "He left."

"Back out the door to the plant?"

She nodded. "Yes, sir."

"What happened next? Did you see him again that day?"

"No, sir. I heard—" She swallowed hard. "More shots. From the plant. But then, nothing. For a long time. It seemed like it was totally silent for a long, long time."

"What did you do?"

"I just lay there. I couldn't move. I was scared. My leg hurt. I just held Brenda's hand and lay there. Until the ambulance guys came."

"Did Brenda say anything? Did she squeeze your hand or anything?"

She shook her head, not trusting her voice at first. The memory made her eyes stream and her lip quiver again. "No-o. She didn't move again."

Jake stayed quiet for a respectful moment.

"Thank you, Ms. Chee. I know talking about this hasn't been easy. It's important for us to know what happened that day. Thank you. Now, Ms. Chee, if you would answer any questions Mr. Vendue has for you." Jake bowed slightly and took his seat.

He'd taken Susan Chee's testimony right up to the edge but hadn't skated over it. Amazing. In bifurcating the trial, the judge had ruled that Jake couldn't introduce evidence of the victims' injuries until after the jury decided whether Perforce and Uplift had caused those injuries. In a hard-fought pretrial motion, Jake had won the right to recount the events of the shootings. But he could not talk about the damages suffered by the plaintiffs. A fine line. Arthur Vendue hadn't jumped up with any objections, but then, how could he? He risked sounding disrespectful of the injured and the dead. Cross-examination wouldn't be easy, either. He'd need to keep this short.

"I know this is difficult, Ms. Chee. I have only a couple of questions. I believe you said Ray Vincent Wilma looked funny when he came into the office that morning. What exactly do you mean? Can you describe his appearance for us?" Vendue kept his voice subdued, as if at a funeral. For Susan Chee, this trial had to feel like a funeral, viewing the dead anew.

She waved one hand, as if conjuring the vision. "I don't know. Crazy. His face was frozen, like he had on a mask. He just — looked right through us. Like we were nothing. His eyes were just dead."

"Did he speak? Did he say anything at all?"

She shook her head. "He just pulled that rifle up, from where he carried it, down against his leg. And he—" Her voice cracked.

"Thank you, Ms. Chee. I appreciate how difficult this is. Your Honor." He nodded toward the judge and toward Jake. "No further questions."

Wise to leave it alone. He didn't want her gilding the details the jury already had. Using the rail to help, Susan Chee pulled herself up and stepped carefully down. She wore long pants, and the jury couldn't see where Ray Vincent Wilma's bullet had shattered her lower leg and left her with an artificial foot — one of the injuries Jake wasn't allowed to mention.

Funereal. Something about this courtroom kept bringing that word to mind. The subdued lighting. The elegant appointments. The gentle funeral director air both the attorneys had assumed with Susan Chee. Soon the jury would be dozing off — the black gentleman with the soft gray fuzz of curls would be the first, I bet, with me right behind him.

"The plaintiff calls Ivan Gretel to the stand," Jake said.

"Ivan Gretel." The clerk of court intoned, a Bible in his hand.

A long-limbed man in a green tweed jacket loped down the center aisle. His shock of prematurely silver hair shone in the light over the witness box as he sat after being sworn in.

"Dr. Gretel." Jake approached the stand, which lawyers are allowed to do in South Carolina. I'd seen a North Carolina trial on television once and wondered how the heck the lawyers tried a case sitting at their tables, asking "permission to approach the witness" every time they had an exhibit. How do you do battle for your client sitting on your bum?

Jake leaned convivially against the railing that enclosed the witness chair.

"Doctor, would you please state your name and credentials for the record."

"Certainly. I'm Ivan Gretel. I hold a Ph.D. — a doctor's degree — in psychology as well as a medical degree in psychiatry. I practice and teach in New York City."

He rattled off an impressive list of chairs, publications, honors, and awards. About the only thing he lacked was being an Eagle Scout, a college football player, or a Southerner. He talked to the jury rather than to Jake, which gave him a relaxed air, like a kindly, intense uncle who'd been into peace, love, and granola in his younger years.

"Dr. Gretel, I asked you to review the medical records and other materials pertaining to Ray Vincent Wilma, did I not?"

"Yes, you did."

"I paid you for your time to review those records and to share with me your opinion and to come here to testify?"

"Yes."

"What instructions did I give you when I asked for your help, Dr. Gretel?"

"You said you wanted me to review Mr. Wilma's records and give you my professional opinion. We agreed that you would pay me for my time." He turned toward the jury, with one finger raised to emphasize his point. "And you are only paying me for my time. You are not paying me for my opinion. My opinion is based on what I find in the records, not on what someone wants me to say."

"Did I in any way indicate what I hoped your opinion would be?"

"Certainly not."

"You gave me your opinion after you'd reviewed the records in this case, did you not?"

"Yes."

"You also gave a deposition to Mr. Vendue, in which he questioned you about your opinion?"

"Yes."

"Dr. Gretel, in your psychiatric practice, as a physician and as a teacher of future physicians, have you had opportunity to work with, to treat patients with issues similar to Ray Vincent Wilma's?"

"I object." Arthur Vendue spoke sharply to cut off any reply as he stood. "Improper foundation."

Judge Bream hesitated only a moment. "Counsel is in process of laying the foundation, I presume. Overruled. You may answer the question."

Odd objection. Maybe Vendue just wanted to break Jake's stride, even though Jake wasn't on much of a roll yet. A couple of the jurors shifted in their seats.

"Yes, I have treated such patients."

"I'm not asking you for your opinion at this time, but are you prepared to offer an opinion in this case?"

"Yes, I am."

"Dr. Gretel, this case deals with the complicated, fascinating field of brain science, about how our brains work and how our brains make us work. It deals with what can go wrong with our brains, what can interfere with how they work. You are here as an expert witness, Dr. Gretel, to help us understand this complex science. What is neuropsychiatry?"

Ivan Gretel swiveled his chair toward the jury, leaning slightly forward, his lean runner's face intent.

"Frankly, scientists don't really agree on what makes our brains work, on what makes us tick. I like to think of it in terms of three schools of thought." Dr. Gretel's voice and posture clearly said he was interested in his topic and on getting his message across. His passion was hooking the jury.

"The first school says we are nothing more than a mass of chemical reactions. Even our most cherished and powerful emotions, such as love or compassion, are simply biologically pre-programmed responses to stimuli. A second group of scientists says no, no, we're both body and soul — we're both biological functions we can understand and metaphysical things we can't measure or fully understand.

"A third, more complex set of ideas says that we are a mass of constantly creative forces, that our brains and, consequently, our thoughts and emotions, are endlessly varied because each of us is endlessly evolving."

Gretel kept his attention on the jury, like a teacher making sure his pupils were following him. "Each of these views has its proponents, each has its Nobel Prize winners. Basically, we agree that the brain is very complex, but we diverge on how it operates."

Jake let Dr. Gretel elaborate on the brain science theories, then, in summary, asked, "Dr. Gretel, in your professional opinion, do drugs work? On the brain, I mean. We know, for instance, that penicillin kills bacteria that cause strep throat. Can other drugs fix the problems in our heads in the same way?"

Ivan Gretel leaned forward into the microphone. "No." He pronounced it with finality. "In my opinion, psychiatric drugs uniformly oversimplify the problem because they oversimplify the brain science. Psychiatrists rely too much on their prescription pads and too little on getting to the real root of a patient's problems. Finding the real cause often means long hours in counseling sessions, peeling back layers to uncover what, in a particular patient's background, led him to develop a particular response to his environment, his circumstances."

Jake let that sink in. "Dr. Gretel, you're trained in both psychology and psychiatry, aren't you?"

"Yes, I am."

Jake wanted to remind the jury that this guy knew what he was talking about. "Is that unusual?"

"There are others, certainly, but it's relatively uncommon."

"What's involved, training in both?"

"There's certainly no single path to get there. I first went to med school and decided to specialize in psychiatry. On

184

our psychiatric rotation — rotations are when med students work for several weeks in each area of medicine to get a feel for what each specialty entails. On rotation, I became both fascinated and frightened by what I saw in the psych ward. People trapped in their own madness or depression. I wanted to be able to help them. So psychiatry became my specialty.

"But then reality struck. It didn't take long, dealing with real people and real problems, to realize that not everything could be solved with a pen and a prescription pad. I knew there had to be something more. That's when I returned to school, to earn my Ph.D. in psychology, in counseling."

The passion in his voice was palpable. "That's where you learn how to talk to patients, how to help them find the real cause of their problems. That's much more effective than drugging them with the latest miracle pill, hoping to dull the pain enough but not too much, so they can live productively. A tough — and ineffective — balancing act."

"So you don't believe in using psychiatric drugs?"

"No, no. I don't go that far. Some problems we regard as being all in our heads are, in fact, chemical imbalances that can be resolved with medication. But we've become too fond of the notion of better living through chemistry. Popping a pill won't solve everything. It can't."

"You've developed a national reputation for being opposed to psychiatric drugs, haven't you?" Jake knew he only had to provide Gretel with the slightest hint of the direction he wanted him to take, and Gretel was off and running.

"I suppose I have. I do believe strongly that, for instance, drugging children rather than letting them explore the full range of their energies and ideas is a travesty. Some say if Johnny's too difficult to handle and won't sit still, just give him a pill As many as half of all college freshmen arrive from high school with a prescription for psychotropic drugs."

"Half?" Jake seemed genuinely surprised.

"At least. Drugs for depression and for hyperactivity are the most common. I don't know about you," he turned toward the jury rather than Jake, "but I remember my teen years as a time of huge mood swings, a time when I and everyone else I knew explored the full gamut of our feelings, our emotions. Why dull that or try to erase it? Where does that leave you later? Of what are you robbed? Coping skills? A rich range of experience? Life itself?"

Jake let silence soak in a moment before changing tack. "Dr. Gretel, can you explain to us how Uplift works, or how you as clinician would use it?"

"I wouldn't use it, except in extreme cases. Uplift is the epitome of the type of drug I find most troublesome. It's designed to take the edge off life, to address anxiety and depression, but it's marketed to the worst instincts within us all."

"In what way?"

"Well," Gretel sounded exasperated. "The message is 'pop a pill and you're better.' It doesn't encourage — or even allow — you to explore the reasons why you're depressed, so you have some hope of correcting those problems. It's perceived as a 'get happy' pill, protecting patients from reality."

"How does it — can you explain how it works? In simple terms. I know you've tried to explain it to me, but I'm not sure I really get it."

Gretel chuckled and leaned back in his chair, the professor chatting with an erstwhile student.

"Frankly, it's a concept that even scientists, neurobiologists, can't claim to fully understand. Researchers have identified chemicals in the brain that affect mood. Serotonin was a major breakthrough, though there were others. The chemical messengers carry neurotransmissions, or messages, between the neurons in our brains. For some reason, in patients who are depressed, it seems the tissues reabsorb or take up these chemical messengers, rather than let them continue to circulate, carrying messages. That's the best way I know to describe it."

"So these drugs add more of the messengers back into the brain, kind of like pouring gasoline in a car tank, so the car can run?" Jake drawled out his questions, strolling around in front of the witness stand.

"No, not exactly. These antidepressants don't add more chemical messengers to the brain. Instead, they keep the brain from reabsorbing what's already there. That's why they're called reuptake inhibitors."

"Reuptake inhibitors. That's a mouthful."

Gretel smiled.

"So when the doctor prescribed Uplift to Ray Vincent Wilma, he thought it would keep enough stuff sloshing around in his head to keep him from getting depressed?"

"Ye-es. More or less, that's the idea."

"Was Ray Vincent Wilma depressed, from what you see in his record?"

"Yes. There's every indication that he was. He had trouble sleeping, he didn't eat regularly, he had trouble maintaining relationships. I personally feel that his two broken marriages are clinically significant, much more important than his treating physician apparently thought."

"But lots of people are depressed. They don't go around shooting people. What happened here?"

"In my opinion, Mr. Wilma was one of the unfortunate patients susceptible to Uplift's most dangerous side effect. He became agitated. He felt more and more hopeless, more and more trapped by his situation. The agitation caused by the drug fed on itself and on his weakness. Simply put, he snapped."

"And shot ten people before he killed himself."

"Yes. He primarily wanted to kill himself, but he didn't want it all to be a waste—"

"I object." Vendue finally got to his feet, having let the questioning wander too far down a speculative path. "Your Honor, Dr. Gretel did not treat this patient. He can't know what was in his head. This is purest speculation."

"Sustained. Though that horse was pretty much out of the barn, counselor."

Jake changed directions quickly. "Doctor, are you familiar with the *Journal of Psychotropy*?"

"Yes, I am."

"Is that considered a reputable, reliable medical journal, one to which folks in your field turn for information?"

"Yes. It's one of the premier journals."

"Are you familiar with an article entitled 'A Report on Clinical Use of Reuptake Inhibitors in a Small Population'?"

"Yes, I am."

"Now, reuptake inhibitors, that's Uplift and drugs like it."

"Yes."

"Small population here means the physician studied a few people, not that he studied some short, skinny people."

Gretel chuckled, though no one on the jury did. They were intent on the testimony.

"So this writer — he's a doctor — studied Uplift in a few of his patients, and he found what?"

"In reviewing the literature and in his own practice, the author found a small percentage of patients on Uplift became agitated, severely agitated within one to four weeks of beginning the drug. Added to their underlying depression, this agitation increased their risk of suicide."

"So he found that some patients are more likely to commit suicide if they start taking Uplift?"

"Yes."

"That means they're likely to kill themselves, not that they're likely to kill other people, doesn't it?"

Jake had a real talent for making his questions sound like a conversation, one in which he himself needed to be convinced.

"Few suicidal patients kill others. Most often, the harm is directed at themselves alone. But in some, those with underlying, unaddressed rage issues, with a feeling of being cheated or wronged by life or by others, they may choose to take someone else with them when they go."

Jake started to pose his next question, but Gretel continued. "Frankly, this is why I'm so opposed to the use of psychotropic drugs. You can't pop a pill and solve complex issues that have taken a lifetime to develop. It doesn't work, and we end up with a tragedy like this. Uplift is dangerous because it lets people become dangerous."

Gretel obviously believed what he said, and that was scoring points with the jury. Jake decided to cut to the finish.

"Dr. Gretel, in your professional opinion, given Ray Vincent Wilma's history and the circumstances surrounding the tragedy at Bradt Industries, what was the most likely cause of Mr. Wilma's actions?"

"The drug Uplift. Mr. Wilma had been depressed, had had problems at work, with his coworkers and with his family. Ongoing problems. He had developed coping mechanisms. But, within a few weeks of filling his prescription for Uplift, he goes on a shooting spree. Quite simply, Uplift pushed him over the edge."

"Thank you, doctor. Please answer any questions Mr. Vendue has for you."

No one, especially Jake, could say "Vendue" without drawling it out. Everything about Arthur Vendue himself was a cultured, slow drawl. Arthur Vendue had a Charleston pedigree at least as long as Jake's. But, where Jake came across as a thick-bodied, combative copperhead, Vendue reminded me more of a salt-marsh egret. Vendue moved toward Ivan Gretel with deliberate grace. I wondered if egrets eat snakes.

CHAPTER TWENTY-TWO

Monday afternoon

"Dr. Gretel." The way Arthur Vendue said it, the name flowed as thick and warm as molasses out of a cook pot. "We appreciate you bein' here today, down from New York. I hope you've had a nice visit."

Gretel just smiled and shifted in his seat, ready to face cross-examination.

"Dr. Gretel, you've said you're not a big fan of psychiatric drugs."

"No, and for the reasons I stated earlier."

"You've gone on record, in your writings and especially in your book — I believe it's called *Stop Doping Your Kids?*"

"Yes."

"—that you don't think people's mental problems can be alleviated with drugs."

Gretel waited, making sure Vendue meant for him to reply. "Boiled down to its essence, that is correct."

Ivan Gretel and Arthur Vendue had met before, in a deposition, so they'd had an opportunity to take measure of one another. But in a courtroom, with multiple sets of eyes and ears fixed expectantly on every word, the stakes are raised; any surprise or miscalculation is magnified. They circled one another cautiously.

"Then it's fair to say you don't support the idea that we humans are merely a mass of chemical reactions?"

"No, I don't believe that. I believe we're much more complex."

"More fearfully and wonderfully made."

Judging from Gretel's confused blink, Vendue's reference to the Book of Psalms was lost on him, but one of the jurors, a middle-aged woman on the front row, gave a nod of recognition.

"You've moved around a good bit in your jobs, haven't you?"

"Yes, I suppose so. Better opportunities come along, you know."

"You are a rather prolific writer, aren't you?"

Whether the cue came from something in Vendue's deliberate drawl or from some imperceptible response by Gretel, I couldn't say, but Vendue had stopped circling. He was closing in.

"Yes, I suppose I am. One of the curses of an academic career: publish or perish."

"You've written many, many articles, in medical journals, as well as in magazines and newspapers the rest of us might read, urging people to avoid drugs like Uplift, haven't you?"

"Yes"

"So this has consumed most of your interest and energy for several years now, hasn't it?"

"Yes" Gretel knew the value of just answering the question, no more. He had pulled the microphone near his mouth so he wouldn't have to bob back and forth to give his short answers.

"And the summation of all your articles and books on the subject is really that people shouldn't numb themselves, shouldn't try to avoid psychological pain. Have I paraphrased that accurately?"

"Yes. They should work through their issues, with drugs as a last resort."

"I believe you said earlier today that people should open themselves to exploring the full range of their emotions. Is that accurate?"

"Yes."

"I made a note here. I believe you said 'drugging children rather than letting them explore the full range of their energies and ideas is a travesty.' Does that sound correct?"

"Yes."

"And you believe that, don't you?"

"Yes."

Arthur Vendue wasn't a man who wasted time or wandered aimlessly, unprepared. He was carefully laying a path, dropping stone by stone into place. Ivan Gretel knew enough to be wary, but so far, he could only agree, stepping on each stone in turn, following Arthur Vendue's line of reasoning like a trail of bread crumbs.

"That's been a constant, long-held belief of yours?"

"Yes." He paused. "But, like anything we know or believe, our ideas have to grow and develop. In our professional lives especially, we test our ideas, learn. We don't leap full-blown into the world, knowing everything we know today."

"Certainly. But this idea, that we should fully explore our energies and ideas, our emotions, that's been a common theme in your writing, hasn't it? Certainly for the last twenty years, since you finished your Ph.D."

"Mm-hm. Yes, I would say so."

Vendue had been asking questions without notes in hand, but now he strolled to the defense table and picked up a small, stapled sheaf of papers.

"You expressed that view in an article you wrote for the *Psychiatric Explorations Journal* twenty years ago, didn't you?"

Gretel shifted in his seat, looking almost like he was rocking onto the balls of his feet, ready to parry an attack. Vendue didn't let him speak.

"In this article," he held a photocopy aloft, "you argued that children — particularly boys — should be allowed to give free rein to their emotions and feelings. Didn't you state that boys — young boys — should be allowed to 'explore their sexual feelings with older boys and young men'? Didn't you write that was healthy?" Vendue's voice grew louder with each phrase.

Gretel had taken hold of the microphone, ready to reply. He didn't appear surprised by the question. Unfortunately, Jake was surprised. He was doing a good job of hiding it from the jury, his face frozen, looking only mildly interested in what was happening on the stand. But the way his jaw muscles worked told another story.

"We all have ideas we — explore. The purpose of academic writing is to propose and test ideas. That's not something I still advocate."

"So you're saying that, today, you're not telling young boys they need to have sex with each other?"

"No—"

"You are familiar with an international organization that, today, actively advocates that boys should have sex with men, to 'explore' their sexuality, as part of maturing sexually?"

"Yes—"

"You in fact have written articles for their website. Recent articles."

"Not so recent, no—"

"One reason this group is based outside the United States is that the activities they promote are illegal in this country. Isn't that true?"

Gretel could only shrug.

"So your advocacy of 'exploring the full range of energies and ideas' extends far beyond whether we should use drugs for psychiatric problems, doesn't it? It extends all the way to child molestation, doesn't it?"

Vendue had lost his gentleman-planter air and had become a street-corner preacher. Jake's jaw muscles bunched so hard, I expected to hear a tooth crack.

"Certainly not."

"No further questions, Your Honor." Arthur Vendue took one last disgusted look at Ivan Gretel and turned on his heel.

The judge, implacable, asked Jake, "Any questions on redirect?"

"Your Honor . . ." Jake rose slowly to a weary half-crouch.

"Counselor, the hour is late. With your permission? I'd like to adjourn until tomorrow."

Jake sank back into his chair. I'm sure he would've preferred not to send the jurors home with the words "child molestation" ringing in their ears, but he apparently didn't have a handy way to redeem Gretel's credibility. Jake hadn't had time to read everything Gretel had ever written, and Gretel hadn't had the good sense to warn him. Unfortunately, the only thing the jury would remember about Gretel — Jake's star witness — was "pervert." Jake might as well wait until tomorrow, when some of the shock had worn off both him and the jurors.

CHAPTER TWENTY-THREE

Tuesday morning

The next morning, before the jury was called in, Jake informed the judge he had no redirect for Ivan Gretel. The judge informed Dr. Gretel he was excused, a routine pronouncement meaning his services were no longer required and he was free to leave if he wished. Jake didn't want the jurors even laying eyes on Gretel again.

After court had adjourned the day before, Jake hadn't wanted to hang around rehashing the day's events. He'd sullenly stuffed a few papers in his briefcase, mumbled a few words in my direction and left the courtroom, leaving Lila to pack up. I didn't know what he'd done after a tall tumbler of bourbon, though he'd likely called Ivan Gretel at his hotel room and told him not to get within rifle range of him or he'd put a hole in him. That's what I would've wanted to do.

This morning, Jake swung back into the courtroom, swapping jokes with the bailiff and clerk and generally looking like his old self. Water under the bridge. A new day.

"The plaintiff calls Dr. Lee Standers."

Lee Standers wore a brown sports jacket, his hair standing at attention in close-shorn bristles, his brogans run-over at the heel. Standers had spent years peering into a microscope — at least twenty of those working on the compound that became Uplift. He looked the quintessential lab scientist, out of place in anything but a white lab coat and unused to dealing with organisms that didn't reside on glass slides or fit into mice cages. Standers' single-minded pursuit of a cure for depression had won him numerous awards and accolades.

Calling employees of the company you are suing is an unusual tactic, one I'd never seen used before. But this was an unusual case, and Jake figured this was the best way to introduce some important evidence.

Jake walked Standers through a recitation of his credentials. Impressive — and lengthy, which meant the jury probably didn't follow much of it.

After the jury had a chance to learn just who Standers was, Jake asked, "Doctor, what prompted your work on chemical factors in the brain? Why are you interested in this area?"

"Well, um, it's a puzzle. I thought we could solve it."

"Why this particular puzzle? Why were you interested in studying the causes of depression?"

"Depression is a devastating disease."

Jake waited him out, trying to keep a pleasant expression so the jury wouldn't suspect he wanted to choke more informative answers out of Standers. "And . . . ?"

"My mother had — was depressed. For much of her life."

So much for communicating a personal, passionate interest in the drug you developed.

Jake led the scientist, sometimes with painful exactness, through the development and approval of Uplift. At times, Standers' commitment to his subject peeked through. But he remained linear and acetic, not one of the most compelling witnesses I'd ever seen. Jake pushed the testimony quickly, not wanting the groundwork he laid with Standers swallowed up in tedium.

Arthur Vendue stood to cross-examine. "Dr. Standers, you're familiar with the various theories about how the brain operates, how we respond to chemical levels in our brains."

Standers nodded. The judge said, "Please answer into the microphone." Everyone in the courtroom was ready to scream at Standers, in unison, to answer into the microphone because the judge had had to remind him after almost every question.

"Doctor, could you please share with us your personal view of how our brains work and what theory you think best explains it."

"Well. I like to paraphrase a mentor of mine who always told us that, behind every crooked thought, there lies a crooked molecule." He stated it almost as a proclamation, as if that explained everything, with succinctness and clarity. Succinctness, yes. Vendue pushed for clarity.

"What does that mean to you?"

"Well — um . . ." He raised his eyebrows, straining for the words.

"Does it mean that we are made up of chemical reactions? That even our mental responses and processes can be reduced to chemicals?"

Dr. Standers nodded, then caught himself, much to the collective relief of everyone in the courtroom. "Yes, sir. That's why drugs like Uplift work."

"Thank you, doctor. No further questions."

Standers' testimony had been dispatched as a proclamation, as if that explained everything, with succinctness and clarity. Quickly enough — painfully but quickly — so that Jake had time to call Dr. Leslie Mercer before the lunch break. This witness would take some time.

Calling Leslie Mercer as part of the plaintiffs' case was a risk. Mercer had once served as Perforce Pharmaceuticals' chief spokesperson. As an adverse witness, a media-savvy scientist might prove a challenge. Jake hadn't asked the judge to declare the Perforce witnesses hostile, which would have let him be more leading and aggressive in his questioning. Instead, Jake planned to emphasize their commitment to Perforce, but he took them as his own witnesses. He didn't want to appear unnecessarily antagonistic in front of the jury, at least not this early in the trial.

Jake took Mercer through his credentials, which were flashier though not as history-making as Lee Standers'. Mercer's appearance also presented a sharp contrast to Standers'. His peppered gray hair swept back from his forehead in a luxurious peak, his face fleshy and tanned, prosperous-looking.

"Dr. Mercer, you were involved in the development of Uplift. Is that correct?"

"Yes." His voice boomed with self-confidence. "Not as closely as Dr. Standers, certainly. The credit for this breakthrough discovery goes exclusively to him. But I did help shepherd it through testing and the FDA approval process."

"That's where your real expertise lies, isn't it? In, as you say, shepherding new drugs?"

"Yes. I like to think that's where I make my best contributions."

"But you've also served as Perforce's spokesman, haven't you?"

"Yes, I have served as both the chief medical officer and as the corporate information officer, dealing with media outlets, shareholders, and other interested parties."

Mercer reminded me of a plump, self-absorbed pigeon. The questions and answers droned on. I have to remember, whenever I enter a courtroom, that what happens here moves at its own deliberate, excruciating pace. Question. Pause. Answer. Question. Explanation. Pause. With the subdued lights and voices, somehow it was even quieter than church. No rustling church bulletins or hymn books. I always have to take a deep breath and remind myself to go with the flow.

Of course, moments of intense emotion pop up, raised voices, tears, pounding gavels. Common in made-for-TV dramas — or staged-for-TV California trials — those moments are rare in real courtrooms. Most of the time, it's quiet, respectful, almost worshipful.

"—of course I believe in this drug. We're in the business to help people. Statistically, fifteen million Americans suffer from depression. They're not just blue or sad, but truly depressed. As a result, they have problems in their jobs, their families. They can't get their work done; their sex lives are unfulfilling or nonexistent. Some can't even go out of the house or get out of bed. It's a devastating, crippling life."

Mercer was wound up, so Jake let him keep going.

"The most telling fact for me is this. I once watched a patient dying of AIDS, a young mother. Pain wracked her every breath. Her immune system breakdown allowed everything imaginable to attack her body. But she struggled mightily to live. Despite the inevitability of her death and the pain of her life, she struggled heroically. For every last breath.

"On the other hand, severely depressed patients can appear perfectly normal, but life seems so worthless to them that one in six of them commit suicide. One in six. They don't fight for life, they don't value life. They kill themselves."

Mercer almost raised himself out of the witness box. With his bouffant hair and the fiery conviction in his voice, he could've been a TV preacher. Instead, he was a witness from the other side — and not doing a lot to help Jake's case.

Jake stepped in, cutting off any more diatribe. He wanted the jury to know about depression, but he didn't want to give Mercer a chance to paint Uplift as the miracle cure for desperate people.

"Dr. Mercer, can you tell us about the FDA approval process for new drugs? Just an outline of the steps, so we can better understand it."

Jake's questions effectively sat him alongside the jury. The way he approached witnesses, the jury couldn't guess he usually knew as much or more than the expert did. What worried me was what he hadn't had time to learn in this case.

With more detail than the jury wanted or needed, judging from their expressions, Mercer tracked through the new drug path, from pre-trial testing to full approval. Despite his televangelist zeal, Mercer could be tedious. I watched the jurors and studied the expressions on some of the observers sitting around me. If Jake's goal was to get the Perforce witnesses to bore the jury stupid, he was succeeding.

"—final approval was granted in April. The FDA was so impressed by the thoroughness of our testing, they expressly commended us for it. Needless to say, we were quite pleased with the FDA's commendation because that's the level of excellence Perforce strives for."

Jake looked like a bird dog on point. A subtle attitude shift, one the jury probably didn't notice. Mercer was feeding Jake just what he hoped for. Jake fished for more.

"So it's uncommon for the FDA to—"

"I object!" Arthur Vendue had been waiting for a time when it would look like he was objecting to Jake and not to his own company spokesman. He popped out of his seat. "This line of questioning is improper, Your Honor."

"Sustained."

The jury couldn't tell how loaded that mild exchange was or how much history it carried with it. Vendue had undoubtedly told Mercer to avoid bragging about the company's reputation. Talking about commendations from the FDA strayed into the tricky territory of reputation evidence.

Jake would use any opening the defendants provided as an excuse to push the judge to allow the Tixtill evidence. If a Perforce witness bragged about the company's reputation for thorough research, the judge might well allow contradictory testimony about their criminal conviction — testimony Jake desperately wanted the jury to hear. At the same time, Vendue had to handle his objections carefully, so the jurors saw him objecting to Jake, not criticizing one of his own people.

Jake and Mercer continued their give-and-take until Judge Bream finally called an afternoon break. My rump felt flat and square from sitting, my head felt like cotton candy, and my seatbelt bruises and battered muscles ached. Jurors can't concentrate for such long hours, and I know the lawyers were having trouble.

After the jury filed out, I sat down next to Jake to give him my impression of how Mercer was coming across.

"Enough yet to get Tixtill in?"

I shrugged. "Truthfully? I doubt it, but Mercer likes to brag. He may push the door wide enough yet."

I felt like a boxing manager, icing my guy down and pepping him up before he went back into the ring to slug it out some more. I left Jake slumped in a chair, flipping through marked copies of Mercer's deposition.

Outside, I checked my cell phone and made a return call to my mom.

"Avery, honey, I don't mean to pry. But . . ."

"Hi, Mom." Mom doesn't beat around the bush. "What's up?"

"Well, Melvin Bertram. Have you — do you have it worked out to share office space with him, when you get back?"

"We're talking about it, Mom. That's all. Neither one of us knows if that's — what we want to do yet."

"Oh. Well. It is best to walk all the way around something like that before you decide."

"So why are you asking?"

"Just a rumor. That he was offering the old Bertram place for sale. I guess it's just a rumor. Somebody got something confused, I'm sure."

Melvin selling his family home place, the building we'd talked about turning into two offices? For the rumors to be circulating, Melvin must be talking. Just not to me.

"Any other news from the home front?" I changed the topic. I didn't want to dwell on the Melvin rumor because I wasn't sure how I felt about it.

"—old Mrs. Waller? Lives in that house at the edge of the city cemetery?"

"Uh-huh." I faintly remembered the lady she was talking about.

"Her husband used to care-take the cemetery. He passed a few years back, but she still lives in the cottage. There's a big something brewing because she's fed up with kids hanging out there late at night, drinking and doing who knows what else, to quote her. Of course it scares her, having people lurking about in what amounts to her backyard. So she's taken to wandering the cemetery at night, dressed in black. She sneaks up on them."

"That's kind of freaky." I smiled, imagining a frail little lady haunting the graveyard.

"It gets worse. She sneaks up on them and blasts down on an air horn. You know those loud things? Your dad said it was attached to a little can of compressed air."

And banned at high school football games for its risk to eardrums, if I remembered correctly. "An air horn?"

"Yep. Now the neighbors are complaining. They say it sounds like a runaway semi-truck squalling through in the middle of the night. The sheriff went out last Saturday and arrested the lot of them, Mrs. Waller and all. Said the judge could sort out which devil started the ruckus."

Sheriff L. J. — Lucinda Jane — Peters. A high school classmate of mine who'd have been voted most likely to break the law until she'd lucked into her real calling — county sheriff.

"Doesn't seem fair to be arresting a little old lady who's just trying to protect her property and her peace of mind. If you ask me, she needs a good lawyer."

"Whoa, Mom. No way. I'm busy here—"

"I know, dear. I know you're busy right now. I'm just saying there's folks that have good causes, that need protecting. Here in Dacus, just like in other places."

"Mm-hmm." Nothing more committal than that. I knew she wanted me to do what I felt called to do; she just hoped that meant I'd be back in Dacus. I still wasn't sure, and the middle of this trial offered no clear space to think very far ahead. Representing demented little old ladies gliding through graveyards deafening pot smokers, randy couples, and Goths — I wasn't sure that looked like a career path.

"Gotta go, Mom. I'll keep you posted."

I would have to talk to Melvin. Maybe he'd dug up something helpful for Jake's cross-examination. And maybe I could learn which way the wind was blowing with him, in case it carried a sign about what I should be planning.

Mercer was already back on the stand when I slipped into my seat. I tuned part of it out while I watched the jurors' reactions, like watching TV with the sound muted. My conversation with Jake during the break had reminded me just how exhausting a trial can be, especially when the shots aren't falling quite right. I realized any commentary I gave Jake would need to be very pointed, very specific. He would be too drained to take in much else.

Jake stiffened and drew my attention back to Mercer.

"—gathered the finest cadre of research scientists in the field. Their attention to detail, their dedication and the thoroughness of their testing are all hallmarks of a Perforce product. We're justifiably proud of the extremely high quality of our testing—"

"I object." Vendue tried to mask his ire, but his sharp tone startled a couple of jurors. It would've startled me too, but I had been watching him to see if he'd heard his chief medical officer straying once again into forbidden territory.

"Sustained." The judge didn't even wait for an explanation from Vendue. He didn't reprimand Mercer, which would only reinforce his message in the jurors' minds. Instead, he peered at Mercer over his reading glasses, his lips pursed, trying to convey his disapproval without wasting time sending the jury out.

Mercer looked unconcerned. I couldn't figure out why he kept wandering over the edge, touting Perforce's sterling reputation. His testimony was strong, without bragging about Perforce's record. Was it a perverse need to make sure people knew what Perforce had accomplished while he was in charge, while his predecessor had gotten the company in trouble with the FDA? Or was he simply so wrapped up in the sound of his own voice and his own accomplishments that he was oblivious to its effect?

He had skated up to and over the edge several times in his testimony. Jake would now be primed to make another motion before the judge to introduce evidence of Perforce's Tixtill black eye.

I still wasn't convinced the Tixtill evidence had anything to do with Uplift or this case. I also wasn't sure Mercer's testimony, with his mentions of Perforce's good research reputation, opened the door wide enough for Jake. But I could tell from the smirk at the corner of Jake's mouth and the added bounce in his movements that he was convinced. He knew whatever changes Perforce had put in place to prevent another Tixtill fiasco wouldn't matter to the jurors. They would likely reduce it to its essence: bad is as bad does. If they'd hidden problems with Tixtill, they might have hidden problems with Uplift.

Jake kept questioning Mercer but couldn't lead him into any other missteps. Vendue took Mercer on cross, which lasted until the evening recess at 6:00.

After the judge sent the jury home, Jake made his move. "Your Honor, based on the testimony yesterday and today, I'd like to renew my motion to introduce testimony related to Tixtill. The company's own witness has opened the door to reputation evidence—"

"Counselor, I was quite certain that would be your motion. I'll take it under advisement and rule later. Court is adjourned." His gavel cracked and he pushed back his chair.

Jake would've preferred arguing now, while his adrenaline pumped from the points he'd scored with Mercer. He'd have to maintain the fire he felt — difficult, but judging from his face as he turned to me, not impossible. At least the judge hadn't summarily ruled against a new motion. Yet.

I declined Jake's half-hearted offer of dinner. We were both tired and needed some quiet time. Dark had fallen quickly under the gray sky. I strolled toward East Bay, planning on dinner at Blossom or Magnolia, when my cell phone buzzed.

"You may have to come up here to get your great-aunt out of jail." My dad's voice had a wry edge of mirth. "Grady Phelps is threatening to sue her for, I believe he said grievous bodily harm."

Grady was the route mail carrier in downtown Dacus.

"Don't tell me she whacked him with somebody's cane."

"Worse. Leon—" her Siamese cat "—jumped off the window ledge and attacked his head."

"Oww. That's gotta hurt. How did Leon manage that?" I pictured the floor-length windows lining the front of the house where my three great-aunts lived.

"Grady was on the side path and Leon came down from the kitchen window. Right onto his head. Managed to get pretty good purchase and wouldn't let go."

"What was Grady Phelps doing on the side path? The mail slot's in the front door."

"That's what Aunt Letha wants to know. She claims he's always lurking about in places he doesn't belong, gives her the creeps. Grady wants to know where his toupee is. Leon drug it off in the bushes. Grady's claiming the thing cost three thousand dollars."

"Leon stole his toupee?" I had to stop walking and lean against a building. I was laughing so hard, I teared up.

"It's really not funny." My dad chuckled. "Leon scratched him up pretty bad. You know that hurt."

"Yep." Especially on skin pulled taut over a bald head. "That toupee looked like straw sweepings from the Feed & Seed. Where's he get off saying it's worth three thousand dollars?"

"Maybe he's adding in all the glue he's had to buy over the years to fasten it down."

We both lost it at that. A couple on the other side of the street glanced at me and kept walking.

"I'd better get over there," Dad said. "I promised Aletha and your mom I'd crawl around under the shrubs and see if I could find it."

"Be careful under the kitchen window, Dad."

"I'll wear a hat." He chuckled and hung up.

Men needed to figure out lots of women find bald heads sexy. Grady Phelps is no Sean Connery, but that toupee was a joke. At the risk of looking drunk and disorderly, I laughed out loud, imagining Grady Phelps wearing Leon as a large, angry toupee.

CHAPTER TWENTY-FOUR

Tuesday morning

Before adjourning court the day before, Judge Bream had made it clear the lawyers had better plan on moving the testimony along. He gave new meaning to "speedy trial."

The judge also had ordered the attorneys to report early so he could hear motions once again on the admissibility of the Tixtill evidence. Jake came prepared and put up one heck of a fight, but the answer — once again — was no. Judge Bream didn't shut the door completely, though he'd have to slam Jake's head in the door — several times — to dissuade him from raising the issue, should future testimony provide a basis. Jake was nothing if not a scrapper.

Jake then rested his case. Forbidden by Judge Bream's bifurcation of the trial, Jake wasn't allowed to introduce details about the shooting victims' injuries. Even though he couldn't fully show the jury what had happened that day at Bradt Industries, he'd hammered doggedly on the liability evidence, trying to weave a compelling reason why the jury should blame Perforce for what happened. Ivan Gretel's testimony that Uplift made some depressed patients agitated, made them unable to control their impulses, had been the cornerstone of Jake's case. Jake could only hope time would weaken the damaging effect of Vendue's cross-examination of Gretel. And Jake hoped to inflict some damage of his own, now that Vendue was putting up witnesses.

Langley Hilliard was the defense's first witness. I'd somehow let Hilliard grow in my mind, imbued with all manner of ogre-like qualities. On the stand, the ceiling spot overhead shining on his silvery hair, he looked — ordinary. Ordinary height and weight, ordinary sagging old-man face. Predictably ordinary expert witness, with enough gray hair and credentials to convince a jury he knew what he was talking about.

I'd spent the months since last October despising him. Watching him now, after Blaine Demarcos's description, I could grudgingly see that Hilliard had to believe doctors were invincible — or at least immune from admitting their mistakes. As ludicrous as it seemed to me, maybe he'd practiced so long that, once upon a time, his faith in his power to heal was the only medicine he could offer his patients.

Another part of me saw him as I'd seen him last fall — a lying, self-serving old fart.

Last fall, I'd watched Hilliard use his prior witness stand experience to lead a little girl's greenhorn attorney by the nose. *No, I don't see any indication in the record that the physician violated accepted standards of care.* He had glibly stretched and misdirected the truth, believably skewing everything in favor of my client, winning my case for me. To my ears, he had lied to do it, and I'd snapped.

As I had mulled on that day when the judge's gavel cracked down so fiercely on the tirade I'd provoked in Hilliard and on my career, I saw not just Hilliard, but myself. I'd goaded Hilliard until he began screaming, I'd baited him to catch him in his lies. The judge had declared a mistrial, and the insurance company had settled. My client had been relieved because he hadn't wanted the humiliation of a trial in the first place, but I was out of a job and back home in Dacus.

Now I'd come full circle, back to a courtroom facing Langley Hilliard. Only this time, I could only watch as I'd watched replays in my mind of our last meeting. This time he was on the other side, and I had no control over what would happen. I'd given Jake everything I could dig up to discredit Hilliard. Now I could only sit and watch it play out. This must be what ballplayers feel when they're relegated to the sidelines, an ache to be a part of it, a need to believe they could make a difference, and maybe a bit — tiny, but real — of relief that it doesn't depend solely on them anymore.

Hilliard had sat in many witness chairs in many courtrooms. He knew the drill. Defense firms paid his fees because he was good. A bit pompous, but he knew how to talk to a jury. Hilliard didn't respond well to sarcastic challenge, but he could take the usual attacks and parries of plaintiff's counsel as an experienced hand.

Arthur Vendue led Hilliard through his testimony, the gist of which said that Uplift had been thoroughly tested, that depression and anxiety disorders are common but complicated and difficult to treat, and that depressed people sometimes go over the edge and kill themselves and others.

"Doctor, do you have an opinion, with a reasonable degree of medical certainty, about whether Uplift caused the events at Bradt Industries?"

"Yes, I do. The events were precipitated, with a reasonable degree of certainty, by Mr. Wilma's underlying mental instability. There's no indication that what happened was caused by the drug Uplift."

"Could you elaborate on the basis for your opinion?"

"It is well documented that Ray Vincent Wilma had a history of depression and mental problems. He'd been institutionalized once before. Both he and his mother had, at various times in their lives, made suicide attempts. He'd made plans and issued threats about 'making the bastards pay' for more than a year before he even began taking Uplift. And there's nothing in the history of the drug to indicate that it would have any connection with this sort of — melt down."

"What do you feel gives you the experience to render this opinion?"

"Most notably, I've spent many years as chief medical officer in charge of Barnard Medical's research program. I'm fully familiar with the FDA and NIH — National Institutes of Health — guidelines on human subjects testing and drug research protocols. Perforce met all the requirements in bringing Uplift to market and continues to appropriately monitor and report side effects or other occurrences now that Uplift is in broad use in the market."

"In your expert opinion, Uplift did not cause the events at Bradt Industries?"

"No, based on the history of the drug, it did not. Mr. Wilma's underlying mental disorder is a better, more consistent explanation of what happened. Uplift unfortunately couldn't prevent the tragedy from occurring, but it also didn't cause it."

"Thank you, doctor."

Despite Judge Bream's unhidden bias for hurry, Arthur Vendue had spent all morning letting Hilliard's testimony unfold for the jury. We'd run past the normal noon recess time, so I was ravenous.

In the courthouse snack bar, I paid for my cheeseburger, Diet Pepsi, and chips, and took a seat. Uncharacteristically for me, I didn't have any notes or papers in front of me, nothing to read. Bringing something with me had taken too much effort. Just thinking takes too much effort when I'm hungry. I just stared into space, munching.

"Wow!" A guy in work clothes sitting nearby thumped his fist on the counter. "Did'ja see that? Whoa-oh." He almost fell off his stool. All eyes turned toward the wall-mounted TV set he was watching. The guy dishing up cheeseburgers pointed the remote control to turn up the volume. The jerky camera movements of a live report took a few blinks to decipher, but the diner who'd been watching the story provided color commentary for us.

"Some guy's strapped a bunch of dynamite to hisself and is holding a bunch of people hostage. Apparently he's in love — see that little girl there? With the tits? She's the one."

A brunette in a tight-fitting T-shirt huddled between an officer and a woman, their attention focused on what looked like a small fast-food restaurant. The camera filming the shots we were watching stood a bit to the side and behind the officer. The camera zoomed in on a sign: Burger Hut. *Uh-oh.*

A figure repeatedly jostled into view from off-camera, microphone extended toward the teenage girl.

"Miss Cole, could you tell us—"

Unexpectedly the screen filled with a blur and something large and square smacked the reporter in the back of the head, cutting off his question.

"Whoa-oh!" Our local color commentator continued. "What a shot! She clocked him out!"

The camera followed the reporter as he stumbled to the ground, then again profiled the threesome: the police officer, the teenager — and my mother.

Mom adjusted her purse strap back over her shoulder and put her arm protectively around Miranda Cole's shoulders.

Whoa-oh. No wonder I hadn't heard from her this morning.

"—standoff here in Dacus is now three hours old." The voice-over on the television finally got louder than the background noise in the snack bar. "Sources say the man inside is wearing what appears to be a fishing vest with several sticks of dynamite and a shoebox attached to the vest with duct tape. He has threatened to blow up the building and the four workers reportedly inside if his demands are not met. He insists on talking with Miranda Cole. It's not clear whether that's a family member or someone else."

A man appeared in the glass front windows of the Burger Hut, looking like a B-grade movie robot, his arms sticking out of a stiff, square vest which was shiny gray and lumpy. Apparently he'd never heard of SWAT snipers.

He leaned closer to the window and waved wildly toward the camera — and Miranda Cole. Miranda shook her head and buried her face in my mother's shoulder. The camera beside Miranda and her protective bodyguard showed a pale, pleasant-looking teenager with thin, shoulder-length hair. A nice-looking kid, but hardly the face that launched a thousand ships. Obviously enough to launch a lunatic dressed in duct tape, though.

Seeing it on TV elevated it to gut-clenching reality, to real danger. I'd sometimes worried about my mom getting in over her head, mixed up in something dangerous as she went about saving the world. But it had never been a serious fear. She'd always seemed surrounded by guardian angels, though I wasn't actually able to spot any of those angels on the TV screen.

Weren't they standing too close to the building — and the bomb-laden Lothario? They were at the edge of the parking lot. How far would a bomb blast carry?

My mom reached to take something from someone out of camera range. A portable phone. She handed it to Miranda, speaking too softly for the camera to overhear. The nut ball appeared in the window, holding what must be a phone to his ear, waving with his other hand. The rest of us just watched.

"Pick him off, how 'bout it?" Our helpful commentator encouraged the screen. "Hell, send the dame with the loaded handbag in. She could take him out. All those cops standing around with their fingers up their butts."

He must have felt the cloud of animosity gathering in the room behind him because he shut up without turning to look at the Highway Patrol officer sitting three stools down from him or the two city cops at the table behind him.

Then the camera's focus shifted. The stiff-legged man in a lumpy vest waddled out the Burger Hut door holding his hands high in the air, his hair greasy and sticking up in twigs on his head. He shambled three steps, waving goofily at Miranda, then three cops converged and took him to the ground.

The camera lost its close-up in the jostling crowd, and I took that as my cue to leave. I'd been suckered into watching those breathless "breaking news" marathons before, always full of inane speculation. I already knew more than the commentators did — more than I wanted to know.

My legs wobbled a bit as I headed toward the elevator — pent-up adrenaline from too much tension and too little I could do about it. Where does she find these people?

CHAPTER TWENTY-FIVE

Wednesday

After lunch, Jake rose to cross-examine Hilliard and wasted no time. One of his first volleys attacked Hilliard's expertise. He'd let the judge certify Hilliard as an expert witness, based on his research experience, and he'd let Hilliard testify about psychiatric matters with minimal challenge, even though Hilliard was an ob-gyn without any training in managing depression. Now Jake lobbed one over the wall.

"Dr. Hilliard, you are a board-certified obstetrician and gynecologist, are you not? That deals with birthing babies and female reproductive issues, doesn't it?"

"Yes."

"So psychiatric diseases aren't really your specialty, are they?"

"Well, you certainly deal with issues such as depression when dealing with new mothers. Postpartum depression is a big concern, you know." He wouldn't let Jake rattle his cage that easily.

"I don't think Ray Vincent Wilma was suffering post-partum depression, was he?"

Hilliard didn't grace that with a reply.

"You aren't certified in psychiatry, are you? Or psychology?"

"No, I'm not."

"Dr. Hilliard, have you, through Barnard Medical, ever done research for Perforce Pharmaceutical?"

"Yes." Hilliard shifted in his seat. "Perforce is a major drug manufacturer. We've served as a test site for their clinical phase research in the past."

"Whenever Barnard served as a test site, that would've been like those situations you talked about earlier, where they would pay you to find patients to take an experimental new drug, and your physicians would let the folks at Perforce know how it worked, whether it took care of the problem or caused side effects or whatever?"

"Yes, simply put, that would've been our relationship with Perforce."

"And you, as a physician, got paid for your work with Perforce, when you were doing these tests?"

"It's common for drug manufacturers to reimburse physicians for their time and effort in executing a research protocol. In the past, I've had patients enrolled in studies sponsored by Perforce, and there would've been some payment to account for our administrative time in seeing the patients and writing the reports to Perforce. We see so many patients. I don't recall exactly which studies reimbursed what amounts. Patients are only referred to drug studies if we feel they may benefit. It's done all the time."

"If you feel the patients may benefit, you say. But that's not really the reason patients are referred, is it? I mean, patient benefit may be low on the list of reasons you might encourage someone to sign up for a drug study, wouldn't it?"

"I'm not sure I know what you're asking." Hilliard's response was stiff.

"Patients are told they shouldn't count on an investigational drug to make them better, aren't they? They're told the best reason for participating in a drug study is to do their civic duty, to help find cures for other people, aren't they?"

"In some cases—"

"Is that just you doctors' way of telling them, we don't want you blaming us if this doesn't work out too well? Is that why you don't promise them any results?"

"We can't promise a patient a certain outcome. You lawyers would be on us in a flash."

"So you all just find it best not to stick your necks out, don't you?"

Hilliard didn't answer.

After a short staring match, Jake moved a step closer to the witness stand, coming in from the side. "Do you at least tell your patients that you get paid? Or is that something else they really don't need to know, that you doctors get paid whether the new drug helps the patient or not?"

"We're paid for our time, time spent seeing the patient and filling out reports."

Jake took several slow steps toward the jury, crossing in front of Hilliard, studying the ceiling as he walked. "How much money do you usually get paid for these patients? You get paid per patient, don't you?"

"It varies according to the size of the study grant or the reimbursement schedule worked out by the pharmaceutical company."

"Well, give us an idea, a ballpark."

"I don't know."

"A hundred dollars for each patient? Ten dollars? Five hundred? What?"

"Maybe a hundred dollars."

"And maybe more?"

"Maybe."

"That's not the only way you doctors get money for one of these studies, is it?" His voice was only a touch quieter. Hilliard leaned forward as if to hear better.

"I'm not sure what you mean."

"Sure you do. You doctors make money working with drug companies, big money. Not just a hundred dollars a pop for seeing patients. What are some of those ways, doctor?"

"I don't really know—"

"Sure you do." Jake and his banty rooster attitude flew at Hilliard. "Are you familiar with a drug company called Rabb & Company?"

Hilliard's eyes narrowed. He'd known this was coming. After I blundered into the relationship between Perforce and Rabb & Company, Hilliard would've been expecting this. Denials wouldn't play well with the jurors when they found out what Jake knew. Even with forewarning, Hilliard acted defensive, as though he had something to hide.

"Yes, I'm familiar with it." He sounded peevish.

"What exactly is your relationship with Rabb & Company?" Jake now sounded conversational, but his body language said he was closing in.

"Rabb is a small pharmaceutical company. It is one of many companies for whom we've conducted research."

"You've done more than merely provide a research site for Rabb & Company, haven't you? More than just another hundred-dollar-a-pop project, haven't you?"

"I'm not sure—"

"Dr. Hilliard, don't you have a drug in development, one that's about to pass the last hurdle and become eligible for investigational drug status — IND, I believe the FDA calls it. Eligible to begin formal testing?"

"My colleagues and I have numerous projects under development—"

"You've already begun testing this product on humans, haven't you? Even though it hasn't formally entered that phase."

"That's perfectly permissible under—"

Arthur Vendue sat quietly scribbling on a notepad. He wasn't demanding that Jake let the witness finish his answers. Vendue figured Hilliard could take care of himself.

"Doctor." Jake stopped pacing. "Doctor, you've been working on this drug for some time, haven't you? You're very close to signing a contract for the further development and licensing of this drug, aren't you?"

"Well, yes . . ."

"A contract with Rabb & Company. Isn't that right?"

"Yes."

"The same man is the principal stockholder in both Perforce Pharmaceutical and Rabb & Company, isn't he?"

Had this been a movie, a thundering crescendo would've sounded.

"I believe the companies are related in some way, but I really don't know much about business set-ups . . ."

"You don't know much about business set-ups?" Jake's voice boomed. "You certainly knew that a man named Pendleton Rabb was involved with both Perforce and Rabb & Company, didn't you? You certainly knew Perforce's attorney would be writing you a check for your time spent testifying here today, didn't you? And you hoped that same attorney would be writing you an even bigger check for your new drug, didn't you?" Jake's voice rattled a light fixture overhead.

"I object, Your Honor." Vendue rose half out of his chair, his voice calm. "Counsel must let the witness answer the questions."

"Sustained. Mr. Baker, please confine yourself to one question at a time."

"Dr. Hilliard, you're expecting to be paid for your testimony today, aren't you?"

"For my time in testifying, not for my testimony."

"You're also expecting to sign a contract with Rabb & Company that will pay you royalties — you expect substantial royalties, if the drug is successful, do you not?"

"Well, we certainly hope—"

"Both Perforce Pharmaceuticals and Rabb & Company are run by Pendleton Rabb, is that not so?"

"I-I believe so. As I said, that's not my area of expertise."

"You've already admitted that psychiatry isn't really your specialty. You're telling us Perforce's drug Uplift had nothing to do with Ray Vincent Wilma going crazy and killing people. At the same time, you're hoping Perforce will pay

217

you a lot of money for your drug. You think your excitement over that deal influenced your enthusiasm about Uplift in any way?"

"Certainly not. I, sir, am a professional. I'm trained to be objective. I—"

"Certainly, Dr. Hilliard." Jake's tone should have sounded a warning bell for Hilliard. "Dr. Hilliard, you testified that you've conducted drug trials for countless drugs for many companies for many years. Is that correct?"

"Yes, I have." Hilliard gave a short answer, hoping to make himself a small target while he figured out where this next tack was headed.

"But this drug you've developed is the first drug you've taken completely through the approval process yourself, isn't it?"

"Yes."

"You've watched other physicians, at Barnard Medical and elsewhere, make lots of money on drugs or medical devices they've developed, haven't you? It can be very lucrative, if a new drug is successful, can't it?"

"Yes, but it's also very expensive to get it through the process. Not all drugs make it through. Not all drugs are successful."

"I'm sure it's very expensive — which is why you desperately needed Rabb & Company to bankroll your project. That's why that licensing contract is so important to you, isn't it?"

Hilliard paused before answering. "Yes. The financial support will be helpful."

"More than helpful. It's vital, isn't it? You don't have the money on your own, do you?"

"No."

"Dr. Hilliard, you've watched others get rich while you collect paltry fees at a hundred dollars a pop, haven't you? This project of yours is your one big chance, isn't it?" Jake emphasized each word. "It's your one chance to play with the big boys, isn't it?"

Hilliard paused too long.

"Isn't it?" Jake's voice was quiet, persistent.

"It's important, yes."

His grudging reluctance was what Jake wanted the jury to see.

"Thank you, doctor."

After I'd blundered all over Atlanta, I was surprised Arthur Vendue had allowed Jake to pursue the Rabb & Company link so rabidly. Vendue's questions on redirect drilled in on the fact that Pendleton Rabb really didn't run Perforce Pharmaceuticals, trying to raise doubt about the implications Jake had drawn. But Hilliard knew so little about the corporate structure that his replies did little but muddy the picture even more for most of the jurors.

Had Jake been too subtle about Hilliard's conflict of interest? In the jury's mind, would Hilliard's greed outweigh Ivan Gretel's sexual perversions? I doubted it. Sex trumps money most of the time.

Could the jurors really grasp what Hilliard's conflict of interest might mean? If one of those juror's doctor got a kickback for prescribing a drug or if the drug company took the doctor and his family to Hawaii and charged the juror higher prices to pay for the trip, the doctor's conflict would seem real. But patients never find out. "Conflict of interest" always sounds sterile and distant — until you know it's taking money out of your pocket or putting you in danger. Was Jake making that clear to the jury? Studying their faces, I wasn't sure.

I scribbled some notes to myself. Jake's closing argument needed to hit the greed factor harder. It was all he really had. He hadn't tried to introduce evidence about Tunisia Johnson's death. Not much he could've done to get that in, but I would've loved watching Hilliard squirm, trying to explain his relationship to a dead Black prostitute. Former prostitute.

I winced inwardly at my callousness toward Tabbi Johnson's mama and wondered if Cas Kirkland knew anything yet about the autopsy results.

CHAPTER TWENTY-SIX

Wednesday night

That evening, after another late adjournment, Jake slumped at his office desk, its usually spotless expanse littered with paper. In the dim lamplight, he rocked his heavy gold fountain pen over his thumb, repeatedly thumping the cap on the legal pad in front of him. His head rested in his other hand. He didn't notice that I'd entered until I cleared my throat.

"Jake, I've got a few notes. For your closing."

Jake tilted his head to look at me but didn't straighten up or untangle his fingers from his hair.

I knew where he was. Arthur Vendue had rested his case. Tomorrow the attorneys would make their closing arguments. It all came down to this, the power of his words, his ability to tell a story so the jury could write the ending he wanted. In his heart, he would feel it rested with him alone. My stomach knotted at both the memory of past trials and at the projection of me sitting in his seat now.

A lot of people were counting on him. His clients needed money for medical care or for retirement benefits they were no longer able to earn. For all of them, more than money, they needed vindication. They needed someone to acknowledge that having their world torn apart had been unfair, that it hadn't been their fault. They needed to hear someone say, "You didn't deserve this."

Judging from the pale yellow circle of light around him and from Lila's absence, I surmised Jake and I had one thing in common. Some attorneys like to have folks around, circling in orbit as they prepare their closings, providing energy from which they can draw. Jake apparently preferred solitude, the long dark night alone to search for the words. I intruded anyway. I wanted to earn my keep.

"Greed, Jake. Highlight their greed. You've laid the groundwork. The jury can understand it. They've seen Perforce's attorneys, all the dark suits on their side of the room. They've seen your clients, their Sunday-go-to-meeting clothes, a couple of canes, a wheelchair. Lots of Kleenex tissues. They know what you need them to know, Jake. You just need to make it simple. You know how to do that. Greed."

Jake slumped back in his chair, his pen still. "Yeah."

"You need anything? Food? Liquor? I could find you a loose woman."

That earned a small smile and a wave of the hand. "No, but thanks for stopping by. I'll see you tomorrow."

"Get some sleep, Jake. Greed."

He nodded, and I left.

I never could pull all-nighters. Finding all the best words wouldn't help if I were too sleep-stupid to utter them. Jake didn't need my advice about that, though. He knew his own rhythms, what worked for him.

I had no idea where to find a Moon Pie, so I wandered toward Market Street in search of some warm pralines. Good thing about a tourist town, the sweet shop stays open late.

Jake knew what neither of us would say out loud: his case stunk. He had clients with horrible injuries, but he had a dead bad guy with no money. Even though too much about Perforce raised questions, the jury probably wouldn't stretch distrust of Perforce into money for his clients.

The jury had to decide whether Ray Vincent Wilma was crazy or Uplift made him crazy. To defend Perforce, Arthur Vendue had done a good job painting Wilma's mental instability. Vendue had worked hard, dug deep into Wilma's past. At best, for Jake to question Perforce's shenanigans with Tixtill and its willingness to work with a slimeball — or dinosaur, depending on your perspective — like Hilliard was smoke; we just hadn't had time to find the fire. I had to admit Jake had smelled the smoke early and had finally gotten my attention. If Perforce would lie and falsify results with Tixtill, why not with Uplift? This deal with Hilliard smelled bad. How could they be trusted? Too many oddities floated around Perforce and Rabb.

I could also see the argument on the other side: the relationship between Tixtill and Uplift was tenuous. Perforce had paid for its Tixtill sins and shouldn't have to keep paying just because Jake Baker wanted Uplift tarred with the same brush. No matter how many lives Ray Vincent Wilma ruined, sometimes stuff just happens with no deep pockets to pay for picking up the pieces.

The pralines — I'd treated myself to two — were warm and buttery and comforting. I nibbled slowly, strolling down the almost empty sidewalk. While I was arguing with myself, how much of my "objective" analysis was colored by my defense attorney days? Could I ever really believe in a plaintiff's case? If not, working with Jake long term would be a fraud. I also had to admit no defense firm would ever hire me again. Defense firms rely on the fat checkbooks of corporate defendants and insurance companies, and they don't take risks. Blowing that medical malpractice trial in October and now hooking up with Jake Baker — even temporarily and even on a losing case — wouldn't make me less of a risk.

In my mind, the rambling, turreted Victorian on Dacus's Main Street and its gingerbread trim and shaded wraparound porch had grown into something of a symbol, a reassurance that I had somewhere to go, that I wasn't entirely adrift, marginally employed, and without a clue what came next. Growing up in Dacus, I'd known the monstrosity perched on a slight rise above the sidewalk as the Baldwin & Bates Funeral Home. Melvin's family had moved out long before I was old enough to pay attention to much beyond the toy department at the five-and-dime store, so to me, it had always been a funeral home.

I'd long resisted any suggestion about moving back to Dacus, to a small-town general practice. I was surely destined for grander things, with leased BMWs and retainers with lots of zeros on the end. Now that Melvin might be reconsidering his offer of an apartment and an office, I was surprised at my melancholy.

I wasn't sure I could go home again, though I did miss my family. And, during the last few months camping out at my grandfather's lake cabin, I realized I missed the mountains in a visceral way that surprised me. The cinnamon smell of damp rotting leaves, the ice in the morning air, curvy roads, red clay, people who talked in slow, twangy drawls. I'd discovered you can go home again — and home is a place as well as people. Places can, despite changes, stay reassuringly the same. Some people unfortunately are also the same, but it was the ones who wouldn't let me change that I worried about. The place couldn't be separated from the people — and all the people weren't my family.

* * *

Back at the inn, I couldn't watch TV or read, and it was too early to sleep. I put on earmuffs and bundled into my jacket and sat on the porch, watching the dwindling traffic pass the Battery. A misty rain shower came up, just enough to make the street shine in the reflected lights. I might have dozed off amidst my daydreams and random thoughts. The street below became just another shadowy dream — the pavement shiny wet, dim streetlights, no traffic, something out of an old movie in black and white and grays. A figure turned the corner, a baseball cap low over his eyes, his face upturned.

I knew he was scanning the upper floor of the inn.

I moved from half-sleep to adrenaline surge as I watched him study my windows. The time that passed couldn't have been more than seconds. He must have seen movement on the porch because he stepped off the curb onto the glistening street about the time I recognized him. Cas Kirkland.

I wrestled myself out of my cocoon of chair and blanket and lumbered down the dark stairs to the side door.

"You always let strangers in off the street at this hour?"

I couldn't read his eyes under his baseball cap.

"I don't know. What hour is it?"

He followed me, the stairs creaking heavily under his weight.

"Coffee?" He offered me one of the two cardboard-wrapped cups he carried.

"Thanks." Black. Not my favorite, but it was the thought that counted.

He shucked off his coat and fumbled in the pocket. "Here's some cream and stuff. Didn't know what you liked. And it's decaf."

"Thanks." And I meant it. A guy who thinks of everything. The room wasn't set up for making coffee. Fire codes were probably strict in eighteenth-century mansions, so this was a real treat.

As large as the room was, it also wasn't set up for someone Cas's size. He claimed the wing chair, looking out the bay window. The coffee warmed me; I'd sat outside too long and gotten chilled.

"You always roam the streets this late?"

"Just finished a shooting at a liquor house past the bridges. That was so much fun, I knew better than to try to sleep."

He stopped talking, but he had more to say. I didn't interrupt.

"Kids. They actually had kids living in that cesspool. Neighbor said they thought it'd decoy the cops, keep suspicion off 'em. Sad thing is, it worked for too long a time." He took a long swig of his coffee. "So, where've you been?" His voice was almost too casual.

"In a trial."

He didn't respond and I didn't elaborate. Reminded of it, a small wave of melancholy returned. "And what have you been up to? Besides liquor house shootings."

We sat with our backs to the carefully made bed. I had dimmed the lights, so we could see outside, but then had to tamp down the awkwardness I felt sitting in such an intimate space with a stranger.

"The preliminary autopsy report on Tunisia Johnson came in today." He still wore his baseball cap — the Toledo Mudhens.

"Anything interesting?" I asked calmly. I wanted to shake him. *So? What's it say?*

He sipped his coffee. "Lots." He kept staring out the window. "For starters, that scene was staged. Somebody moved her body after she died. Lividity patterns are harder to mark on black skin, but the autopsy showed pressure markings on her buttocks and back that didn't correspond to her position at the scene."

"So she was killed somewhere else?"

"She probably died somewhere else. The time of death has been screwed up, so now we're not at all sure she was murdered."

"What?" I turned in my chair to face him. He didn't look over at me.

"The ME says she died of a thromboembolic stroke."

"A stroke? So it's not a murder?"

"Maybe not, but we've got a hell of a suspicious death scene. Somebody moved the body, staged that kinky stuff. And," he paused, "something else odd happened to that body between the time she died and when we found her."

He took a gulp of coffee, building suspense. A born witness.

"The ME can't be sure," he said, "but the body may have been put on ice for a while."

"On ice?" I sloshed a drop of coffee on my hand.

"Refrigerated. The decomp hadn't progressed as far as we'd expect, given the time since she disappeared. They've called a bug guy at Clemson to look at the insect deposits, to help us narrow the time frame. But that's a long shot."

He stared out the window. "The last time her family saw her may not help much. She could have been on the street for a while before she died. Or she could have died the day she disappeared and been iced down before she was put in that room for us to find. Without something to better pinpoint her whereabouts, we may never know for sure when or where she died."

"How about her stomach contents?"

"Only fluids, mostly coffee, in her stomach. That won't help much."

"Where the heck would somebody refrigerate a body?"

He shrugged. "She was small, she could fit in somebody's deep freeze. Or a meat locker. A commercial refrigerator. Even a refrigerated truck. Or a deer cooler. Deer coolers aren't abundant in downtown Charleston, but they're sure plentiful a few miles north of here. That's deer-hunting territory. Just say there're plenty of places around to keep a body cold."

He leaned his head back on the chair, his chin in the air, his throat exposed.

"You said the sex scene was staged."

"Yep. The lividity patterns are one key. But no sign of recent sexual activity — no semen, no bruising. Of course, with Tunisia's history and with the impotence rate of a lot of sex sickos, the absence of signs may not mean much. The chafing from the ropes occurred after death. No bruising under the skin."

This clinical discussion of the death of a woman I'd never met made me queasy. Tunisia Johnson could have done plenty of kinky sex in her former line of work, but I couldn't believe — didn't want to believe — that she'd left the white-fenced yard and, more importantly, little chocolate-eyed Tabitha, to hit the streets for more of that.

"She was so young, how could she have a stroke?"

He shrugged. "The ME says she needs more time on that one."

The coffee burned into my empty stomach. "She's sure that's what killed her?"

"The ME said that without something clean, like a gunshot wound, cause of death becomes a process of elimination. Doc loves to lecture me while she slices and dices."

"Can she eliminate anything else?"

"Doc will check the victim's family history. Got to wait on the tox screen. That'll eliminate alcohol and a raft-load of drugs. They took bladder urine and heart blood at the autopsy, but the screen takes time, and it won't eliminate everything."

"Any leads on who might have — I started to say killed her. This is so weird. Who would have staged something like that?"

"Not a clue. Some of the street cops are asking around her old neighborhood. Until the autopsy is complete, we can't really afford a lot of time on this. It's likely not homicide, so we can't work it long. We got too many of the real thing to fool much with this one."

"It's — scary. Warped. You might have a real sicko on your hands here."

In the faint light from the window, he shrugged.

We both sat there in silence. A car slished by outside, slowly.

"Cas." I wasn't sure he was awake until he stirred slightly. "Surely she would have had some warning signs of a stroke?"

Another shrug. "I don't know. Maybe."

I glanced at him, my guilty conscience stinging. Talk of a stroke had reminded me I'd never really talked to Cas about Mark's research journal. Before, I thought it was a crazy tangent, of no use to him. Finding Tunisia's body changed the equation. Cas didn't stir as I swung my legs off the window seat and padded over to the desk where I'd left the journal and Tunisia's records in a stack.

On Tunisia's first study visit, Mark had noted her vital signs in his research journal: height, five feet one inch; weight, one hundred pounds; blood pressure, 148/88. An idea formed, something I should have recognized earlier.

I flipped through Tunisia's record, then picked up Tabitha's chart, looking for what I dimly remembered. In his notes on Tabbi's last visit, Mark's cryptic scrawl explained everything: SOB and acute HA, shortness of breath and a bad headache. Tunisia's blood pressure had risen to 164/110.

"Cas." His head was back, his feet on the window seat. I got no reply, so I spoke louder. "Tunisia had an appointment with Langley Hilliard at Barnard Medical the day she disappeared. Well, at least the last day her family saw her. Her grandmother or her aunt told me that.

"The day before, she told Mark Tilman she was having trouble breathing, that she was having severe headaches and her vision was blurred. Mark told her to stop taking the experimental medication and to see Hilliard. If Hilliard saw her, he surely would've recognized the importance of her symptoms."

I paced the small room. "Cas, it has to be the research project Tunisia was enrolled in. Hilliard was studying some kind of intranasal contraceptive, one that Pendleton Rabb and his pharmaceutical company were interested in licensing. The exact symptoms she reported are printed in every packet of birth control pills as severe warning signs. Damn."

Cas wasn't listening to a word. He'd fallen asleep. Granted, my life as a defense attorney irrevocably altered my view of medicine and its practitioners. I no longer doubted their fallibility. But how could Langley Hilliard miss such clear danger signs, symptoms that must have killed a young woman very shortly after she last saw him? How the hell could he have missed seeing it earlier?

More importantly, could he have saved her life if he'd done something?

Bits fell into place: her grandmother's thick body and heavy arms, Tunisia's disorientation, her headaches and blurred vision. Together, everything pointed to a stroke risk.

The fact that she was Black and — I flipped to her record — had started the study with a slightly elevated blood pressure screamed stroke risk. With her absentee mother's medical history unknown and so many risk factors, why had she been allowed to enroll in the study? Even worse, how could Hilliard have missed the warning signs when she saw him for her two-week checkup?

Langley Hilliard had seen Tunisia only two weeks before she'd brought Tabbi in to see Mark Tilman, two weeks before Mark was concerned enough about her symptoms that he told her to stop taking the medication and to see Hilliard again.

Langley Hilliard might have a plausible explanation, but I could only come up with one: first, he'd signed her up because he desperately needed study subjects for his pet project; later, he hadn't wanted to report negative results on the eve of signing the licensing agreement. So he ignored problems when they presented themselves. Either that or he was just rock-stupid and had missed the signs.

Hilliard was far from stupid.

What had Pendleton Rabb's lawyer said about the contract? They'd reached an understanding a couple of weeks ago, but they hadn't signed anything — because Mark Tilman had called Rabb headquarters.

What could Hilliard have hoped to gain? Sooner or later, something had to happen to Tunisia, using the contraceptive with those symptoms.

Something had happened. Tunisia Johnson had died. How could it benefit him to ignore her problems? Why not just drop her from the study? Why try to cover up? Rabb's attorney had mentioned an audit of the research records. Perhaps dropping Tunisia from the study would have waved a red flag at the wrong time.

Langley Hilliard would certainly benefit from a successful contraceptive, once developed. Could he be so greedy, so blinded by dollar signs dancing before his eyes, that he simply ignored what he didn't want to see?

Of course Hilliard was capable of deluding himself. That's what made him an effective witness, particularly when the facts on his side were weak and his first hurdle was convincing himself of their merit.

What had I told Jake? The cornerstone of the Uplift lawsuit was greed. Pure, plain, green-eyed greed. I needed to check a couple of things tomorrow. How long before a blood clot developed? How long before it hit the brain? What would tip off a physician that a problem existed? What was the standard medical response? I had to think of somebody to call.

I paced about in my bare feet, careful not to wake Cas. I tried not to look at him. It somehow embarrassed me to see him sleeping, his mouth slightly open, his neck exposed. Thank goodness he wasn't snoring.

I hesitated to wake him. He might be one of those ex-military types who'd break my neck if awakened suddenly.

I stretched out on the bed, not bothering to undress. I thought I'd lie there contemplating the ceiling until morning, but I didn't remember another thought until 6:00 a.m.

CHAPTER TWENTY-SEVEN

Early Thursday morning

The next morning, Cas was gone. Maybe it had been the door closing that woke me. Sheesh. Had I snored or talked in my sleep or drooled? He hadn't even heard my brilliant deductions about Hilliard and his complicity in Tunisia's death.

I called the station. He was out. I didn't bother leaving a message. Plenty of time to fill him in after I'd double-checked a couple of things.

I showered and tried to rub the grit out of my eyes, but succeeded only partially.

Fortunately for me, Dr. Redfearn in Dacus is an early riser. Semi-retired, he was waiting for the rest of his patients to die off quietly. Despite his quirks and oddities, he's still one of the best doctors I've ever known.

"You home, Avery?"

"No, sir. Just calling to—"

"You heard about the excitement in town yesterday?"

"Yessir—"

"Your mother, you know. Deranged man with the hots for some little girl. Don't know her, you know. Lots of new folks in town. Much too young for him, even if he hadn't been somewhat unlatched. Not sure there's more of that these days, but you sure do hear more about it. Folks used to have the decency and good sense to take care of their own."

"Yes, sir. I was—"

"Where was I? Your mother. She talked this fellow out of blowing up the Burger Hut. Not that the place would be such a loss. Dreadful food. Can't figure out why the Rescue Squad trucks always park around there, unless they're waiting on a ptomaine outbreak. He had enough dynamite strapped to his chest to blow a crater in the entire block. Not to mention himself and all those kids.

"There was your mom. Right there on the evening news. Sent a crew all the way from Greenville to cover it. The national news even picked it up. 'Course they showed such a short piece that anybody seeing it would think the whole town wasn't anything but toothless wonders. Except your mama, who wouldn't talk to them.

"She swatted one of those reporters with something. Heard it was her purse. Or her fist. You know how folks are, tellin' a story. Rarely get it right."

I leapt in as soon as he took a breath. I still hadn't talked to Mom — and she hadn't called. "Dr. Redfearn. I had some quick questions I wondered if you could help me with. An embolic stroke."

"Goodness, darling. That's not something I can help you with over the phone. That's serious—"

"It's a case I'm working on, Doc. I just need to pick your brain." I kept talking over his *oohh*. "How quickly does it progress? How do you know when somebody has one? How would you treat it? How risky is it for someone taking birth control pills?" I got all my questions out at once. He'd remember them — and be more likely to stay on the subject without straying than if I introduced them one by one.

"Somebody on birth control pills?"

"Well, a hormone-based contraceptive delivered intranasally."

"What's the blood pressure reading?"

"164/110, at the last check."

"That right there is cause to assess somebody. Any risk factors for stroke? Other than living in South Carolina, which is risk enough."

I ran down the list, describing her grandmother and the missing pieces of her medical history.

"Honey, she's an extremely high risk. I wouldn't keep her on something like that."

"Even if the drug was expected to produce fewer side effects than oral contraceptives?"

He harrumphed. "That's what they always claim, isn't it?"

"Suppose she took this stuff and developed severe headaches and had trouble with her vision. How long would that take to develop?"

"I'd expect to see signs within the first two weeks."

"Two weeks?"

"Mm-hmm. Then I'd take her off it immediately. A lot of Blacks, particularly downstate it seems, are more at risk from oral contraceptives. You got to be careful."

"Thanks, Dr. Redfearn. You've been a big help."

"You gonna tell me what this is all about? Or do I have to wait to see you on the evening news, like your mama?"

I didn't laugh. I promised to fill him in later.

As I crossed the street to my car, I called Tunisia's grandmother's number. I hoped she too was an early riser.

"Miz Linnie Ann? This is Avery Andrews. I met you — yes, ma'am. I was so sorry to hear about Tunisia. I hate to bother you, but it's very important. Tunisia had been using a nasal spray. Could you tell me, was she still using it right before she disappeared?"

"Well, now." Linnie Ann paused. "Tunisia didn't really take much of anything. Had been like that for a long time. Wouldn't hardly even take aspirin or nothing, but she had been using some kind of spray. Here's the bottle. Let me get my glasses. Yep."

"Was she still using it the last time you saw her?"

"As a matter of fact, the day before — well, when she took Tabbi to the doctor for her ear infection, she said Dr. Tilman had tole her to quit using it."

"But she was using it up until then?"

"She was. She said she needed to go back over to the clinic to see another doctor the next day about it."

"Who was that? Do you know?"

"The one here on this bottle, that wrote it for her."

I exhaled as she read it out for me. "Hilly-yard," she pronounced it. "L. Hilly-yard."

"Thank you very much. That'll be a big help." I didn't know what to say, what to offer in exchange for intruding on her grief.

"Um. Miz Andrews? I was wondering. Have the police — have you heard anything? They haven't tole us . . . Bessie says I'm bein' too nice and not askin' enough." Her voice trailed off.

"I don't know much yet, ma'am. As soon as I do, I'll let you know. You've been a big help."

"They said they'd probably release the body by the weekend, so we could plan the funeral."

Oh, dear. I was chasing shadows while she faced much more practical — and painful — tasks. "I'd appreciate you letting me know about the arrangements. And just as soon as I know something, I'll call you. You still have my number?"

After we said goodbyes, I thought about marching straight into Langley Hilliard's office to confront him with what I knew. Now that the trial testimony had ended, the judge couldn't rap my knuckles for contacting him. Then I hit on another plan. Better gather all my ammunition first. I dialed Linnie Ann again and asked if she'd sign a representation form for me as Tunisia's next of kin.

CHAPTER TWENTY-EIGHT

Early Thursday morning

I stopped by Jake's office to pick up a medical records release form and drove to Mt. Pleasant to get Linnie Ann's signature.

My plan carried high stakes and I needed to think through each move. A call to Gatekeeper Deb confirmed where the research records were stored — at a small clinic office on a side street near Barnard Medical. I recognized the street address; Langley Hilliard and other staff physicians had private practice offices in the vicinity.

In the shrub-sheltered lot behind the brick building sat only two cars: a Mercedes sedan and a Honda. Patients hadn't started arriving yet. The young woman behind the sliding glass window in the office matter-of-factly looked over the release form, went to pull the file folder, and offered to copy the slender chart while I waited.

"Would you mind if I look through it first?"

"Sure," she said, with only a moment's hesitation. "You can sit back here." She walked around to open the waiting room door for me and left me alone in an examining room with the folder. She had more pressing duties before the day's patients filled the waiting room.

Most of the sheets in the slender file were multi-paged consent and patient history forms. I thumbed quickly through those looking for the physician's notes. Exactly as I'd suspected, Langley Hilliard had been Tunisia Johnson's physician contact for the Rabb study. He'd conducted the initial intake interview with her, had seen her vital signs with the slightly elevated blood pressure. Not that I'd needed this puzzle piece to see the picture, but it was nice to know it fit in place so neatly.

"Avery! You are an early bird!"

I jumped, startled. Blaine Demarcos stood smiling in the doorway.

"Sorry. Didn't mean to surprise you. Annie said you were here."

"Dr. Demarcos. You work out of this office?"

He nodded, hands in his pockets. "Several of us use this office for research patient follow-up. It helps keep things centralized."

I hadn't expected to see Demarcos but, as Barnard Medical's head of research, what lay in my hands would soon be his problem.

"We need to talk." No need to drag this out. "About Tunisia Johnson. Did you know the police found her body?"

"I — no, I hadn't heard." His face had frozen in an attentive cast. I plowed on.

"Did Dr. Hilliard say anything about Tunisia, about her reporting any problems to him? Anything that you can remember? It's very important."

He shook his head slowly, his lips pursed. "No, he didn't say anything. What would he have said? She was progressing just fine, no complaints."

"He told you she was fine?"

Demarcos nodded. "We give routine updates on patients. Maybe not in so many words, but that would've been the gist of the conversation."

"So you know she was fine because Hilliard said she was fine." I fought to keep the sarcasm out of my voice.

"Certainly — and because I saw her myself."

"You saw Tunisia Johnson?" I kept my questions slow and measured, casual. "When?"

"Umm. About two weeks ago, I guess. When she saw Dr. Hilliard."

I tried a smile. "You have a very good memory."

"She was Dr. Hilliard's patient, so he had full responsibility for her, of course. But she was such a lively, funny young woman — sassy is a good word, I guess. We both enjoyed her visits, Hilliard and I. She had a great way with a story."

She wasn't the only one. "This was a couple of weeks ago. What was that, just a regular visit?"

"Her regular two-week checkup." He nodded, indicating the file I held. "That's only part of her file. If you have time, we can go across to the medical records office so you can have everything that pertains to Ms. Johnson. That might help give her family some — closure."

"Sure." Might as well humor him. Did he have any idea what he was saying? He'd learned about Tunisia's headaches and shortness of breath when Hilliard did, two weeks after she started using the contraceptive. Neither of them had done anything to help her, their inattention all because of the timing of their licensing contract.

Hilliard and Demarcos let her die. I might believe one of them made a stupid mistake and overlooked her symptoms, but not both of them.

I still couldn't see them arranging Tunisia's disappearance — and her reappearance in that obscene, humiliating stage set. What had happened?

I calmly walked with Demarcos to the back door and waited while he locked it behind us.

"Darn," I said, looking at my watch. "I just remembered. I've got a meeting at Jake Baker's this morning before court. I didn't realize how close to time—"

"I doubt that." He turned to face me. His voice had a bitter edge.

I raised my eyebrows but didn't reply.

"I heard a bit about the courtroom fiasco this week. From what I hear, Baker'll be off somewhere licking his wounds." His whole demeanor changed, his smile unpleasant.

"Hilliard, I sup—"

"No. I haven't seen Langley. No, in fact it was a security fellow from Atlanta. They've been keeping something of a watch on you since your pathetic visit to Atlanta."

I forced myself not to glance frantically about. Only two cars sat in the parking lot. Ever since my swamp adventure, I'd felt a bit skittish. Shrubs surrounded the parking lot and blocked the view from the street or nearby buildings. I wasn't likely to spot someone skulking about, spying on me. But then, I hadn't spotted anyone since Sunday, when I'd left Atlanta.

"Oh, yes. He followed you here. But don't worry. He's gone to catch a shower and some breakfast. Seems you caught him a bit unawares by leaving so early this morning, after such a late night. Some strapping fellow with a shoulder holster under his jacket, he said. You really should be careful about those late-night rendezvous, hmm?"

Apparently the guy from Atlanta hadn't recognized Cas Kirkland as a cop, even though he'd noticed the holster. No point in trying to defend my honor. I had more than that at stake here.

"I really do need to be going." I stepped off the sidewalk. I'd learned in a self-defense class years ago to keep my keys in my hand so I could enter my car quickly, better to avoid any unwanted problems in lonely parking lots.

"I don't think so, Avery." Demarcos held, not keys, but a cute, dull black automatic, its unblinking eye pointed at my midsection, probably in the vicinity of some major blood pathway.

"For Pete's sake. What do you think you're doing?" I sounded like my mother.

I must have lacked her authority because it didn't faze him. He locked my arm against his, wedged the gun against my side hidden from any passersby, and marched me across the parking lot toward the street.

I kept hearing the larger-than-life voice of the ex-FBI guy who had taught me self-defense: never leave the first crime scene. Never let the perp take you to the second crime scene. Chances are, you're dead if you do.

The FBI guy's other advice — run, scream, fall down in a faint, fight back — didn't seem workable in this case. Demarcos wasn't going to run away in search of an easier victim. There was nothing random about this.

"Though you probably won't find my company as entertaining as your houseguest last night—" He stopped to look both ways before crossing the narrow street.

No cars appeared on the little-used side street at this early hour, but Demarcos clutched my arm and froze, staring down the sidewalk. A shabby group of men emerged from an alleyway twenty feet to our right. Four guys shambled toward us, surprisingly regimented considering the early hour and their apparent state of incoordination.

"Good morning, fair lady." The self-appointed leader doffed his horn-of-plenty hat. The scavenger I'd met behind the hospital a few days ago.

The one immediately behind him, dressed in grimy green fatigues and a beret, didn't hear the unspoken command to halt and marched vigorously into the leader's bent-over backside. Curses, stumbling, and a few smacks with the horn-of-plenty and the beret were exchanged before everyone righted themselves and order was restored.

"Good morning," I said. Demarcos dented my ribs with the gun muzzle.

"And to you, sir," the ever-polite troop leader nodded curtly. His eyes, a startling crystal blue, seemed to see through whatever he looked at.

"Come on." Demarcos spoke low and close to my ear.

I turned to the peculiar crowd on the sidewalk as Demarcos strong-armed me into the street. I held horn-of-plenty's gaze and mouthed the words *help me, please help me,* as plainly as I could. I didn't dare break and run. Demarcos was scared and unpredictable, and I didn't know how these four would respond or how much help they would be facing a gun.

Horn hat man drew himself up straight, but he didn't make a move. The swaying threesome behind him didn't seem to notice. Demarcos and I disappeared behind the shrub-covered wall that surrounded the back path to one of the Barnard hospital buildings.

Demarcos held me tighter than any lover would in a street embrace. The smell of stale coffee on his breath and the acrid odor of his fear made me queasy.

The alleyway, overgrown with shrubbery, ran between two brick walls. Except for distant traffic sounds, we easily could have been miles from town.

The crumbling back entrance of the building — which building, I didn't know — had suffered the ravages of an ivy coating. Beside the door knob, a red light smaller than the end of my finger blinked at us. Demarcos fumbled for the card that unlocked the door and pulled it shut behind us.

I knew better than to hope someone waiting inside could help me. I wasn't sure how panicked I should be. A gun was serious. But, after all, not too much had been said so far, nothing irretrievably confessed.

Demarcos led me down a dim hall filled with pungent Charleston basement smells. The hallway dead-ended in a brightly lit corridor that echoed with the throb of engines or air compressors.

Demarcos, by firmly placing his hand in the small of my back, indicated that I should enter the door in front of us. That gentlemanly, proprietary gesture I'd always enjoyed from men would never be the same again.

The room held an office furniture graveyard — a scarred metal desk, one wooden chair, a rusty metal folding chair, and a dented green filing cabinet with one drawer sprung out about two inches.

"Do you mind telling me what all that show was about?" I aimed for a blend of righteous indignation and playfulness.

"What's this about some guy from Atlanta following me? Just let me in on the joke so we can both laugh."

If I hadn't been watching him closely, I doubt I would've noticed. But, on close inspection, he seemed to vibrate from some unseen current, as if pulled into the engine noises echoing through the building.

"If this is some prank over me wanting to see Tunisia's record, okay. Just let me in on it. Now that her body's been discovered, her family is probably satisfied. They're not the kind of people who will ask a lot of questions or think about suing. The whole thing's moot."

"Sit down and shut up."

The gun pointed. His hand trembled.

"Dr. Demarcos, I really don't understand. But I'll be leaving now. Maybe we can talk more later, after you've—"

"Sit down, dammit." He shoved me into the wooden desk chair so hard it rolled backward. My head smacked into the wall.

"I don't understand." He mimicked me with a high-pitched, prissy tone. "Dammit. Do you think I'm stupid? Mark Tilman might have been stupid. I can assure you, I am not."

His voice got louder and more agitated. The mental ward lockdown upstairs held saner people.

"Tunisia Johnson was nothing but a two-bit street whore. If we hadn't helped her off the street, she would have been dead a lot sooner. You're going to tell me I should turn over a fortune, what I've worked my entire professional life for, because some whore has high blood pressure? I don't think so." He articulated the last sentence with deliberateness.

I'd seen the need to confess compel stupid admissions. Despite my attempts to offer him a graceful exit, he would tell me all about it whether I wanted to know or not.

"Everything's going just fine. The study results are moving as we expected. Then that bitch shows up with her damned headaches. We were so close to a deal, and Hilliard had to screw it up. If he'd done something more when she first came in. But no, he missed it, then tried to keep it quiet."

Demarcos rubbed his forehead and leaned against the desk, facing me. In a room this small, our knees almost touched.

"I thought Hilliard had taken care of it. Dropped her from the study. By the time I saw her, she was too far along. Can you believe it? I'm in my office, talking to Pendleton Rabb's damned lawyer, negotiating with that son of a bitch. Rabb's lawyer is playing hardball — wants to delay the agreement until he checks a few more things," he mimicked mincingly. "And what happens? Hilliard comes into my office looking like Mount St. Helens just erupted in the parking lot. The bitch died. Right in his office. Can you believe it?"

Demarcos gesticulated with both his gun and his empty hand.

"She came into his office for an appointment and died. Right there. While I'm negotiating a deal that'll fix me and Hilliard for life, she dies. Right there in his office." He shook his head, still unable to believe the unfairness of life.

"So what were we to do? I ask you. We can't have this go on any official record and queer the deal. We're talking a lot at stake here."

His voice trailed off. Was he trying to convince himself or me?

"When the first glitches showed up, we knew it was something we could correct. More to do with the population we must resort to using here than anything else. We could have corrected the problem in our protocols for later trials. But the big fish had already bitten and we didn't have much time to reel him in. Pendleton Rabb wanted a new contraceptive so bad he could taste it. He needed it. Something that would be successful, profitable. Something his dad and granddad hadn't developed, that was just his, to make his mark. He was ripe."

Demarcos pinched his fingers across his upper lip, then wiped his hand down his pants leg. I sat quietly and let him rant.

"We only had to patch things together until Rabb signed on the dotted line. Of course, the FDA would be another hurdle, but we could fix that. Then she dies. Right there in Hilliard's office. How, I ask you, can somebody have such luck? Hilliard went ape-shit. He comes squawking into my office, asking if we should call the police. Can you imagine?"

He quit talking. The rest of the story must be too awkward to repeat aloud.

I gently prompted him. "What did you do?"

He kept staring at the wall, as if I wasn't there. "Stored her in the morgue. She only had to chill for a few days, until everything finalized and Rabb signed. Just a few days. We got a call a week later. Rabb agreed to our terms and would fax us the signed contract.

"We decided to move that night. We couldn't keep her hidden in the morgue icebox forever. So we moved her, figuring her history would ensure that no one asked too many questions or got too many answers.

"We moved her into this very room, waited until the coast was clear, then rolled her out to the parking lot and into a borrowed wagon. With the college kids and their stunts, we figured no one would pay much attention.

"Then, wouldn't you know. Those assholes call the very next morning to change their tune. No faxed contract. Rather than a lump-sum payment and royalties, they pick that day to start talking about an equity position, stock options. Hell. I'm a doctor. I'm not even supposed to know what an equity position is, much less be offered one, part ownership in a drug that should be worth millions."

He sighed deeply. "It was too late to do anything about the body. All we could do was wait and hope it wasn't discovered too quickly. I've been sick since we got that phone call. A lump sum would've been better, don't you think? I can't help but think if this thing blows up, stock options won't be worth much. What's the use sharing profits on something no one's going to be able to buy?"

"I don't know, Demarcos. Things don't look all that bad. After all, what have you really done? It's not as though you killed her." *You sorry son of a bitch.* "You weren't covering up a murder or anything. Any malpractice claim would be a civil case, not a criminal one. Your malpractice carrier would take care of that, and your premiums won't even go up. The prosecutor in Charleston has better sense than to take on a couple of Barnard Medical's golden-haired boys over some silly misdemeanor offense for moving a body. So what's your problem? Nothing a good lawyer can't get you out of."

I tried my best salacious shark grin, but it lost most of its effect when Langley Hilliard burst through the door.

CHAPTER TWENTY-NINE

Thursday morning

Langley Hilliard insinuated himself between me and Demarcos, crowding the small room even more.

"Good gawd almighty, I'd hoped it was some sort of juvenile prank. Have you lost your mind?" Langley Hilliard raved. "You call me at the crack of dawn, saying you've got a lawyer to dispose of? Have you lost it, you little asshole?"

In the small room, Demarcos and I couldn't do much except turn away from the random spittle drops that flew from his lips.

"Dr. Hilliard." I tried to put that school-marm bark in my voice, the one my mother uses so adeptly. He shut up. "I was just telling Dr. Demarcos that your investment doesn't look as much at risk as you might have thought. With some quick work, we can probably put together a good defensive position—"

"What the hell are you talking about?" He whirled on me, spit flying in my face. His pupils dilated and I could feel the heat his skin radiated. "Defensive position? What the hell, a defensive position? What kind of defensive position do you suggest for murder?"

"Langley." Demarcos cautioned. "Langley. We've just been talking about Tunisia, about—"

"That whore. I suppose you know they've found her. She's only been there two days. Nowhere near long enough. They'll be asking questions."

"Langley—"

"—just like that little asshole resident."

For a moment, the room fell silent, as if we had sucked all the air out of the room and left nothing to carry sound.

"Langley. Shut the hell up."

The sharpness of Demarcos's tone took some of the wind out of Hilliard but didn't shut him up. He turned to me, his back still to the door.

"He just asked too many questions."

Mark Tilman. The whiny petulance in Hilliard's voice, their self-absorbed focus on the inconvenience over Tunisia's death made the bile boil up the back of my throat.

Demarcos and I had politely avoided mentioning Mark until Hilliard uncorked the bottle. Now none of us could neutralize it.

"If he'd just known his place. Imagine, a resident with such impertinent questions. We simply had no choice. Perhaps, though," he ran a hand over his silvered hair, smoothing the strands that had shaken loose, "if those men you hired had done their job more competently, the questions would have ended there. As they should have."

"You supercilious fart." Demarcos exploded. "How dare you?"

Hilliard's expression was one of a schoolmaster who'd just been hit in the eye with a spitball.

"Hilliard, you've screwed this deal every which way. About the time I get one of your screwups under control, you stick your wrinkled prick into another one. Don't look at me like that, you pathetic old fool. The only reason I had you anywhere near this project was your name, your connections. Connections. Ha."

246

Demarcos's derision was bitter and humorless. "The only thing you've connected us with is the gas chamber. Or is it the electric chair in this unenlightened backwater state?"

Hilliard pushed against my knees as he tried to get away from the venom in Demarcos's face, forcing my chair a little tighter into the corner. Demarcos pinned him against the filing cabinet.

"You killed that whore by ignoring an impending stroke. Good gahdamighty. How stupid. Then your shifty-eyed evasions when Tilman came asking questions just made him ask more questions. I handled that the only way I could. Now you still can t keep your damned mouth shut. How can anybody—"

"Don't yell at me, young man. You called me this morning, somebody asking too many questions, for me to get over here. How am I the one to blame for not keeping quiet? I guess now you plan to call those same two ne'er-do-wells you had 'take care' of the Tilman problem. They burned an entire house down to get rid of a stupid notebook and failed at that. They certainly didn't prove effective with her the last time," he gestured at me, "or we wouldn't be here now, would we?"

The stuffy little room grew very cold.

"I've been meaning to ask you, Blaine. Just what makes you think you can trust those two hoodlums? I have a sneaky suspicion that, about the time we think things are settled, those two will be back to haunt us."

"Shut up, you senile old bastard. I'm not the one who screws up everything he touches. They can be trusted. Money doesn't satisfy someone nearly as much as keeping them alive does." Demarcos looked pleased with himself. "You're the one who'd be stupid enough to pay somebody, expecting that would keep him quiet. No, I offered him his sister's life. And his own death, if he ever breathed a word. Reward and punishment. Life and death. Most beings, even those of limited intelligence, respond to that."

Like the Blaine Demarcos I'd met at the hospital a few days ago, he was smooth, in control.

"But you're right. We can't risk another botch-up. Hilliard, go check down at the end of the hall. Make sure everything's clear."

Surprisingly, Hilliard complied. He peeked into the hall before slipping out, the door clicking shut behind him.

After Hilliard left, Demarcos's smile made me more nervous than his gun. He'd settled on something since Hilliard had arrived. That smile, his relaxed sureness, said I wasn't going to like whatever he'd decided. He studied me closely. And smiled.

"Hemp's sister, the one who raised him, is by my good graces enrolled in a promising new breast cancer study. I have his picture, taken with Tunisia Johnson's body all trussed up in the abandoned building where she was discovered. And," his grin broadened, "he thinks my name is Langley Hilliard."

On cue, Hilliard opened the door and joined us again.

"Langley, we'll need to take care of this one ourselves. I called you so you could stay with her while I make arrangements. Use this if you have to, Langley. Remember, your life depends on it."

Demarcos could have been guiding a med student through a routine procedure, for all the emotion in his voice as he handed Hilliard the pistol. The short four-inch barrel would provide plenty of accuracy in this small space, even with Hilliard's shaky reluctance.

Demarcos favored me with another smile. He was betting I couldn't convince Hilliard that he was being set up. Another of his games, to prove he was smarter than the rest of us.

The door closed behind him.

Did I have time to persuade Hilliard? Or only enough time to make him happy to help Demarcos off me.

"Hilliard, he's setting you up. He—"

The door burst open and slammed against the wall. The sound that followed seared through my head. A gunshot. The pain pulsed so intensely that, for a second, I thought I'd been shot through both ears.

The strange sight at the door disconcerted Hilliard, who didn't seem to realize he'd fired his own gun.

"There you are, dear lady. In the future, if you seek assistance, it would be wise to make sure that assistance can find you." His horn-of-plenty at a rakish angle, the crystal-eyed leader of the scavengers posed in the doorway.

Behind him, Blaine Demarcos looked more startled than anyone. A strapping fellow in smelly fatigues held him immobilized in a headlock while the guy with the beard grasped his arm with one hand and a hypodermic syringe with the other. Demarcos's eyes bulged and he made slurping sounds at the back of his throat.

I slipped the pistol easily from Hilliard's shell-shocked grasp.

"By the time we had a plan of attack, you'd disappeared into a locked building. Next time, just a wee bit of assistance from you — more specifically, leaving the door unlocked — would expedite the mission. We followed your trigger-happy captor there in. He obliged us by being much less careful with the door. Stephen here grabbed it quick. Good work, my man "

He patted Stephen expansively on the shoulder. Stephen's beard, a full, luxurious thatch of wiry red, quivered proudly.

"Of course, while fearing for your safety, we had to reconnoiter and formulate a new plan of attack. As the localized activity accelerated, with first your captor and then your abductor popping in and out, we decided to act, whether precipitously or not."

"Your timing was impeccable. As was your valor, your skill, and your luck. An outstanding operation, men." I still sat wedged into the corner in the wooden chair.

Blaine Demarcos's face turned shades of dark red tinged with purple as the chest of the man holding him swelled with pride and the headlock tightened.

"Perhaps, sir, you could let Dr. Demarcos have a breath there," I said.

Demarcos gulped air, but that was the only freedom his guardian would allow.

I'd left my cell phone in the car, so I chose the most public route to the lobby and a pay phone. My guys were a valiant lot, but likely no match for some thug from Atlanta or the two thugs from the swamp or whoever else might lurk about the fringes of this peculiar operation. I regretted that no local news team happened to be cruising the hospital as we emerged onto the side street and marched around the corner to the front entrance of the hospital. That footage would've made the evening news for sure — maybe even wider coverage than Mom at the Burger Hut.

Not one soul acted as though they even noticed us. Not one person acted as though a parade led by a man wearing an upturned horn-of-plenty and brought up in the rear by a gun-wielding lady lawyer was the least extraordinary.

Within minutes of my call, cop cars jammed the circular drive at the hospital entrance. They drew a bit more notice than our parade had, even though sirens and flashing lights aren't anomalies around a busy hospital.

Just to make sure the story drew the kind of attention I knew it deserved, I called the area TV stations and local paper as soon as I got off the phone with Cas Kirkland. The first news crew arrived in time for some footage of the two prominent physicians being driven off to the station to be booked. Shots of the officers putting a hand on each head to keep them from banging the door frame would be particularly nice. Rob — the horn-of-plenty man — was well-spoken on camera. He'd probably been a sales guru in another life.

"Don't suppose," Cas said, appearing beside me as I finished my last phone call, "it ever occurred to you to drop a dime for me. You know, fill me in. Bring me up to speed."

"Believe me, if I could have called you instead of Rob and the gang, I would have." If I'd known the extent of Demarcos's involvement, I'd certainly never have wandered into his office.

He loomed, his hand on the wall beside the telephone and his armpit at my eye level. "Regardless of what you might think, Miss Hotshot, we've been busy, too — with a tip and a court order for Blaine Demarcos's cellular phone records. We found two calls made to one Hemp Simpson, a convicted felon we picked up on a probation violation. He kept his mouth shut; we couldn't get him to tell us what time showed on his watch dial. But his cousin sang like a canary. A word of advice, Avery. Don't have dumb friends. It's worse than being dumb yourself."

"I'll remember that."

"Both those cell phone calls were made prior to a couple of traffic accidents — one off a marsh road on James Island, the other near Cooper Street in Mt. Pleasant." He paused to make sure I was with him.

"The cousin tumbled to both of them. Said Hemp — the doofus with the cell phone — was the neck-breaker who's afraid of snakes. His cousin was your whiner. Of course, I'd like to try you on a voice lineup, see if you can ID them."

I nodded. Knowing they'd found the two guys from the swamp somehow made all this nonsense more real. Knowing they had killed Mark Tilman made it intimately more frightening.

"The whole thing is odd, though," Cas said. "Before, those two had been strictly small time."

"Demarcos dropped some hints. Something about a sister — probably Hemp's — needing to be enrolled in a breast cancer study. Demarcos helped her get in, in exchange for a couple of little favors."

"You gotta be kidding." He stared down at me. "Damnedest pay-off for a hit I've ever heard. Hemp mentioned his sister was in the hospital. She raised him, you know."

"Demarcos took blackmail photos of Hemp with Tunisia's body. To keep him in line down the road."

"You going to tell me how you tumbled to this?" Cas and I stood at the far side of the lobby, away from the gentle but endless tide of people washing in and out of the front doors of the hospital.

"Stumbled is a more accurate description. Mark sending his research journal hinted that something was wrong. He was worried about Tunisia. Of course, she'd died before I first talked to Mark. Then Mark died that night."

Cas graciously didn't jump me about not giving him the research notebook earlier, and I graciously didn't point out he'd been sleeping when I'd mentioned it to him. "The cousin who's singing about what happened in the swamp is laying it all on Hemp, who's keeping quiet. But it squares with what Dauber Dothan saw that night."

I nodded, feeling sad. "The next link was Rabb & Company. They delayed signing a contract with Hilliard. Belatedly, what Tunisia's grandmother said about her headaches and how puny she felt clicked with me. I thought Hilliard was in it alone." Or that's what I wanted to believe.

My stomach heaved, as if trying to churn off the unpleasant taste of truth. "Demarcos did a good job covering his tracks, shifting blame to Hilliard, and Hilliard was involved deeply enough that the blame was plausible. Demarcos stumbled when he admitted seeing Tunisia at her last appointment with Hilliard. Until then, I didn't suspect him." I guess that's why psychologists warn about the halo effect; we really do endow handsome people with handsome characteristics.

Cas stared at me a moment, waiting to see if I'd gotten it all out. "Come on, counselor. I'll take you to your car or wherever."

Wherever was a thought. Where had I left my car? Demarcos's office, across the street. I sure didn't want to leave my Mustang there.

CHAPTER THIRTY

Early Thursday afternoon

Jake's voice through the phone sounded tired. "The jury's coming back."

"Not this soon?" I checked my watch. It was almost noon. Surely the jury hadn't finished its deliberations this quickly. "They probably have a question or want the court transcriber reread a portion of testimony."

"Who knows."

That morning, I'd left the hospital and scooted into the courtroom soon after Jake had begun his closing argument. Jake was in top form and delivered a doozie. Passionate and to the point, he had woven the strands of evidence together into a narrative that could persuade a jury. I watched them but, like most juries, this one remained inscrutable. Vendue's closing had also been stylish and well-presented, though it lacked the fire and the dramatic drawl Jake had used so well.

I'd offered Jake a couple of points to emphasize on his rebuttal to Arthur Vendue's closing — Jake had reserved part of the time allotted to his closing so he could have the final word before the jury retired to deliberate his clients' fate.

A few minutes after noon, I eased open the courtroom door and peeked through the crack. Folks were inside, but I couldn't see whether the judge was on the bench. The door swung wider, pushing me back a step. Wendell, one of the bailiffs, motioned me inside with a grin. "We hadn't got started yet. The jury's fixing to come back."

I padded quietly down the center aisle, struck again by how church-like it was — hushed voices, subdued lighting, life and death. Jake nodded in my direction as I took a seat behind him, but the judge entered behind the bench and his order to bring in the jury cut off any conversation.

Not much to say, at these times. You've done all you could do. No, that's not true. There's always more you could've done, given the time, the money, the brains. But now, all that's left is waiting to see if you did enough.

I carefully watched each juror's face as they filed in. Not one looked in Jake's direction, not one looked behind him, to where the plaintiffs sat. Bad sign. Jurors always look at the plaintiffs if they're bringing them good news. They look at the ground or the defense table if they're bringing in a defense verdict.

Jake's back was rigid, his arms resting on the table as the judge went through the preliminaries.

"Madame Foreperson, do you have a verdict?"

"Yes, sir, we do." Her voice was quiet, her eyes unreadable behind her glasses. She handed the paper to the clerk.

"The jury finds for the defendant, Perforce Pharmaceuticals."

I didn't hear anything else. All the "is this your verdict?" questions, all the "thank you for your service, this is what makes America great" speeches. Finds for the defendant. I used to love hearing those words. Now they meant we'd lost. I couldn't bring myself to look around for Ada Jones.

Up until those words, I'd thought of this as Jake's case. Now, suddenly, it felt personal. I had wanted to fight for Ada Jones. I'd wanted to humiliate Langley Hilliard. What must Jake be feeling? How much money had he sunk into this case?

If I'd unmasked Langley Hilliard sooner, would that have changed things? Doubtful. Would it have mattered to the jury that Perforce, through Rabb, was involved with yet another questionable drug, a drug that killed Tunisia? The tougher question: should it matter? Did Tunisia's death and the problems with Tixtill, did any of that have anything to do with Uplift?

The objective part of me said no. Too many variables. But if they'd known about Tunisia, about the lies and the conflicts of interest, would they have blamed Perforce for what went wrong in Ray Vincent Wilma's brain? Maybe not. Drugs help, drugs hurt. Sometimes drugs do nothing — or don't do enough.

I still didn't believe Uplift had made Ray Vincent crazy enough to kill people. He'd been crazy enough already. But Perforce cut corners, looked the other way when physicians fudged test results, manipulated test rosters to get the results they wanted — and that made me doubt everything they did.

If the jurors had known the whole story, would they have written a different ending? That's what troubled me — should they have known?

It didn't matter now. It was over. Lila was packing the laptop and files. Jake's clients were sitting frozen in their seats, looking lost. The jury had filed out, the courtroom was mostly ours, a place of stunned mourning.

Jake wisely disappeared through the back door, going somewhere to collect his thoughts and lick his wounds in private for a while. He couldn't offer any consolation at the moment. Lila took on that role. She whispered quietly, to first one group, then another, that Jake would talk to them in about half an hour, after the courtroom had emptied of others.

I wanted to throw up. Jake might enjoy knowing about Hilliard's arrest, but I decided Lila could best decide the timing. I gave her a nutshell of the morning's events and left.

The sunlight had faded behind thick clouds, leaving only wan winter light. Everyone else in Charleston's lunch hour rush appeared surprisingly oblivious to what had just happened inside the fourth-floor courtroom.

My voice mail announced three new messages. The first call reminded me I was overdue for a dental appointment. The call after that was a real surprise.

"Avery Andrews. This is Rowly Edward, your friendly and accommodatin' Atlanta cabbie. Just tumbled across an inter-resting piece of news you might see in the papers in the next few days. Picked up an airport fare — fellow said he was in town doing a little legwork on a case against Rabb & Company for a big California plaintiff's lawyer. About some new contraceptive they're testing. He claimed their research was coercive and highly suspect, several women had gotten sick or died. He positively smacked his lips on the words 'cover-up.' They expect lots of media attention, he said, hot on the heels of those stories about how the government experimented on human guinea pigs. Thought you'd be inter-rested."

I liked the idea of a high-profile California lawyer sharking the waters around Pendleton Rabb. What connection did that have with Hilliard's contraceptive? Did Rabb have more than one in the works? I jotted a note to call Rowly later and fill him in, find out what else he'd picked up and how the country music or PI careers were going.

I wandered up Meeting Street and turned into Washington Park. It felt even gloomier under the trees, but I needed to sit and think. I clicked the phone off. This jury hadn't believed Uplift made Ray Vincent Wilma crazy. But a jury would have a much easier time believing Hilliard and Demarcos killed Tunisia. Even though the police held them on criminal charges, those would be mild compared to what Jake Baker could do to them in a malpractice suit. The money Jake could win would help Tabbi.

For the first time since the trial had begun, I felt optimistic. We'd have time to do a thorough investigation, see what Rabb knew and when, catch the company in the net, maybe collaborate with the California lawyer. Dear Lord, maybe I was turning into a plaintiff's lawyer after all.

I scribbled a note to call Tunisia's grandmother and fill her in on what had happened — or as much as would make her memories easier. I'd tell her to keep my phone number, just in case Tabbi ever needed anything. Maybe see how she felt about suing bad guys.

My phone buzzed and a reedy voice asked, "Is this Avery Andrews?"

"Yes, it is." Who the heck was this with my cell phone number?

"This is William Wink. You aren't in the Yeller Pages. I had to get your number from this guy. He said you could help me."

He didn't give me time to ask what guy.

"I hear you're a lawyer, and I think a lady lawyer would be a good thing on this case. Can't see any of these other Dacus fancy pants taking this serious enough."

Dacus. That narrowed it down, as if his Upstate accent hadn't been hint enough.

"You know Miller's Dry Goods? On Main Street?"

"Yessir." Everyone just called it Miller's, but its old sign and old name now had a renewed cache, as craft and "junque" stores replaced the businesses moving out to strip centers.

"You know it's supposed to be haunted?"

"Un — no, sir. I'm not sure—"

"Just let me finish. I'm paying for the call, aren't I? Jabe Miller opened that store after dubya-dubya-two, but it didn't take off like he hoped it would. Folks had cars and gas by then, so they could drive other places, if need be, get better stuff and not pay three prices like Jabe charged. So Jabe hit on an idea to boost business. The old sumbitch started telling everybody his store was haunted. Big tales about spooky sightings and noise and things flyin' around. 'Course, folks aren't stupid. They started askin' Jabe who'd want to haunt his store, so he re-searched it," pronounced as if it was a dirty word, "and come up with my daddy."

Mr. Wink gave a dramatic pause, letting the revelation sink in. "Ever since, the sumbitch has been telling people my daddy's hauntin' his store."

I'd grown up in Dacus, walked past Miller's untold times. This was the first I'd heard of a ghost. What do you say to the irate son of a purported haint?

"I want it stopped. Now his son's taken over. Apparently thinks all that rusty, dusty junk they've never been able to sell is now in fashion. They've added ice cream and a candy counter. His idiot son's gone out and contacted *Southern Living* magazine and who knows who else to tell them the tale. Claims folks can get a whiff of my daddy's pipe tobacco. Even had some kinda crackpot psychic come in and go all tithery at the manifestations. Bullshit. My daddy didn't smoke a fool pipe and he ain't manifestin' nothing, and he sure as hell hadn't decided to spend eternity entertaining tourists in Miller's Dry Goods."

He paused finally to catch a reedy breath. "I-want-it-stopped. You got any idea how that makes me feel, him touting that nonsense about my own daddy? My mother, God rest her, was mortified enough when ol' Jabe started up on it. She had a come-to-Jesus meeting with him about it, and he toned it down. But Sonny Boy, having a word with him just got him wound up that much tighter. I-want-it-stopped."

"That's a very — interesting situation, Mr. Wink. What — um — would you like to do?"

"You're a lawyer, aren't you? I thought for sure you lawyers would have some useful something you could do. I-want-it-stopped." His breath whistled over the phone line. Then his voice was quieter. "My daddy was a good and decent man. He deserves better than to be turned into a side-show freak by the likes of Jabe Miller and his idiot son. I owe him that much before I pass on."

I was turning possibilities over in my head. A dead person can't have his character defamed. But what about false light invasion of privacy? An interesting puzzle.

"Mr. Wink, I've never heard of a situation quite like yours, but just because I don't know the solution right off the top of my head, doesn't mean there isn't one." My family had never done business at Miller's. I bet Aunt Letha could give me a few reasons why. "Could we meet at Maylene's tomorrow morning? Talk over some options?"

"Don't know what good more talking will do. I-want-it-stopped. But sure, I can meet you. Seven not too early for you, is it?" He offered it as a challenge.

"No, sir. Seven would be great." I'd have time to drive home, do a little research, mull on some things. I also needed to see Melvin, talk over where we stood with the office plans — or if there would be any office or any plans.

Mr. Wink said good-bye and I opened my last voice mail. The message began mid-sentence. "—used to talking to these things. I wish you were home more often. I worry about you out at such odd hours. I need to talk to you." No mention of the Burger Hut. "Glad you'll be home soon. Would you look over some paperwork? For a local group providing residential care for the mentally challenged. There is some neighborhood opposition. Well, actually, it's Nellie Norris who's opposed it most loudly. So naturally that means Aunt Letha is solidly behind it."

I added *call Mom* to my list. I was looking forward to heading home, if only to catch my breath, hike in the mountains, regain my footing, and find out what happened to Miranda and her dynamite-toting paramour.

I wondered if William Wink was kin to the Wink Realty folks. If so, he could afford to pay me. Somehow he didn't sound the type who showered money about. Imagine the publicity, though — a ghost-busting lawyer. I couldn't wait to hear what Aunt Letha had to say about this one.

THE END

POSTSCRIPT: DRUG RESEARCH AND TESTING

Pharmaceutical researchers work tirelessly to expand knowledge and increase the options for diagnosis, treatment, and cure of diseases. Each year, more than 80,000 drug trials are conducted at over 10,000 test sites in the United States, representing thousands of volunteers who participate to help others. No drug is tested or sold unless it meets rigorous requirements and is approved by the Food & Drug Administration (FDA), the federal agency charged with regulating both drugs and medical devices.

Most patients enter studies because they have a disease with no good treatment options or none of the available options work for them. Some just want to help others. Drug trials carry risks, and patients must give their *informed* consent before participating in a clinical trial. Effective informed consent means the patient is warned of the risks and told of alternatives and knowingly accepts the risks.

Any Adverse Event (AE) must be reported to the FDA. The FDA weighs AEs against the drug's benefits in deciding whether to allow the drug to be marketed and, if so, with what warnings. A Serious Adverse Event (SAE) must be reported within seven days; if these risks are severe and widespread, the study will likely be halted.

Under-reporting AEs and SAEs is an oft-cited problem; researchers are only required to report "unexpected" bad reactions, not expected consequences of the illness, so some investigators choose to blame problems on the underlying illness rather than the drug.

Payments made to investigators present another potential conflict of interest: in 2002, according to the drug-trial information group CenterWatch, 40% of the $10 billion drug companies spent on clinical trials went to the investigators conducting the tests (*Informed Consent*, by Kenneth Getz and Deborah Borfitz, Boston: Thomson/CenterWatch: 2002, p. 23). An investigator can earn tens to hundreds of thousands of dollars conducting research trials, depending on the size and number of studies conducted.

Drug companies routinely send study monitors to research centers to oversee ongoing studies. The federal government also monitors studies that it funds. The greatest risk to patients occurs in studies that are funded by sources other than the federal government or a pharmaceutical company, because of the lack of knowledgeable external oversight.

Investigators who fail to comply with research standards and government requirements may become subject to closer monitoring, may be blacklisted and not allowed to conduct future studies, or may be criminally prosecuted.

The FDA recently began requiring that researchers disclose any financial interest in the drug under investigation, including any finder's fees, stock ownership, patents, licenses, or other interest. However, only the FDA is told of the financial interest; the patient is not.

Of the thousands of studies conducted, only a small minority of drug investigators have violated ethical codes or regulatory requirements; few allow conflicts of interest or their own financial gain to blind them to their patients' interests. It happens, but it is rare. The FDA website lists those researchers who have been blacklisted (www.fda.gov, search for Investigators Inspection List).

If you are considering participating in a drug trial, do your homework. The federal government lists clinical trials currently being conducted (www.clinicaltrials.gov) and information on how to enroll. Some pharmaceutical companies, in response to charges of hiding negative results, post clinical trial results on their individual sites.

The CenterWatch website (www.centerwatch.com) provides information, and the book *Informed Consent* provides a user-friendly review of how and why to get involved, as well as questions to ask to protect yourself.

The thousands who volunteer each year for clinical trials provide a valuable service, but it is your responsibility to educate yourself before you or a loved one becomes involved in a research study.

THE JOFFE BOOKS STORY

We began in 2014 when Jasper agreed to publish his mum's much-rejected romance novel and it became a bestseller.

Since then we've grown into the largest independent publisher in the UK. We're extremely proud to publish some of the very best writers in the world, including Joy Ellis, Faith Martin, Caro Ramsay, Helen Forrester, Simon Brett and Robert Goddard. Everyone at Joffe Books loves reading and we never forget that it all begins with the magic of an author telling a story.

We are proud to publish talented first-time authors, as well as established writers whose books we love introducing to a new generation of readers.

We have been shortlisted for Independent Publisher of the Year at the British Book Awards three times, in 2020, 2021 and 2022, and for the Diversity and Inclusivity Award at the Independent Publishing Awards in 2022.

We built this company with your help, and we love to hear from you, so please email us about absolutely anything bookish at feedback@joffebooks.com

If you want to receive free books every Friday and hear about all our new releases, join our mailing list: www.joffebooks.com/contact

And when you tell your friends about us, just remember: it's pronounced Joffe as in coffee or toffee!